Irish Crown

NASHODA ROSE

Irish Crown
Published by Nashoda Rose
Copyright © 2018 by Nashoda Rose

ISBN: 978-1-987953-18-3
Toronto, Canada

Copyright © 2018 Cover design and Photography by Sara Eirew
Model: Mike Chabot
Content Edited by Kristin Anders, The Romantic Editor,
www.theromanticeditor.com
First Editing by Hot Tree Editing, www.hottreeediting.com
Formatted by Champagne Book Design, champagnebookdesign.com
Proofing & Editing: Elaine York/Allusion Graphics, LLC ,
www.allusiongraphics.com)

Warning: Irish Crown is for 18+ due to language and sexual content.

*Any editing issues are my own. I'm Canadian and may use the Canadian spelling rather than US.

Books by
NASHODA ROSE

Irish Crown

Tear Asunder Series
With You (free)
Torn from You
Overwhelmed by You
Shattered by You
Kept from You

Unyielding Series (Tear Asunder spin-off)
Perfect Chaos
Perfect Ruin
Perfect Rage

Scars of the Wraith Series
Stygian
Tyrant
Credo
Take

What's Coming?

Ugly Perfects
Vic Gate
Ardent (Scars of the Wraiths)
Edge of You (Tear Asunder)

www.nashodarose.com

Dedication

To the readers.
For the readers.
Thank you for waiting.
Thank you for believing in me.

Prologue

Eva

SATED. COMPLETELY AND UTTERLY SATED. THAT WAS THE WORD THAT sat warm and cozy in my belly as I lay curled in a half-moon on his bed.

The white sheet fell across my breasts, then dipped low down my back to pool at the cusp of my ass. With one arm crooked under the plush pillow, the other was slung over my hip, palm resting on the indented mattress where the heat of his body still lingered.

My skin tingled at the memory of his mouth.

His velvet tongue.

The weight of his muscled body on top of mine as he held my wrists above my head and pressed me into the mattress with hard rhythmic thrusts.

He brought me to the edge of falling into a sea of daisies, the velvet petals fluttering deep in my core. Then he'd soften.

Not his body, no, that was like a cement graffiti wall, but his movements.

Slow. Tranquil. Deep.

He leisurely peppered kisses across my flushed skin. Grazed my nipples with his teeth before drawing them into his mouth and sucking.

He watched. He waited. He knew when my body needed more.

When I couldn't take the slow any longer, that's when he'd give me more.

Harder. Deeper. Faster.

Seven hours in bed. We napped. We drank red wine and snacked on leftover pizza with extra cheese and mushrooms because that's all he had in the fridge. But mostly, we had unbelievably, amazing sex.

He didn't know it, but he made me laugh before I even met him when he missed the soccer ball and fell on his ass at the Treasured Children's Centre charity event yesterday. It was obvious he'd done it on purpose, so one of the kids could get the ball and try for goal.

It was sweet. And yet there was nothing physically sweet about him.

He looked every bit the badass. Tattoos scrawled across his skin everywhere except his legs, right shoulder, and face. His russet hair was long on the top, not overly, but chin-length with a slight wave, and the sides were shaved.

Yesterday, he'd worn the long pieces tied in a bun. A bun I'd ripped out when my fingers raked through it the second we walked into his place, and he pushed me up against the steel door and kissed me for the first time.

No. He didn't just kiss me. He devoured me.

Possessive. But giving.

Controlling and yet guiding.

His lips perfectly melding with mine even though he was over six foot to my five foot four.

His square jaw had at least a week's worth of stubble, and my chin, neck, and cheeks burned from it, and I bet I'd wear his imprint for days.

And that was fine by me. I liked the feel of his coarse stubble when he kissed my neck. My mouth. I liked it a whole hell of a lot between my legs too and he'd done that a number of times last night, and this morning.

I'd never been a sexual person. I liked sex. Liked it less after my a-hole ex-boyfriend. But of my top ten things to do, it would be my fifth. So, yeah, I'd rather spend an evening with my girls drinking wine or eat crème brûlée or read a good book.

But sex just blew away crème brûlée, a book, wine with my girls, and I wanted more of that. More of him.

I was crazy thinking I'd get more, but there was something between us and I swear he felt it too. He'd said that I was rare and he'd never had rare before, and he liked it—a lot.

I'd never gone home with a man after one conversation. It was never worth it. It took me a while to become comfortable enough with a man in order to strip naked and have sex with him.

But he laughed with the kids playing soccer, high-fived them when one scored a goal, and it was obvious he was good with kids, and that was important to me. It said something about a man. My ex wasn't good with kids and that should've been my first red flag, but I'd been twenty-two and swept away by his charm.

I was a safe kind of girl, and what went with that was knowing exactly what would happen before it happened. I had sticky notes for everything, and when I made plans, I stuck to them.

My dad had worked most of his life on an oil rig, and he said I'd have been good at it because you had to be reliable, responsible, and dependable, or it could cost a life. So, I got all that from him.

Now retired, he lived just outside of the city on a farm. Not a working farm, but an old house with a few acres, some chickens, and two great dogs my friend Charlotte had rescued, Blue and Midnight, to which he swore never got on the furniture. But whenever I visited, they were always on the couch or curled in his old recliner. He'd become the local handyman in the community and was pretty damn good at it.

My job was the unplanned part of my life. Often hectic. And I never knew what would come through the hospital emergency doors, so I was prepared for anything and everything. It was why I liked to keep every other aspect of my life organized.

Sleeping with a man I barely knew was uncharted territory. But I was thinking this was the best territory I'd ever been in.

I rolled onto my back when I heard the shower turn off. Steam leaked under the door and filled the air with the delicious scent of coconut and papaya.

I slowly slid my foot up the side of my calf, imagining his rough hand.

We hadn't really talked much after that first kiss. More like moans, groans, and the numerous swear words that emerged from deep in his throat in a raspy growl. There'd also been a few abrupt instructions like "open your legs, pet" or "on your knees, baby."

I swallowed, pressing my thighs together at the memory.

The bathroom door opened and my heart skipped a beat as Deaglan emerged in a fog of steam with a towel slung low around his hips. Pearls of water clung to his skin, and the black ink on his tattoos was vibrant over his muscled shoulder, chest, and arms. He flicked off the light, then strode across the room toward me.

God, there wasn't an ounce of uncertainty in his stride.

Deaglan was a work of art. A sculpture I'd been lucky enough to explore every crevice, hill, and valley. Granite hills and rock valleys.

I sighed, hugging the pillow closer and waiting with bated breath for him to come back to bed.

I didn't have to work today, so I kind of hoped he'd do that thing with his tongue again.

My body quivered and I bit my lower lip.

He sat on the edge of the mattress, and without a single glance my way, he said, "Pet, I have shit to do."

I tensed.

Then the daisy heads snapped off and the velvet petals shriveled up in my belly.

Uh, what?

Suddenly, that hot, raspy Irish accent didn't sound so hot.

Okay, I wasn't expecting a proposal or anything, not by a long shot, but I did expect a morning kiss and a possible number exchange for a possible second date. Or rather, first date.

He didn't even pretend like he'd call.

God, was I that naïve?

I sat up, taking the sheet with me. "Excuse me?"

He bent, picked up his cargo pants from the floor and tugged them on.

"I called a cab. It'll be here any second."

My heart slammed into my chest. He called me a cab? Was I supposed to think this was okay because he called me a cab?

Because it wasn't. It totally wasn't.

There was a brief honk outside.

Oh. My. God.

Jesus, when did he call me a cab? When he had his finger in my ass during the last throes of passion?

Deaglan walked shirtless across the room, if you could call it a room because it was more like a garage in a warehouse or something. He actually had a motorcycle parked beside the couch.

He stopped to grab his wallet off the black leather armchair next to the matching black leather couch, then opened the steel door and disappeared outside.

The tingling, heated skin and euphoria of our sexual escapades for the last seven hours burst like a dart to a water balloon.

What a complete dick. I didn't even know how to react as I sat frozen in bed with disbelief.

I realized that despite our conversation we had sitting on the picnic table at the charity event last night, I had no idea who Deaglan was. I didn't even know his last name or what he did for a living.

Not that it mattered any longer.

I didn't want to know.

All I wanted was to get out of here and never see this asshole again.

Tossing back the sheet, I scrambled out of bed before Mr. Insensitive returned.

I found my knee-length, yellow sundress under the bed next to one of my light blue sandals with the pink soles. My strapless bra was on the seat of his bike and I found my other sandal next to the front tire.

My eyes frantically darted around for my white lace thong.

Shit. Where did I put it? Or rather, where had Deaglan ripped it off? I couldn't remember anything except his hands sliding up under my dress as he lifted me off my feet and shoved me against the wall.

Then it was a frenzy of mouths and hands and body parts.

My cheeks heated thinking about it, and my sex clenched.

Damn it. I so hated myself right now.

I saw my robin egg blue purse on the armchair, and I walked over, grabbed it and hitched it over my shoulder.

I scanned the garage one last time for my white thong, but it was nowhere to be found. Lost along with my dignity.

What had I been thinking going home with a guy like him? He was hot. Sexy as hell, and I'd noticed the abundance of girls gaping at him last night.

But I liked that he walked right up to me and introduced himself.

He'd been a little cagey, but sweet, playful and definitely cocky. And physically, the complete opposite of my ex with his tattoos and ruggedness.

He didn't hesitate to introduce me to his friends, Connor and Deck, who also wore cargo pants and looked badass, and their wives, Alina and Georgie, who were super nice.

Georgie was hilarious, had pink-streaked hair, owned two coffee shops, and was five months pregnant. Alina was a photographer, sweet and also pregnant. Alina and Connor had a little girl, Skye, who sat on the picnic table beside me and drank her apple juice while a barn cat perched on her lap. She talked about Simon, her cat, that slept with her every night until she fell asleep and then trotted off to her daddy. Then she whispered that her daddy didn't like orange cats, but Simon liked him anyway.

I discovered Georgie is Connor's sister and that they are friends with Chess and Tristan Mason, who had opened the Treasure Children's Center for abused kids.

I walked across the cement floor toward the door, then stopped when Deaglan appeared, blocking the doorway and my escape.

A flash of heat warmed my skin at the thought of what this guy must think of me. Not that I should care, but I did because I didn't normally do this sort of thing and he probably thought I did. And yeah, even after two years of building myself back up, I still had those haunting uncertainties. The tight little ball I'd shoved in the far corners of my mind unraveling and making me doubt myself.

I straightened my spine and crumpled up the ball.

"Cab will take you wherever you need to go," Deaglan said as he shoved his wallet in the back pocket of his cargo pants.

What I felt like saying was "go fuck yourself," but instead I said, "Thanks."

I clutched the shoulder strap of my purse so hard the leather crackled.

Don't take it out on the purse.

He stepped closer, and I knew he was about to touch me. What I didn't know was whether it was to kiss me or toss me over his shoulder and throw me out. I was leaning toward the latter with the way things were going and I wasn't about to give him the opportunity.

"See ya," I said, hoping he'd move out of the way.

He didn't.

Shit.

I stepped past him and my body brushed against his. Then, with as much dignity as I could muster, I walked out the door.

Unfortunately, Deaglan followed with his hand on the small of my back.

I approached the cab idling in the alley. I didn't know where we were, but there was no chance in hell I was taking a cab he paid for.

He opened the passenger side door, but before I could escape, his fingers curled around my wrist. "Eva...."

"Don't," I said quietly.

He hesitated a second, then nodded and released me.

I slid onto the tattered vinyl seat and ignored him as I took my cell out of my purse and tapped on the screen.

Deaglan stood there a second before closing the door.

"Where to, Miss?" the driver asked.

"Uh, if you could wait a second, please." I glanced out the side window and waited until Deaglan disappeared into his place.

I opened my door. "You can keep whatever he paid you. I don't need the ride. Thanks anyway." I'd call Uber as soon as I was far enough away from Deaglan's place.

"You sure? It's not the safest area, Miss," the cab driver said, looking in the rearview.

I smiled. "I'm sure." Besides, I carried pepper spray in my purse.

I shut the door and walked down the alley as the cab sped away.

Deaglan could kiss my ass.

One

Eva

"MR. JOHNSON. PLEASE, YOU NEED TO TAKE YOUR PILLS," I urged, holding out the white cup with the four, multicolored pills at the bottom.

My smile fake.

My control teetering.

And my emotions like the metal ball in a pinball machine. Because the cab driver had been right two days ago. The area hadn't been safe for a woman alone at six in the morning wearing a sundress. And my pepper spray didn't do me any good when it was in my purse. The purse the guy was trying to grab.

"Get that poison out of my face." Mr. Johnson waved his hand and it knocked the cup from my hand and the pills scattered across the floor.

Patience, Eva. Mr. Johnson is a sweet old man who is just scared.

This wasn't Mr. Johnson's first time in the Emergency Room. It was his fourth in the last seven months, mostly because of his diabetes, but six months ago he broke his hip after falling off his grandson's skateboard. What an eighty-four-year-old was doing on a skateboard, I had no idea. Mr. Johnson had been uncooperative then and even more so now. But today he wasn't here for his hip or his diabetes.

He was here because his wife called an ambulance when he complained of chest pain. Mr. Johnson insisted he had the strongest "ticker" in this place, and his self-diagnosis was heartburn.

It wasn't heartburn, although I wish it were.

The doctor had ordered more tests and requested him to be seen by the cardiologist.

I liked crotchety old Mr. Johnson because he was refreshingly candid and told you exactly what was on his mind; however, today I wasn't up for it.

What I wanted was to go out with Ally for a glass of wine, then go home and soak in a bath of Epsom salts until my skin turned to tissue paper.

I breathed in a lungful of air and silently prayed for patience. I loved my job. I'd wanted to be a nurse ever since I was five and my mom brought me to the Emergency Room when I broke my arm falling off the top of the playground slide. I'd been terrified thinking my arm was going to fall off, but Nurse Becky sat with me the entire time and explained everything to me. Then she distracted me with games on her phone that she helped me play because I only had one hand. That day, I told my mom I was going to become a nurse and make people feel less scared, too.

I cared about every patient who walked through the hospital doors. And normally, I'd have the patience to easily convince Mr. Johnson to take his pills.

But not today.

The thought of bending to pick up the now scattered pills on the floor had me groaning, because it was going to hurt.

The thug's fist slamming into my ribcage had left bruises.

After he'd grabbed me and punched me, he'd got in my face and I'd gagged on the smell of heavy cigarette smoke clinging to his clothes with the mixture of peppermint and whiskey on his breath. It had happened so fast that my brain didn't register anything except the spider tattoo on the back of his right hand.

He'd tried to grab my purse, and maybe I'd been stupid for refusing to give it to him, but after what I went through with my ex, Curran, I swore to always fight, no matter the consequences.

So, I fought. And I knew a bit about self-defense because I took a course two years ago.

"Eva? You nearly ready?"

I jerked my head to the doorway and saw my friend Ally in her blue scrubs with a stethoscope looped around her neck and blonde hair tied back in a loose ponytail.

We'd met on the first day of nursing school at Ryerson College four years ago. She'd run into biology class ten minutes late wearing pajamas and carrying her anatomy books instead of bio. We were partnered up and somehow, despite our drastic differences, we became best friends.

"Give me ten minutes?" I replied. We were grabbing lunch in the cafeteria.

She frowned, her eyes on my wrist. "What happened to your wrist?"

I glanced down. My shirtsleeve under my scrub top had slid up.

Shit. Purple, yellow, and red marred my skin.

Luckily, my attacker hadn't expected a girl in a flowy yellow sundress to fight back, and at first, I hadn't, because I'd froze in fear as memories were triggered.

It was when he trapped me up against the wall that I'd reacted. I raised my knee into his groin as hard as I could. A ragged cry escaped his throat as he released me, staggering backward, hands to his crotch and bent over in agony.

Then, I ran.

I shoved my sleeve down to cover the thug's handiwork. "It's nothing." I had no intention of explaining why I'd been in an alley in a shit part of town on the weekend.

At least not yet.

I needed a glass of wine, or two, before dropping the bomb on her about the thug in the alley and the explosive sex with Deaglan.

My dignity was still swishing around in the sewer from Deaglan's "I have shit to do, pet," dismissal and wine was a must before spilling to Ally.

Ally's eyes narrowed and her pink glossed lips pursed. It was a sure sign she didn't believe me. "What happened?"

I crouched to pick up the scattered pills. "Honestly, it's nothing."

Ally was fast approaching by the sound of her sneakers squeaking on the linoleum floor.

Mr. Johnson leaned over the side of the bed to peer at me. "You okay?"

"Yes, Mr. Johnson. It's just a bruise," I replied.

Ally crouched to help pick up the pills off the floor. "Did someone grab you?" she whispered.

I reached for a red escapee tablet under the bed and a sharp pain ripped through my ribs.

I winced. Ally noticed.

She grabbed a wayward pill near the bedframe and plopped it in the cup, then stood. "That's it. Let's go. We're talking."

"I'm fine," I insisted.

"You want me to get Dr. Richard?" Ally asked, crossing her arms over her chest.

My eyes snapped to hers. Dr. Richard was the attending on duty. He had that Dr. Sloan from *Grey's Anatomy* arrogance, but with no bedside manners. He also treated nurses like his personal slaves.

It's why I'd said no when he asked me to go on a date several months ago.

And I certainly had no intention of taking my clothes off for him to examine me, and Ally damn well knew it.

"I'm a nurse. I self-diagnosed," I said.

The bed creaked as Mr. Johnson shifted his large frame up onto his side so he could see me better because I was still crouched looking for

4

the last pill. "That Dr. Richard fella needs a hot iron prod up his ass, if you ask me. Don't like him. Not one bit."

Ally laughed.

I grabbed the last pill and put it in the paper cup to dispose of. Unfortunately, the five-second rule did not apply in a hospital.

I stood. "Mr. Johnson, let's worry about you right now." I glared at Ally, attempting to get her to leave. "I'll have to get you some new pills, but please, you need to take them."

He grumbled something about it only being heartburn, then stopped as his eyes swung to Ally and back to me. "I'll take the pills if you let your friend check you over."

Brows lifting, I looked from Mr. Johnson's stern expression to Ally, who was trying hard not to smile by firmly pressing her lips together, but semi-sort of was anyway.

"And you'll take your pills at home, too?" I negotiated.

He snorted with a frown, but there was a twinkle in his eyes. "You drive a hard bargain. Yeah, I'll take 'em, but I don't need them. It's heartburn. Ate some chili. The wife makes it real spicy. And damn, it's the best chili you'll ever eat. I'll have her bring some over." He looked at Ally. "You, too."

I patted his arm. "Okay, Mr. Johnson. You have a deal."

He nodded as if satisfied.

"I'll grab the pills. You finish up." Ally left the room and went to get more pills from the pharmacy while I checked Mr. Johnson's vitals, and he told me how he'd wooed his wife away from the quarterback in grade twelve by bringing her wildflowers and putting them in her locker every day for six months. He said she was more impressed with how he got in her locker than with the flowers because she changed the code to her padlock several times.

When Ally returned, I took the pills and passed them to him. He tossed them back without any water, then said, "Now go with your girl."

I lowered my hand to the bed, squeezing his arm. "Your wife is a lucky woman, Mr. Johnson. The doctor will be by to check you again and sign your release papers."

"About damn time," he grumbled, but there was a twitch at the corner of his mouth and a spark in his green eyes. I bet Mr. Johnson charmed plenty of girls with those eyes and that smirk. And it obviously wasn't just his ability to pick locks that won his wife's heart.

Ally snagged my hand and pulled me down the corridor, then yanked open the storage room door and towed me inside.

She flicked on the light and crossed her arms. "Okay, let's see."

I sighed then lifted my scrub top and long-sleeved shirt. That was when the barrage of sounds emerged from her throat, then a multitude of curses.

"What the..." Curses. "Jesus Christ, Eva, what happened?" Her gaze bounced from my bruised ribs to my face. "Is he back? That pathetic piece of dog shit bastard. We're calling the police. He is going back to jail where he belongs," she said through gritted teeth as she reached into her scrub pants pocket for her cell.

"No. Don't." I lurched forward and grabbed for her arm, instantly regretting it when my ribs protested. But I didn't need the police knocking on Deaglan's door to check my story and to see if he heard or saw anything.

She ignored me and tapped her phone.

"I swear, if you tap one more number, our friendship flatlines," I threatened.

Her head jerked up, finger hovering over the screen. "I'll give you one minute to explain, and then I'll decide whether I take the risk and call the police."

I half smiled. Ally knew I'd never defriend her or my other two friends, Kendra and Charlotte, who were sisters.

She lowered her phone, crossed her arms and cocked her hip. "Okay, let's hear it."

"I was mugged Saturday morning."

Her eyes widened. "What?"

"The guy tried to take my purse and we fought—"

"You fought? Over your purse? Jesus, Eva. Why would you do that? God, did you listen to our self-defense teacher at all?"

Our instructor Evan told us on day one in self-defense class to never let someone take you to a second location, and if they just want your purse, let them take it.

"I kneed him in the crotch."

"You kneed him in the crotch," she repeated.

But first, he'd grabbed my wrist and threw me against the wall, then slammed his fist into my ribcage when I tried to get away. "Ally I'm fine. It's just a few bruises." I could definitely handle a few minor bruises after Curran's fists.

She paced the room, head down, brows pulled together. "Eva, I think we should call the police. Tell them what happened and they can try to find the guy."

"They won't find him. It happened so fast I didn't get a good look at him." But I'd never forget that spider tattoo on the back of his hand and the wretched smell of whisky with peppermint.

She scrunched her nose as she paced the length of the storage room.

Ally and I were complete opposites.

My idea of a perfect day off was reading a good book; hers was going to a local festival, a pub, or a concert.

I liked those things, too, but after several grueling shifts at the hospital, I craved boring. Boring was good. Boring was my Zen and rejuvenated me for the week ahead. Right now, I didn't get boring, though, because on my days off, I worked on fixing the century-old house I'd bought eight months ago with the money my late grandmother left me. But I still couldn't live in it because it was a century old and falling apart...and also why I'd been able to purchase it so cheap.

Ally chewed her plush lower lip with the pink gloss, the same gloss that was now partially rubbed off by the chewing.

"Why the hell didn't you just give him your purse?" she asked.

"Because I have everything in it."

"Everything can be replaced," she said. "It's that neighborhood you live in. I bet the asshole lives on your street. God, you need to move into your house, Eva."

I remained quiet because I wasn't ready to explain that it hadn't been my neighborhood where I rented a house until my house had at least a functioning washroom. It had been Deaglan's, although it could've easily been mine and why Ally made the assumption.

The house I rented was in a shitty part of the city, but within walking distance to the hospital, so very convenient. I'd moved in there after I broke up with Curran.

Ally's rubber soles squeaked on the floor as she ran to me. Her body slammed into mine and she threw her arms around me in a fierce hug. "God, you don't need this shit."

I winced.

"Oh, damn, sorry," she murmured as she withdrew to arm's length. "Next time just hand over your purse, okay?" Tears filled the rims of her eyes. "Seeing bruises on you…. Jesus, I thought that bastard was back."

It had been two years since I'd seen or heard from my ex, Curran Carrick. Of course, one year of that he'd been in jail, but he hadn't tried to contact me at all.

Buzzing erupted in our scrub pockets at the same time.

"Trauma," we said in unison, and ran from the room.

Two hours later, we were at the nurses' station filling out medical records. The trauma had been a car accident involving a husband, wife, and their twelve-year-old son.

According to the paramedics, a transport truck carrying a load of tomato sauce blew a tire and swerved into their car on the highway doing a hundred kilometers an hour.

"My stomach is eating itself," Ally said. "Cafeteria's soggy tuna sandwich is looking really good right now."

Cafeteria specials on Mondays were tuna and chicken salad sandwiches on soggy bread. They were soggy because they sat in plastic wrap in a fridge that was too cold.

"We could go to—"

"Holy smokes," Nurse Greta exclaimed.

The two other nurses behind the desk looked up at whatever Greta gawked at coming in through the emergency sliding doors.

One by one their mouths dropped open and eyes widened.

Looked like lunch would have to wait.

"What is it?" I swung around, picturing someone with an ax in his or her chest or an incoming patient with missing limbs.

It was like an ice storm moved in as everything in my body stilled.

There was no medical emergency.

Not even close.

But it was most certainly an emergency.

Mine.

Two

Eva

HOLY CRAP. DEAGLAN. HERE. IN THE HOSPITAL.

There was no way I could mistake the tattooed badass striding across the waiting room. He commanded a room without doing anything except being in it, even a room full of ill patients who had suddenly stopped moaning and were now watching him.

I clutched the tablet to my chest in a sort of prayer-like fashion as I stared at him across the crowded waiting room, breath locked in my throat. Those daisies that had been beheaded, one by one, two days ago regrew, and quivered in my belly.

He stopped, and his eyes scanned the Emergency Room until they landed on me.

That was when the ice cracked and my body went into complete chaos. Pulse zip lining, heart pounding, and tingles tap dancing across my skin in a mixture of anger, alarm, and desire. A lethal combination.

Everything slammed into me like a tidal wave of lava and I couldn't breathe as I gaped at him.

Shit. I never, *ever* thought I'd see this man again.

I wasn't supposed to see him again.

Damn it, I didn't want to see him again.

Least of all in my workplace with an audience, which included Ally, whom I had not yet told about Deaglan.

"Jesus... that is the sexiest, scariest man I've ever laid eyes on," Rachael, one of the nurses from behind the desk, said.

Greta, who was at least sixty, but looked fifty because she was a yoga fanatic, had great skin, and looked after herself, nodded. "Mmmm, total deliciousness."

"Now, *he* would be one wild ride," Tammy, an admissions nurse, said.

He is a wild ride.

And he knew his way around a woman's body. Knew how to make her beg and scream and make her body quiver.

God, he'd made me beg and scream and quiver too many times to count.

Ally shifted closer and whispered, "Uh, why is he staring at you? It's like he's eye fucking you right here on the desk."

I didn't move. Or speak. I lost the ability to do anything but stare for those ten seconds it took Deaglan to make his way toward me.

"Wait a sec," Ally said. "Are you holding out on me? Do you know this hottie? 'Cause he sure as hell looks like he knows you."

I swallowed, and it felt as if I had a stethoscope lodged in my throat. "He's..." A man I fucked. "Uh, well he's an acquaintance. Kind-a-sorta." An acquaintance who had his finger in my ass while his tongue did all sorts of things to my pussy.

"That man isn't looking at you like he's just an acquaintance," Ally said, just before Deaglan halted in front of me.

I forced a smile, despite my urge to spin around and run like hell.

He didn't waste any time as he said, "We need to talk. In private."

We need to talk? In private?

Was he for real? No, "Hey, Eva. How are you?" Not even a simple "Hey."

Was he insane? Or just a completely insensitive asshole?

Okay. This is my workplace. Be professional. Be polite.

My hands curled into fists around the tablet as I forced out, "Sir, is there something I can help you with?"

"Sir?" His brows rose and he smirked, and the smirk was just as annoyingly sexy as I remembered. "Cute."

No, not sexy.

He. Is. Not. Sexy.

This guy kicked me out, then pretty much shut and locked the door behind me. The only thing he did that was nice was call me a cab and pay for it, but really that didn't count because it was all for his benefit to get rid of me.

God, he made me feel... well... like garbage, and I had sworn after Curran to never let another man make me feel that way. I couldn't completely blame him because I'd gone home with him knowing full well that it was a one-night stand.

And I'd had amazing, mind-blowing sex. And that sex had been all about me. He'd made it all about me.

What pissed me off was that despite him kicking me out of his bed, Deaglan still did it for me.

That confidence. The way he commanded a room. How he stands with his legs braced, yet still appears casual.

That smirk.

Those piercing, sun-streaked, ocean eyes.

I never thought I'd like tattoos on a guy, but I'd spent an hour tracing them with the tip of my fingers. When I asked if any of them meant anything, he flipped me onto my back and proceeded to kiss me, which led to him sliding inside me, and I forgot about the question.

Then, it ended.

Like a mirror shattering, so had everything I'd liked about him.

God, what had I been thinking going home with him?

Reality was... I hadn't. I'd had a few drinks, but was far from intoxicated. No, I'd been drunk on him.

"We need to talk," he repeated.

I raised my chin and met his eyes that were now more green than blue, with amber mixed in. "I don't have anything to talk to you about."

"It's not a request, pet."

Pet? Was he for real? Okay, admittedly, I'd thought it was cute with his sexy Irish accent, but I certainly didn't now.

I wanted to tell him to go screw himself. But I didn't. I was still working to yank off that blanket that smothered me with self-doubt.

I cleared my throat. "Sorry, but I'm busy. As you can see, the Emergency Room is swamped so you'll have to wait your turn. One of the other nurses can take your information and you'll be called." Then, I straightened my shoulders and added. "It's triage. That means—"

"I know what triage means," he interrupted.

"Great. It should only be a few hours, so if you'd like to have a seat."

I glanced at my tablet, pretending to read a patient's file, but the words were a jumbled mess of letters because there was no way I could concentrate with that deep, earthy scent wafting around me.

His voice softened, "I'm not leaving until we talk, Eva."

Ally cleared her throat and shifted closer, so she could, not so subtly, kick my foot. I thought she wanted me to introduce her, which I was so *not* doing.

"Rachael," I said to the pretty blonde nurse who would love nothing better than to assist Deaglan. "Do you mind helping, Mr...." I raised my brows, waiting for him to offer his last name.

He didn't.

Deaglan shifted closer. "I asked twice. I'm not doing it again. If you want to do this here, we'll do this here." *Oh, shit.* "Why the fuck didn't you take the cab?"

I stiffened. How the hell did he know I didn't take the cab? I saw his door shut. It was a garage, so he had no windows. And I'd made sure he'd gone into his place before I hopped out of the cab.

"I felt like walking," I said.

"Wait. What are you talking about?" Ally asked.

His jaw clenched. "You felt like walking." I nodded, despite the fact it wasn't a question. "At five in the morning in an alley you know shit about?"

"It was a nice morning."

That seemed to really piss him off as his brows lowered over his hard eyes. "It was a nice morning," he repeated then, "Fuckin' stupid."

I flinched and my stomach twisted. He was right; it had been stupid, but I'd been humiliated. Hurt. My pride left swishing around in the sewers, and taking a cab he had paid for after he'd kicked me out made me feel worse about myself.

Ally nudged me with her elbow. "What's he talking about?"

"I'll, uh, tell you later," I whispered out the side of my mouth, while my gaze remained on Deaglan.

I had a feeling he wasn't accustomed to being waved off like a pesky fly and wouldn't take to it well.

Deaglan had been intense, but still playful, especially with the kids, when we'd met. He'd charmed me with his smirk, and easygoing laughter.

But there was no laughter in Deaglan now. No charm. And I was pretty sure any kids would run for their lives.

"Some guy chased you," he ground out.

My eyes widened and my mouth dropped open. "You know?"

"Yeah, I know."

"But how do you know?"

"I don't like my business being everyone else's, babe. You need to find us a place to talk or I will."

I had no idea how he knew, but he did, and I suspected he was here because he felt guilty I was mugged outside his place. Well, he didn't have to be. It wasn't his fault I didn't take the cab. "There's nothing to say." Then I added, "And since you don't appear to be ill or injured, you need to leave."

Ally stepped toward the desk and reached over the counter for the phone. "Do you want me to call security?"

Deaglan's eyes sliced to her. "Don't fuckin' move, sugar." Her hand stilled on the phone. "Your girl was chased by some lowlife outside my place Saturday morning and she thinks it's cool not to tell me this shit. I had to fuckin' watch it happen fifty-nine hours after the fact."

He watched it? How did he watch it happen?

Ally's eyes snapped to me. "You said you were attacked outside your place."

I looked at Ally and bit my lip. "I, uh… didn't actually say where it happened."

Her eyes narrowed before popping open with realization. "You were with him. Holy shit. You were with him? Like *with him* with him. You had sex with *him*," Ally finally concluded.

Oh. My. God.

My face felt as if it was being held over a hot stove. I shifted my feet, hands gripping the tablet as I glared daggers at Deaglan, who didn't look at all affected by the fact he'd just shared with Ally and three other nurses that I had slept at his place. Well, slept was the wrong word. There hadn't been any sleeping, although there'd been napping, albeit briefly.

"I can't believe you didn't tell me," Ally continued.

"You were away for the weekend and honestly, it wasn't worth telling."

Deaglan snorted, shaking his head. "Babe."

It was so worth telling, but I was still processing the fact that I'd gone home with a guy I'd had one conversation with, had the best sex I'd ever had in my life before he called me a cab and said he had shit to do.

So, I hadn't shared the embarrassing info with Ally. I'd been waiting for the embarrassment to simmer with the assistance of mind-numbing wine.

He placed his hand on the edge of my tablet, plucked it from my hands and tossed it on the counter.

"We're talking," he said. "You have one second before I throw you over my shoulder and find a room for us to have this conversation."

I raised my chin and straightened my spine.

"One." His fingers wrapped around my wrist.

The second his fingers tightened on the bruises, I inhaled a sharp breath.

He frowned and immediately loosened his hold. His gaze sliced to my arm.

He was gentle as he pushed up my sleeve. "What the fuck…"

Then everything in him went explosive. Clenched jaw. Hard, narrowed eyes. Body a missile.

A grenade with the pin pulled.

And it was scary. He was scary. I didn't pretend to know Deaglan, but I hadn't been scared of him the other night.

It was eerie how everything went silent. No phones rang. No patients moaned. All I heard was my heart slamming into my ribcage and his dangerously ragged breath.

"Christ," he ground out. "Didn't see that."

He looked genuinely upset, concerned eyes scanning the bruises then moving to my face. "Didn't see that," he repeated.

No matter what his reaction was two days ago, Deaglan was protective. I'd witnessed it in the way he'd acted at the charity event. It was in how his body shielded mine when we walked to his car and then from the car into his place. How he stayed close, his hand settled on the small of my back. How he helped me onto the top of the picnic table, and when he noticed I was uncomfortable with Georgie's questions about my love life, he'd changed the subject.

"I'm fine, Deaglan. And I really need to get back to work." Or rather, go for lunch, although, I wasn't sure I could stomach eating anything.

He inhaled a long, ragged breath, his eyes remaining fixated on my wrist and his thumb lightly brushing back and forth over the bruises.

He looked up. "Kane," he said.

"Huh?"

"My last name. It's Kane."

Oh. I slid my hand from his grasp and my fingers curled on the hem of my sleeve, pulling it down to cover the thug's handiwork.

I glanced at Rachael, Greta, Tammy, and then Ally, all of whom raptly watched the exchange.

I sighed, shoulders slumping. Privacy was probably a good idea, and I had a feeling the only way to get rid of him was to give him five minutes.

"Room 101 is free," I said.

"Which way?" Deaglan asked.

"This way," I said, nodding to the corridor on the right.

"You okay alone with him?" Ally asked, snagging my sleeve.

Deaglan raised his brows and smirked. I groaned, because I knew what was coming. "Sugar, your girl came back to my place in the middle of the night knowing shit about me. If I wanted to hurt her, I would've by now." Deaglan interlocked his fingers with mine and tugged me in next to him. "She's safe. She'll always be safe with me."

Three

Eva

DEAGLAN'S TOE-SCUFFED COMBAT BOOTS THUMPED STEADILY ON THE hospital linoleum floors, matching the drum of my heartbeat.

We passed numerous patients, nurses, and doctors, and every single one of them gawked at Deaglan as we passed. I probably would've, too. A tattooed, commando badass striding through the hospital drew attention.

I frowned when I noticed Mrs. Hendy, an elderly patient the doctor had sent for radiographs three hours ago, on a gurney in the middle of the corridor.

I pulled free of Deaglan's grasp and approached the gurney.

"Mrs. Hendy. Is everything okay? Is a doctor looking after—"

"Nope." Deaglan's arm hooked my waist.

I stumbled into him, and he propelled me forward down the hall. "But—"

"I don't care. She's not your problem."

I glared at him. "Every patient who walks through the emergency doors of this hospital is my problem. My responsibility."

"Then, right now… I'm your problem."

"Well, I don't look after the emotionally volatile patients," I retorted. "That's the fifth floor."

He smirked, gaze briefly shifting to me as we walked. "You have no idea." Then he tilted his head and drawled, "The other night wasn't even close to my volatile, babe."

My heart skipped a beat, but before I could do the sensible thing and run like hell, he pulled me inside room 101 and shut the door.

The room had a single hospital bed, a window with orange-colored, flowered curtains, a heart monitor machine, and intravenous stand. There was a small bathroom behind the door and a yellow plastic chair beside the bed and nightstand. A television hung on the wall in the corner.

I immediately moved away from him and stood on the far side of the bed, which maybe wasn't optimal because I was trapped, but it was the farthest I could get without climbing out the window.

"Why are you here, Deaglan?"

He leaned against the door and crossed his arms over his broad chest. "A guy chased you outside my place. Now I'm finding out he did more than just chase you. He put bruises on you. Where the hell else would I be?"

"Two and a half days ago. And it was a block away from your place and had nothing to do with you."

"You're not hearing me, Eva. You were *attacked* outside my place, so yeah, it has something to do with me."

"And you're not hearing me. A random mugging isn't your problem," I reiterated.

"You have my tongue on your pussy?" I stiffened as heat blazed in my cheeks. "Have my cock inside you? Were you screaming my name as you came?"

"That has nothing to do with anything," I stammered. God, did that even make sense?

He shook his head as his chin dipped. "Jesus."

He needed to leave before I died of humiliation. "Listen, I

appreciate your concern, thank you for popping in, but as you can see, I'm a nurse and can look after a few bruises."

"This is way more than popping in, babe."

I kept going before I lost my nerve, although I avoided meeting his eyes. "You're not responsible for what happened. So you can walk away with a clear conscious."

"I watched you being chased by some guy fifty-nine hours after the fact," he ground out. "Fifty-fuckin'-nine."

"I got away." I shivered, thinking about how close the mugger was to catching me again.

He pushed off the door and stalked toward me. "And what I saw and what you didn't because you were running, was the knife he pulled from his boot when he ran after you. How he nearly caught you before you ran into the street and he stopped."

The guy had a knife? I had no idea he had a knife. Because he hadn't had it in his hand before I ran.

Deaglan drew close.

I inched backward, but only managed one step before my spine hit the wall.

He stopped in front of me.

I swallowed. "I don't understand. How do you know all this?"

"Security cameras. I have five in the alley."

"Cameras?" That wasn't normal. I understood having a security camera outside your door, but up and down the alley? Was that even legal?

"I deal with some not-so-nice people, Eva. I also don't live in Toronto, so I can keep an eye on things when I'm not here. I used to stay with friends, but they have a kid now, another one on the way, and I don't want my bad shit touching them."

My chest tightened at the idea that Deaglan was involved with not-so-nice people. I didn't need a repeat of being around people like Curran.

God, Deaglan was turning into an epic mistake.

I snagged my lower lip with my teeth, and his eyes flicked to my mouth. He frowned, but his eyes smoldered.

I quickly released it. "So, umm, what *shit* are we talking about? Are you a drug dealer or something?"

He snorted. "I don't deal drugs, Eva. Don't touch them."

I exhaled a breath. I couldn't have been that wrong about him, could I? Yeah, I totally could have. I'd been wrong about my ex. Epically wrong.

"The low-life who attacked you, did he say anything?" he asked.

I shook my head. "No. He wanted my purse."

"I need to know exactly what happened."

"It was a mugging, Deaglan. He grabbed me and threw me against the wall and tried to take my purse." I avoided the part where he slammed his fist into my ribcage so hard I couldn't breathe. "I got away. Nothing happened."

"That's where you're wrong. Something did happen. You have bruises saying it happened. He attacked you where my security cameras failed to record, meaning he knew their exact location, so he'd been in my alley a while checking it out. The only reason my cameras caught him was you got away and he ran after you, and he failed to avoid my cameras because he was more concerned about catching you."

I remained silent, chewing my lower lip as I tried to process what that meant. But it wasn't processing. Not really. Because I couldn't process when he stood so close.

"Then maybe he's an experienced mugger."

"He's experienced, babe. What I don't know is why he was there. And why he'd go after you."

Because I was a magnet for bad guys.

Deaglan stepped to the side and looked out the window. The sun hit the side of his face and I saw the pencil-thin scar on the right side of his jaw. I'd asked how he got it the other night while we lay in bed, but he kissed me instead of answering.

"It was just a mugging, Deaglan," I said quietly.

He turned to look at me. "Outside my place."

"Yeah, but it could've happened anywhere."

"It wasn't anywhere. It was outside my place after you writhed underneath me, screaming my name. After I tasted you and had your sweet mouth around my cock."

I glanced away and walked toward the door, my insides quivering at the memory. "Deaglan, I appreciate your concern, but really, I'm fine, and I have to get back to work."

"Gut says it wasn't random, Eva."

I curled my fingers around the door handle, but I didn't open it. "Maybe your gut is wrong," I said.

I heard his approach, his booted feet slow and deliberate. "It's never fuckin' wrong. I'd be dead if my gut steered me wrong."

I released the door handle and turned, crossing my arms over my chest. "So, you're saying, or your gut is saying, it wasn't random, and he was one of those not-so-nice people you deal with?" I said.

He stopped in front of me, his jaw tight, eyes hard, and there was a slight flicker of unease in them before it washed away. "Yes."

Epic mistake had turned into an Academy Award blockbuster mistake. *Way to go, Eva.*

I glared at him. "Then why would you take me to your place knowing you have not-so-nice people after you?" But really, I was asking myself why I went with him.

"I flew in from Ireland the day before we met. I didn't know anyone was watching my place until today when I replayed the security footage." He leaned in so his arm bridged my head. "And I took you to my place because I knew you were rare the moment I saw you... and I told you I wanted rare." Despite not wanting to like that, I totally did. "It was that stupid goat." My brows lowered. What? "I saw you by the barn patting Rocket's muzzle. You were smiling and talking to the goat like he was a friend of yours."

The three-legged goat, Rocket, was one of the numerous rescued animals at the Treasured Children's Centre. It was a place that helped homeless kids who had suffered traumatic events, and the animals were there to help them. But it went both ways because the kids helped the animals heal, too. My friend Charlotte had brought them Rocket after a farmer had left him dangling by his leg in a fence.

"When you stopped petting him and walked away, he raced after you, then head bumped you in the ass and you went flying."

He had. I had. Rocket had crawled under the fence and I'd heard his little hooves, but was too late to do anything before his head hit my butt and I landed on all fours on the ground.

"You laughed. Wearing those light-blue sandals with the pink soles, and in that sexy, yellow sundress, you laughed, even though the goat put you on your ass."

I sagged against the door. He remembered the pink soles of my shoes?

"I wasn't going to approach you. I saw you weren't a woman to take home just once, because that's what I do, Eva. I'm not interested in anything more. But seeing you chew your bottom lip while you watched me play football. Uncrossing and crossing those long-as-fuck legs...." I hadn't noticed him watching me. Not once had I seen him look in my direction. "Not showy or seductive, but Christ, you were all kinds of sexy. And I wanted to know more about you."

I opened my mouth to say something, although I wasn't sure what, when he leaned closer, and the heat of his body seeped into me. Goosebumps rose and those damn velvet petals fluttered in my belly.

His voice low and raspy, he said, "And fuck, you were into me."

For several seconds neither of us said anything. He didn't touch me, and yet it felt as if his entire body was against mine.

I had been into him. Really into him, and it had been two years since I had felt anything for a man.

I slowly turned and raised my chin, eyes meeting his, and the only thing I could say was, "My friend Charlotte rescued Rocket. He is the sweetest."

His mouth twitched. "Don't say that around Kai. He wants that goat on a spit for jumping on the hood of his car."

I had no idea who Kai was, and right now, I didn't care. I leaned against the door for support as my knees trembled. I didn't know exactly how to take everything he had just said.

God, he thought I was sexy. I didn't care what kind of sexy. Any was good with me because I'd never really seen myself as sexy.

What sat like tar in the pit of my stomach was how he had reacted to me the next morning. "You called me a cab before I was out of bed and still throbbing from you inside me."

He tensed. "I had shit to do."

Oh. My. God. Everything he'd just said about me blew up into a million particles, and I was back to knowing this guy was a jerk. "I get that, Deaglan. I had shit to do, too." Like go home and do a week's worth of laundry. "But having a cab at your door before a girl barely has her eyes open is not cool." But the truth was, even if I had the choice to do it all over again, I'd have still gone home with Deaglan. I'd just have left before he called me a cab. "I think we should forget this ever happened and go our separate ways and chalk it up to a fun night."

"I'm not going to forget sliding inside you and tasting your pussy, Eva."

Tingles flared between my legs. "God, I really don't like you."

"I have scrapes on my back that prove otherwise."

I glared, but on the inside, it was complete chaos as the memory of him above me, hair falling in front of his eyes, my fingernails digging into his back as he drove into me, assailed every sense that I had.

"I was drunk and didn't know what I was doing," I blurted.

"Babe, you had two-and-a-half beers in three hours." God, he knew how much I drank? "You were far from drunk. And if you were, you wouldn't have been in my bed."

"Why not?"

"I may only fuck a woman once, but I'm never with a woman who doesn't know what she's doing."

I knew exactly what I'd been doing when I got into his car. What I didn't know was what I was doing right now by having this conversation. "Are we finished here?"

"Fuck no." He pushed off the door. "I'm telling you, the mugging wasn't random, Eva. It happened outside my place and the guy was experienced. That means it's my shit and my shit is bad, so you need to get this, when I tell you that if the guy wanted your purse, he wanted to know who you were."

"But he didn't get my purse, so he doesn't know."

"Did he follow you home?"

I stiffened. "I hailed a cab afterward."

"Was the cab followed?"

Shit. "I wasn't exactly thinking that a guy trying to steal my money would hop in a cab and follow me, Deaglan."

"If it was important enough, he'd have followed you. What I don't know is if it was, but I plan on finding out."

I swallowed. "Uh, so what are you going to do?"

"I'm going to find out who the fuck he is."

"How do you expect to do that? I can't give you anything more than he smelled like whiskey and peppermint and had a tattoo of a spider on his hand."

"Which hand?"

"Right. On the back." I'd noticed it when he grabbed my purse.

"I'll find him," he repeated.

"Are you going to search the city for a man with a spider tattoo on his hand and smells like peppermint?"

"I'm good at what I do, babe."

I was uncertain if I wanted the answer, but I asked anyway. "And what exactly do you do?"

"Among other things, I find people."

I didn't like that answer. "So, you're like a detective?" I asked.

25

He slowly formed a smirk. "Guess you could say I have that skill."

"What are you going to do when you find him? Hand him over to the police? Because I won't be able to pick him out of a lineup."

"There won't be a lineup," he said. "I'll have a chat with him."

Oh. My eyes widened. *Oh.*

He didn't have to spell it out for me what a *chat* meant.

What did I expect from a commando guy like Deaglan? He lived in a garage. Had security cameras in the alley, and he wasn't clear about what he did for a living.

"Babe, did he scare you?"

"Yeah."

"Did he put bruises on you?"

"Yes."

"Did he pull a knife on you?"

"I didn't see..."—because I was too busy running for my life—"but, Deaglan, I'm fine and he didn't get my purse."

"No one fuckin' assaults a woman and walks away from it." His voice was harsh and gritty as he bit out the words. "And if this guy was in my alley because of me, then you need to understand this, Eva." His voice lowered. "He isn't a good guy. Far from it. And he sure as hell didn't attack you because of a few bucks."

Okay, that scared me a little. Or, maybe a lot.

I'd lived with fear a long time after I escaped Curran and I'd conquered it. Or, at least, I'd packaged it up in a little ball and shoved it into the far crevices of my mind.

I wasn't that girl anymore and I learned to stand up for myself.

But as he towered over me, I was hit with a hint of fear mixed with desire, and the two emotions didn't go well together. They clashed, sending my body into a tornado of hot and cold.

Damn it, I do not like him.

And then to make my inner battle more debilitating, he cupped my chin and raised my head, so our eyes locked. It was gentle and yet, there was firmness to his touch, too.

He bent toward me like he was going to kiss me. "That fear in you, Eva. I'm erasing that."

My breath locked.

A loud vibration erupted from his pocket, and Deaglan's hand dropped and he pushed away from me.

He took his phone from his back pants pocket, hit a button then placed it to his ear.

"Deck." He tensed and glanced at me. "Yeah. Okay." He paused. "On my way."

Ending the call, he slipped his phone back in his pocket. "I need to take off. What time are you off?"

"Why?"

"I'll drive you home. Vic will meet us there."

I had no clue who Vic was or why he'd meet us at my place, but I didn't ask. "I live five minutes away. A walking five minutes."

"And you were attacked thirty seconds from my door."

True, but I knew these streets.

"Eva, whether you like it or not, you're on my radar until I find who attacked you." On his radar? "That means we're doing something about that house you live in. There's no security system and the doors are fuckin' cardboard."

My mouth gaped. "How do you know there's no security system? Jesus, how do you know where I live? And that the doors are thin? How do you know any of this?" A tremor went through me, and it wasn't a good tremor.

"You ask too many questions."

I huffed.

"You do that when I'm fucking you next time, I'll gag you."

A small squeak escaped.

"I'll text you," he said and strode down the hall.

He didn't have my cell number and there was no way he could get it. I paid to have it unlisted ever since Curran. It was under my mother's maiden name, Brighton.

"I don't need you to pick me up." Then I shouted, "And I'm not having sex with you again."

His response was a chuckle. A goddamn chuckle.

Mine was mortification when I realized everyone in the corridor stared at me, including Dr. Richard.

Four

Eva

H E HAD MY CELL NUMBER.

And he used it. Several times.

He also hadn't been nice about it.

So, I ignored it several times.

I also received a text from Greta informing me that "the hottie" was at the hospital looking for me. She'd told him I'd left for the day, which I had because I'd left early in order to avoid him. If he discovered my cell number and where I lived, I was pretty sure he'd find out what time my shift ended.

I'd left the hospital through the side door on Shooter Street and texted Ally that I'd meet her at the pub.

"Tell me everything," Ally said, the second she arrived and slid into our usual booth at O'Sullivan's, which happened to be an Irish pub.

We'd been coming here ever since we were hired at St. Micks Hospital and I wasn't about to change things because of some Irish sex god I couldn't get out of my head.

Two glasses of red wine slid onto the table. "Thanks, Evan." I smiled up at him.

The bartender taught self-defense Wednesday evenings at the local community center and had been our instructor.

"You girls eating tonight? Dana called in sick, so I can take your order." The pub had a packed lunch and after-work crowd, but on a Tuesday evening it was quiet.

"No, thanks," I said, smiling. "I ate at the hospital. Pure liquid diet tonight." I required mind-numbing in order to forget the Irish stud with sexy bedroom hair and a sculpted tatted body who said I was rare and all kinds of sexy.

"Maybe some munchies? To soak up some of the pure alcohol," Ally said.

"You got it," Evan said, and headed back behind the bar.

I raised my glass and sipped, at the same time my phone vibrated in my purse.

I ignored it, like I had for the last hour. The first text from Deaglan was him asking what time I was off. The second was "Where are you?"

The third text was a little more... well, concerning.

You don't want to ignore me.

I sipped again.

Why couldn't I get him out of my head, damn it?

I sipped again.

It wasn't normal the way my belly flipped whenever he was near.

Chug.

God, he didn't even have to be near. Or in the general vicinity. I just had to think about him and there was a shift in my inner core. But I was blaming some of that on fear since that, too, swirled inside me after he'd said the part about dealing with the "not-so-good guys." Or was it not-so-nice guys?

I took another long swallow then set my glass on the table. It was half gone, and when I looked at Ally, she was watching me with a bewildered look on her face.

"Okay, what the hell is going on?" Ally asked. "I saw you run out of the hospital like the angry nuns were chasing you."

The angry nuns were not actually nuns. They're the hospital board members who are complete pricks to the staff and more concerned about the politics of the hospital than the patients.

"Deaglan was coming to pick me up."

"For a date?"

I laughed. "Uh... no. He doesn't date."

Her brows lifted. "You sure about that? He acted like he was into you."

"Trust me, he's not into me." *Anymore.* I was pretty sure he had been the other night, but in the morning, not so much, and now... well, I was more like his guilty conscience. I was "on his radar" until he found the guy who attacked me because he thought it had to do with him.

"Your voice rose an octave and your cheeks turned radish red."

"My cheeks didn't turn radish red."

She grinned. "Ah, yeah, babe, they did."

Shit.

"So, where did you meet this tattooed, combat-boot wearing hottie?"

I slowly turned my glass between my hands. "At the Treasured Children's Center charity barbecue." Ally didn't go because she went to Charlotte's farm up north with Kendra.

"That guy was at a children's charity? He looks like he walked out of a Navy SEAL biker magazine." She leaned forward, palms on the table. "I swear, I came a little when I heard him speak in that Irish accent."

I rolled my eyes. "There is no such thing as a Navy SEAL biker magazine."

She shrugged. "But there could be, and if there was, he'd be on the front cover sitting astride a bike."

"Ten speed or tricycle?"

She laughed. "Very funny. It would be one of those cruising bikes where the guy's legs are forward, long handlebars, and an abundance of black and chrome that's perfect for fucking on."

"He has one of those."

Her eyes widened. "Really?"

I nodded. "Inside his place. Next to his couch."

"Damn, did you do it on his bik—"

"Ally." I kicked her leg under the table as Evan slid a bowl of peanuts and pretzels on the table.

I cleared my throat and smiled. "Uh, thanks, Evan."

As soon as he walked away, Ally was back onto Deaglan. "Tell me everything. What's he like? What does he do for a living? Is he an undercover cop or something? Is that how he knew about the mugging? Are you going to have sex with him again?" She paused a millisecond as she sipped her wine. "You totally should. You haven't been with anyone in two years. You haven't wanted sex in two years and I don't blame you. You needed that time. But maybe a fling with a hottie like him is a good idea. You know, to get back into it."

I sighed, picking up my glass and leaning back in the booth. And this was why I'd waited to tell Ally about him. It was a volley of questions, many of which I didn't know the answer to.

"You finished?" I asked, laughing.

I'd been on a few dates since Curran. Three, to be exact, but none of them had that spark. I'd gone on two dates with Drew, the paramedic, last month hoping the spark would evolve. It didn't.

"I never pictured you with a tattooed, combat-boot wearing guy."

Curran had been the complete opposite of Deaglan. He didn't have any tattoos and wore expensive tailored suits.

I'd met him when he walked into the emergency with blood dripping down his face from a gash in his head. He told me he owned a shipping company and there'd been an accident with one of the container's being lifted onto the ship. I'd only been working at the hospital for a week and was still nervous, but Curran had put me at ease with his polished, easy-going charm. And there'd been sparks, small ones, but enough that when he asked me out for dinner, I'd said yes.

But eventually that polished charm turned tarnished and stained.

Ally grinned. "Does he have a big cock? I bet he has a big cock and knows how to use it."

I choked on my wine. "Jesus, Ally." I glanced over at the bar. Evan poured a beer for the older man sitting on a stool at the far end of the bar. If he heard anything, he didn't make it known he did.

I sipped my wine. "I'm not talking about the size of him or the sex with him."

But after three more glasses of wine, I told her about the sex. Not the details, just that it had been amazing. And the best sex I'd ever had.

Ally was all smiles, until the part where he ordered me a cab before I was even out of bed.

"What? What a total schmuck move. He could've at least waited until you had a pee. Isn't there a rule about that?" Ally said. She slapped her palm on the table. "I should've called security. Better yet, had the angry nuns chase him out of the hospital."

I laughed. I had a feeling security or the angry nuns wouldn't have done much except piss him off.

"So, what? He feels guilty he kicked you right into the arms of a low-life, piece of shit and wants a do-over."

"No. He definitely doesn't want a do-over, and neither do I."

"You could use him for sex." She swigged back the rest of her wine.

"I don't want a fling." I'd just had a one-night stand and that didn't turn out so well.

Ally leaned forward, elbows on the table, wineglass cupped between her hands. "Eva, he obviously cares about you, otherwise he wouldn't have shown up at the hospital. Not many guys after a one-night stand would do that. Bonus points for the amazing sex that was all about you."

But not many guys had security cameras everywhere. Or lived in a garage. Although, he said he didn't live in Toronto.

And Deaglan didn't think I was randomly mugged. He was

adamant it had something to do with him.

I wasn't sure what to think about that yet.

"I don't want to talk about him anymore, Ally." My stomach was in knots from the late lunch tuna on mushy bread. God, that was a lie. My stomach was in knots because of Deaglan.

Ally sat back in her booth. "Did you see the way Nun Helen cocked her hip and flicked her hair in front of Doc Richie Rich in the cafeteria? Do you think they're fucking?" She wiggled her brows.

And this was my friend changing the subject. She was the best. "Oh, gross. That's disgusting." Angry *Nun* Helen was fifty-five, bone thin, with paper-white skin that looked as if it had never seen sunlight.

We laughed, and the Deaglan conversation was now pushed aside and I was on my way to mind-numbing.

Evan brought us another round of drinks and told us to let him know when we needed a cab and he'd flag one down.

We rarely drank like we did tonight, and it was nice Evan was looking out for us.

Before long we were giggling too much from the drinking too much.

That is, until the bell dinged above the pub door and I noticed Evan's spine stiffen and his gaze focus on whoever entered the pub. He set the glass he'd been drying on the bar top and flicked the white rag over his left shoulder.

Then he watched.

It was as if suddenly the air was sucked out of the pub by a high-powered vacuum and I couldn't breathe. The fine hairs on the back of my neck stood at attention like little soldiers saluting, and my skin tingled.

Footsteps approached.

Booted footsteps. And it wasn't just one set; it was two. Or, I thought it was two, but I couldn't be sure because I was kinda seeing double, so maybe I was hearing double, too.

Ally loudly whispered, "Uh-oh," and then, "holy shit, he has a combat-boot wearing friend."

Nope. I wasn't hearing double.

Okay, I could handle this. I could handle him. I was tipsy, but not drunk.

He is just a guy, Eva.

A totally delicious, sexy guy with an attitude who kissed every inch of my body, but he's still just a guy.

In college, I'd survived Professor "intimidator" Graham's anatomy class and did it with an A. But more importantly, I survived my ex-boyfriend Curran Carrick.

I could handle one Deaglan Kane.

The booted feet stopped beside our booth.

I didn't have to look at him to know he was pissed. Even drunk I felt the anger waft off him in molecular heat waves. Maybe I was too drunk to be scared, but for some reason, he didn't scare me.

I inhaled a deep breath, produced a smile, and looked at him. He was a little fuzzy, but the supremely sexy Deaglan was all there in his sculpted magnificence.

I didn't know what I was expecting, considering the guy just did it for me, but I'd hoped after a few glasses of wine my insides wouldn't light up like a meteor the second I laid eyes on him.

They did. And not just any meteor. One that raced toward Earth in a fireball of heat.

"Oh, heeeyyy," I said. "Fancy seein' you here."

His brows lifted. "Fancy?" he repeated.

It wasn't a word I'd normally use, my mom would. "Oh, aren't those fancy shoes?" "Isn't that a fancy house?" She loved the word fancy because she liked fancy things.

My dad did not. He was practical and liked non-fancy things like white dishes, white walls, paper towels without the faded imprints of flowers on them. But he got the paper towel with the imprints because he hadn't been around enough to say otherwise.

"Yep, a fancy pub," I said.

It so wasn't a fancy pub. There were old metal signs nailed to the peeling green wallpaper and every table wobbled. I knew this because Ally and I had sat at every table in this place over the last two years.

I looked at his friend and squinted. "Oh. I know you." He was with that woman with the pink streaks in her hair who owned a couple of coffee shops.

His lip twitched. "Deck," he said.

"Oh, right. Deck."

"I'm Ally," Ally piped in.

Deck's nod was barely a nod, more like a subtle chin dip while his gaze shifted to the bar.

Deaglan glanced over at the bar, too. "Bartender going to give us trouble, babe?"

I leaned forward, sloshing my wine on the table. Deaglan reached out and snagged it from me.

"Bartender?" he asked.

Right. I looked past the two men and saw Evan intently watching us. I turned back to Deaglan. "Are you gonna do something he doesn't like?"

"Depends," he replied.

Shit. I didn't like that answer. "On?"

"On whether you're going to do what I say."

My insides coiled. I didn't like that answer either. I'd never be a man's puppet again. Never.

Ally said, "We've been drinking."

Deck grunted at the same time as Deaglan said, "Got that."

She continued, "So, what she says can't be used against her tomorrow."

I totally loved Ally.

"Let's hit the bar," Deck said to Ally.

She glanced at me to make sure I was good with that and I nodded. She slid out of the booth and followed Deck to the bar.

Deaglan didn't waste time. "You ignored my texts."

I had. I did. "Huh, did you text?"

A mild smirk appeared as his arm draped the back of the booth behind me. "And you ignored my calls."

"Silent feature. I was working." God, he smelled like strawberries dipped in melted chocolate sauce. How was that even possible?

His brows lifted. "Mmm. Or silent treatment."

I sputtered, laughing. "I'm not in high school."

"You're acting like it."

"I'm soooo not."

"You are."

"Not."

"You're drunk."

I am. "How did you find me?"

"I told you, I find people."

"I don't like that," I muttered. I should've shut up then, but I didn't because I babbled when I drank. "You got my number... and you're here. Why are you here when it's a mistake and now it's turned into another mistake and I'm not doing that again and this isn't fair because you are in my head like a stupid..." I gnawed on my lower lip as I thought about it, but I couldn't think of anything logical. Probably because my head was swimming in an ocean of red wine. "...bug."

He coughed with a hint of a grin as if he was trying not to grin. "A bug?"

I nodded. "Yep. You're a bug."

This time he did grin. "Like a ladybug?"

I snorted. "No. Like a cockroach."

He chuckled. "Baby, you're a cute drunk. But you need to go home before you face smack the table."

I index-fingered him in the chest. "I don't do what you have to say. Not anymore and I'm staying."

"I have no idea what you're talking about, but I do know your drunk off your ass." He glanced down at my palm now resting on his chest. I snatched it away.

I pursed my lips and glared, although I wasn't sure how much of a glare it was because squinting made everything disappear, and when everything disappeared, my head spun. "I'm not drunk. I'm tipsy."

"You're drunk and I'm taking you home."

"I'm not going with you, and you know what? I don't like you very much because you didn't let me go pee before I left, and that's a rule, you know. You can't kick a girl out without letting her go pee first." He grinned and that pissed me off even more. I inhaled a deep, ragged breath. "And you're not hot at all." I slurred the outright lie.

"Jesus Christ, how much did you drink?"

"And I still don't like you even if you think I'm sexy and rare."

"You've said that already."

"Don't be obsuse…obus."

"Obtuse?" he offered.

I raised my chin as I glowered at him. "I know big words, you know. Very big and you don't know what they mean." I stretched my arms out wide. "Big ones."

His brows lifted. "Go ahead. Try me."

Wine and words sloshed around in my head as I racked my brain for a medical word. I smiled. "Spheno… palatine ganglion… euralgia."

He chuckled, shaking his head. "Fuck, that's hot."

I scrunched my nose. "You suck."

"I do suck. Hard. Soft. And really, really deep. You know this, pet."

I did. My lower region tweaked, and a moan escaped at the memory. Oh God. I needed to get away. Far, far away. Like down the rabbit hole with Alice and woodland. Woodland? No, Wonderland.

His hand slipped in mine. "Let's go."

My lips quavered as I blew out a puff of air between them. I was tired of arguing and coming up with words and wanted to curl up in a ball and fall into a dreamless sleep.

"Fine," I mumbled. "But only because I want to."

He chuckled.

Deck and Ally appeared beside the booth. "I'll drive Ally home.

She's not far from my place."

Ally smiled ear to ear, her gaze ping-ponging between Deaglan and me. She mouthed the word "fling" before she said, "Deck paid the tab." I opened my mouth to protest, but Ally shook her head. "I wouldn't."

"You can't go with him. You don't even know him," I said to Ally. "We should go together." Because being alone with Deaglan wasn't a good idea in my current, inebriated state.

"Deck's cool," Ally said. I saw Deck's lip tug upward in the corner. "His wife Georgie owns the coffee shop near my house. I go there all the time."

"Oh." Shit.

"Won't find a better guy than Deck, Eva," Deaglan said.

He slid from the booth, taking me with him. My bruised ribs protested, but it wasn't as bad as this morning. Or, it could be the fact that I was feeling no pain.

The room spun as I stood and Deaglan's arm slipped around my waist before I spin-wheeled to the ground. "I think I drank too much."

He made that little *mmm* sound that was delicious and sexy and made my belly flip.

"Hey, Eva, you good?" Evan called while walking toward us.

"Not really," I mumbled as I sagged against Deaglan's side.

"She's good," Deaglan replied.

"Rather hear it from her," Evan replied in a curt tone. His gaze sliced to Deck and Ally and back to me and Deaglan. "Ally says you know these guys?"

I nodded. Whoa, too much head movement. "But I don't like him very much."

"We're fine, Evan. Thanks," Ally said.

Evan moved in and put his hand on my forearm. "Eva?"

Deaglan stiffened, or at least I think he did. I smiled up at Evan. "You're a good guy."

"Thanks, sweetie. You okay leaving with him?"

I peered up at Deaglan, but he wasn't looking at me, he was looking at Evan and it wasn't friendly. "He's trying to find the bad guys."

Evan frowned. "What bad guys?"

"Appreciate your concern, but she's good with me," Deaglan said.

I put my hand to my head as the room violently spun. "I don't feel well."

"Go," Ally said. "I'll talk to Evan and explain."

We walked, or rather, he walked and I stumbled, toward the door. "Let's get you home, baby."

Did he say baby? No. My head was all messed up. "Because you know where I live," I muttered.

"Mmmm, I do. And I didn't like finding out your neighbor was charged with cocaine possession last year. And your other neighbor is a drug dealer."

I knew this, but how did Deaglan know this? "Mrs. Handerlin across the road has dogs that bark for hours when she passes out and leaves them on the back patio, and Mr. Cavendish's cat Ricky, but I call him Garfield, wanders from house to house and meows looking for food, so I give him tuna."

A raspy chuckle and a light squeeze of his fingers on my hip.

Deaglan half-carried me to his car that was illegally parked outside the pub. He helped me onto the plush, black leather seats, then leaned over me, and before I could object, he grabbed the seat belt, drew it across my lap and snapped it in place.

The door clicked closed, and I watched him walk around the front of the car. He folded into the driver seat and the engine purred to life.

I groaned, closing my eyes while leaning my head back as my stomach rolled. "I don't feel that great," I mumbled.

"If you're going to throw up. Tell me," he said.

My eyes flicked open for a second before closing again. "I never throw up." And that would be utterly mortifying in front of him.

But my stomach had other ideas, and five minutes later he yanked over the car and I threw up on the side of the road.

Deaglan held my hair back as I did it.

Five

Eva

I WOKE TO THE SUN FILTERING THROUGH THE WINDOW AND MY HAND TO my head, wondering if it was possible for a head to implode after too much red wine.

What was I thinking last night? I'm a responsible drinker. Mostly.

Girls' nights at Charlotte's farm with Kendra and Ally didn't count because it wasn't in public. The last time I drank like that was when Ally and I graduated nursing school.

Shots of rye whiskey and Beam Me Up Scotties led to singing on stage with a band. I was a horrible singer, but that night I thought I was really good, so good I told Ally I was joining the band.

I pulled the duvet up farther and tucked it under my chin.

My duvet cover was artichoke green with embossed flowers. It came with matching pillowcases with frills and a set of soft cotton sheets. I had an abundance of decorative pillows, and at the end of the bed was a soft white throw blanket that Charlotte bought me last year for my birthday. She'd also bought me a pink vibrator that she'd hid inside the blanket. When I unwrapped it, the vibrator fell to the floor and, to my utter horror, landed at my dad's feet.

I threw back the covers and grit my teeth as my ribs and head protested any and all quick movements. God, how was I going to pull a twelve-hour shift later today?

I swung my legs over the side of the bed and stood.

Crap, too fast.

I glanced down at myself. What was I wearing?

A light blue T-shirt. The one I'd left on the top of the dresser because I never wore it and was planning to add it to the bag of clothes I was donating to the Salvation Army.

Panties. No pajama pants. I always slept in pajama pants, usually the ones with the yellow sunflowers that were way too long and pooled on the floor at my feet.

What happened last night? Did I get undressed? How did I get...

The avalanche of memories crashed down on me. Irish pub. Irish stud. And the words sphenopalatine ganglioneuralgia.

Shit, I'd said that last night. I can't believe I said that.

Deaglan. He drove me home.

Oh God, I threw up in the street while he held my hair back.

Heat blazed my cheeks.

My only consolation was I didn't do it in his car. At least, I didn't think I did.

I remembered waking when he asked about my keys, and then he carried me inside and put me in bed.

Deaglan put me in bed.

I moaned. Shit.

I slipped on my pajama pants that were folded in the bottom drawer of my dresser. I needed a carafe of coffee and an endless jug of water. Although, hooking myself to an intravenous drip sounded awfully tempting.

I opened my bedroom door and the aroma of freshly brewed coffee slammed into me.

My eyes bounced to the kitchen where coffee percolated, and one Deaglan Kane stood in snug, faded jeans and a black T-shirt. Same clothes as last night. At least, I thought so. His back was to me as he fiddled with something on the counter, next to the coffee maker.

He stayed? He was here all night? In my house?

Shit. Was he also in my bed? Did he sleep with me last night? After Curran, I habitually slept on the edge of the bed and I might not have noticed, even if I hadn't been drinking.

"Are you going to stand there all day or would you like coffee?" he asked without turning.

"You undressed me?"

The coffee maker beeped to indicate it was done. "You weren't going to do it yourself."

Since most of the night was fuzzy, he was no doubt accurate in that assumption.

"I could've slept in my clothes."

"You could have. How are the bruises?"

"Like love kisses compared to the pounding in my head." It would take a few days for them to heal, but they were already much better.

He chuckled. "Coffee?" He reached up in to the cupboard above the coffee maker and took down two mugs.

"Yes, please."

He made coffee and knew where my mugs were. I wasn't sure if I liked that he'd obviously been through my stuff, but since I was desperate for coffee and he had made sure I got home safely and into bed, I didn't say anything.

I padded barefoot across the hardwood floors into the kitchen that was barely big enough for two people, but the essentials were clean, and they worked.

Deaglan poured coffee into the mugs.

"You stayed." I was getting to the part of asking whether we'd slept together, but I had to work my way up to it.

"Mmm," he murmured, and set the carafe back. He opened the cutlery drawer and pulled out a spoon.

He had yet to look at me, and from how I felt, it was probably a good thing.

"Milk? Sugar?" he asked.

"Half sugar," I said. "It's on the...." My voice trailed off because he was already reaching for the *fancy* china sugar container my mom bought me a few years ago and had shipped here. The lid was chipped from the shipping, but I didn't have the heart to throw it out.

He dipped the spoon in the sugar and put a half-spoonful of white granules into my mug.

The spoon clanked against the sides as he stirred. He didn't put anything in his, so he set the spoon on the counter and lifted both mugs.

His eyes hit mine as he held out the mug.

My belly flipped twice as I stared at him. God, how could a man look so damn hot this early in the morning? His hair was messy, but then that was part of his hotness.

I did not look hot. I hadn't looked at myself in the mirror yet, but I was pretty certain my face showed how awful I felt.

His brows lifted and I realized I was staring at him.

Right, coffee. I took the mug and wrapped both hands around it. "Thanks."

He nodded and leaned against the counter and sipped his coffee.

I sipped mine.

Did I ask if he slept with me last night? Or did I just ignore it? If I asked and he did, then I'd hate myself. If I didn't ask and he did, I wouldn't know and I'd probably continue to wonder.

And then there was the possibility he didn't sleep at all.

"Babe, just ask," he said.

"How do you know I want to ask something?"

Again, his brows lifted. "You're nervous." He set his mug on the counter. "And when you're nervous, you chew your lower lip, which is sexy as hell, especially since I don't think you even know you're doing it."

I released my lip. The chewing the lip started when I gave up chewing gum. Studying for exams was nerve wracking so I chewed gum and drank a lot of coffee in order to stay awake. When I graduated, I gave up chewing gum, not the coffee, but the chewing habit stayed.

I bit the bullet. "Where did you sleep last night?"

He nodded toward the living room. "Couch."

"Oh." Relief settled over me that he'd been a gentleman and hadn't crawled into bed with me, yet there was a sliver of disappointment that I quickly squashed.

He picked up his mug and sipped again. "I told you I don't fuck girls who don't know what they're doing."

"Or sleep with a girl more than once," I said. Why did I say that?

"True," he replied, and walked with his mug past me into the living room like he owned the place. "Like I said, you're rare." He snagged his cell off the coffee table and tapped on the screen with his thumb.

Rare. God, why did he have to make me coffee and call me rare first thing in the morning?

I leaned my hip against the counter and cradled my coffee between my hands as I watched him. It was hard to not watch Deaglan. Every movement, even just tapping on his phone, had confidence, and it was impossible not to be drawn to it. To him.

And probably why he could easily find girls to sleep with just once.

He slipped his phone in his back pocket and looked at me. "Have shit to do, pet."

I tensed as the same words barreled into me. Except, this time, at least, he was the one leaving. I wondered why he stayed at all. He could've put me in bed and locked the door behind him.

He approached me, and I set my mug on the counter. I wanted both hands to be able to push him away if need be because, with his determined stride and scowl, he had something on his mind that didn't look friendly.

He placed his mug on the round kitchen table between the couch and the kitchen island, or as I liked to call it, the islet, because it wasn't much of an island.

I straightened as he continued his approach. "Thanks for making coffee." His scowl deepened, and I added, "And for bringing me home."

He stopped in front of me, and my eyes dragged up the front of him until I met his eyes. My heart skipped a beat.

He smelled amazing. How that was possible after sleeping on my lumpy couch, I had no idea. There was a lingering scent of his cologne, but it wasn't that. It was him. Deaglan's smell, and it did all sorts of things to my body. I may have been on his radar, but his scent was on mine. Not that I wanted it. But controlling my body's reaction to him was like trying to control a wild mustang.

"You're still on that," he said, getting into my personal bubble.

"On what?"

"The 'I have shit to do'."

I was a girl. I didn't let things go so easily, even if I wanted to. I shrugged, glancing away from him. "I'm over it, Deaglan."

"No, you're not."

I crossed my arms over my chest. "I am."

"You're not."

I totally wasn't. But I didn't want him to know that.

He sighed and shook his head. A few strands of hair fell in front of his eyes. He didn't bother to shove them away; instead, he moved past me and walked into the kitchen and snagged whatever he'd been fiddling with earlier off the counter.

He walked back to me. "You need a new one. This one's had it." He placed the can opener on the island next to me.

Why had he been using my can opener? I knew it was shit because the thing didn't go anywhere when you turned the handle. I had to continuously unclamp and re-clamp the wheel into the can all the way around. I hadn't gotten around to getting a new one with working at the hospital four days a week and working on my house the other three days.

He headed for the front door and slid off the chain.

"What were you doing with my can opener?" I asked.

"There was a cat at your side door screaming half the night. I gave it a can of tuna." He undid the bolt and opened the door. "You working the afternoon shift?"

I nodded, unable to speak.

"Vic is on his way over. He'll put in a security system for you. I'll text you later. Lock the door."

He was gone.

I stood staring at the door.

He fed Mr. Cavendish's cat tuna.

Six

Eva

A KNOCK SOUNDED ON THE DOOR TWENTY MINUTES LATER. I HAD JUST climbed out of the shower and was drying off. I yanked on my panties, then hopped around on one foot while tugging on my jeans, which weren't cooperating because they were snug and my skin was damp. Wet and denim did not go well together.

Another knock. Louder this time.

Shit. "One sec," I shouted, and grabbed my pink, long-sleeve shirt I'd set out on the bathroom counter and pulled it over my head. I still had a towel turban on and it caught in my top.

Another knock.

Impatient much. I headed for the door while pulling it out of the bottom of my shirt.

Pounding.

"Jesus. Give me a sec." I slid off the chain and flung open the door.

The towel dropped from my hand. My jaw fell right along with it and my stomach was somewhere underneath both the towel and my jaw.

I slammed the door again and leaned up against it. Holy crap. Who was that guy? He was huge, and not just in all six-foot-five of him, but broad and seriously built.

"Eva," the rumbling voice said through the door.

Should I answer? He knew my name and was likely this guy Vic, but he didn't look like some tech guy who installed alarm systems. Not that I should know as I'd never had an alarm, and I was pigeonholing a type of tech guy, and that was obviously wrong. But he was seriously huge.

I noticed my purse on the coffee table and slid the chain across before running over and dumping everything out on the table. I found my phone and pepper spray.

Another knock and then a few curses. "One second, please," I yelled.

I scrolled through recent calls and found Deaglan's that I ignored yesterday.

"Eva." He answered on the first ring.

"Uh, yeah. Hey. The guy installing the alarm?" I peeked out the living room window and saw a black Range Rover with tinted windows, not a white van with a logo. "What does the security guy look like exactly?"

"Is Vic there?"

"I think so, but when I opened the door, he was pretty pissed and big and scary, so I shut the door again."

Silence, then, "You shut the door in Vic Gate's face?"

I huffed. "Well, it's your fault. You have me paranoid that it wasn't some random mugger and some not-so-nice guys might be after me because of you."

"And you think that cardboard door with the flimsy lock and chain would stop that guy standing on your front porch from coming in?"

No. Definitely not. "Vic is The Rock?"

He chuckled. "Don't call him that to his face, babe."

I walked to the door and slid off the chain. "And he installs alarms?"

"No. Vic's specialty is extracting information from bad motherfuckers." What? "Open the door, Eva."

Did I trust Deaglan? I obviously trusted him enough to get in his car—twice.

"Eva. Open the door."

"Okay."

"Okay, baby."

The phone clicked and I lowered it and opened the door. "Uh, sorry about that." I offered my best smile, but he didn't return the gesture. "I'm Eva."

Vic jerked his chin up in greeting, accompanied by some kind of gruff sound. I stepped aside and he walked inside with a toolbox in his hand.

Huh. I hadn't seen the toolbox when I'd first opened the door. But then seeing a cement wall in front of me that could easily crush me with a pinky finger had drawn all my attention.

Vic was taller than Deaglan by an inch or two, and broader. He had thick, tree-trunk arms and rock-hard legs outlined by black cargo pants.

"Would you like coffee?" I offered, as he walked around the house checking windows.

"Nope," he replied.

Okay.

He checked the lock on the back door that led out onto a small deck that held my barbecue and two chairs I'd picked up at a flea market Ally dragged me to one afternoon.

He crouched as he examined the bottom of the door. "You have an inch space under the door."

I nodded. "Yeah, I put a towel there in the winter to stop the draft from coming in."

He stood and faced me.

I was in the kitchen ten feet away from him, but I still felt like moving back a few steps.

"Do you own this place?" he asked. I shook my head. "Then the landlord needs to deal with this."

I laughed. "That won't be happening."

When I called the landlord about the fridge making a loud humming sound, he said it was a fridge and hung up. When I called about the rotting boards on the deck, he said weather will do that and hung up. And when I called about the crack in the wall, running from the living room window to the ceiling, he said the house was fifty years old and hung up. My father fixed the boards and the crack. I lived with the fridge sounding like it was on steroids.

The landlord certainly wasn't going to do anything about an inch space under the door that caused a draft in the winter and skyrocketed my heating bill.

"Give his number to Deaglan."

I frowned. "Why?"

He didn't respond.

He slid his hand along the top edge of the window as he continued to check the house. I poured myself another coffee and texted Ally to ask how she was feeling. She had the morning shift at the hospital today, and from the way I was feeling, she had to be suffering.

My phone rang and I smiled, seeing Ally's picture of her sticking her tongue out pop up on the screen. "Hey."

There was no 'hey' back or 'how are you'. She went straight into it. "What happened with you and Deaglan last night?"

I glanced over my shoulder at Vic who had a tape measure out as he measured a window. I moved into the living room and sat on the couch. The second I did, Deaglan's scent wafted into me and my pulse spiked. Jesus, his scent was going to be my downfall.

I propped my feet up on the coffee table and crossed my ankles. "Deaglan was here this morning," I whispered into the phone.

Her screech of "What?" vibrated through the phone.

"Nothing happened," I clarified. "He slept on the couch." That was when I noticed the knitted pink and blue throw blanket folded neatly over the arm of the couch. I never folded it because it was a throw and I casually threw it over the back of the couch.

"Drunk sex is the best," Ally said.

I lowered my voice as Vic measured the kitchen window. "I was way past the ability of drunk sex, Ally."

"Jesus Christ," she yelled. "Get out of the fast lane, asshole." Her pet peeve was people cruising in the fast lane. I didn't like it either, but Ally was vocal about it. "I think you should do the fling thing. He's Navy SEAL biker hot, protective, and that accent is pussy tingling."

"I'm not doing a fling thing. And he doesn't want a fling thing. I don't want a fling thing." I heard a grunt and my eyes darted to Vic in the kitchen. He wasn't looking at me, but he shook his head.

Shit. It was obvious he heard me.

"Why not?"

After Curran, there'd been a permanent roadblock on sexual desire. Even my toys developed a layer of dust in the back of my nightstand. Deaglan bust right through that roadblock.

He was protective and sweet, when he wasn't being bossy.

"Which door do you normally come in?" Vic asked.

My gaze shifted to Vic. "Ally, I have to go. See you later," I said.

I heard her yell, "Who is that?" as I lowered the phone and pressed End.

I stood. "I use the front, mostly, but if I'm driving the side door."

"Two panels," he said. He walked out the front door and went to his SUV.

I dragged my sopping wet hair back over my shoulders and glanced down.

Shirt. Wet. No bra.

Crap. My cheeks burned.

My nipples were clearly outlined like two headlights.

Shoot me now.

Vic walked back in and I ran into the bedroom and slammed the door.

Seven

Eva

"YOU WANT THE TOILET UPSTAIRS OR DOWNSTAIRS," THE DELIVERY guy asked.

"Upstairs, thanks," I replied, and the two guys shuffled by me.

"Dad?" I called up the stairs. "The toilet's here. Can you show the guys where it goes?"

"Sure thing," he hollered.

He was upstairs installing the new showerhead, which cost a fortune, but I always wanted the overhead rain shower, so I splurged.

I closed the front door and leaned against it, my mind instantly shifting to Deaglan, where it annoyingly went every time I stopped for a second and why I tried to keep busy all week.

But it didn't help that Deaglan texted daily. They were short, abrupt texts asking if I was good and he definitely wasn't an emoji kind of guy, but every time my phone vibrated, my heart skipped a beat, which pissed me off.

Last night, after I'd jumped in the shower, he showed up at my place because I forgot to activate the alarm after work. When I came out of the bathroom wrapped in a towel, Deaglan had been standing in my bedroom, leaning against the wall, arms crossed, and of course, looking absolutely mouth-watering in a black tee and snug dark jeans sitting low on his hips.

That's when I discovered he had a link on his phone to my alarm that alerted him when there was activity at my house.

A confrontation ensued because I didn't like being spied on, but Deaglan was calm and stubborn, and told me that until he knew who'd attacked me, he'd have eyes on me.

But this house was Deaglan free. He didn't know about it and I had no intention of telling him.

I picked up the sandpaper and continued working on the bannister in the foyer. Why would anyone paint a beautiful walnut bannister purple?

My dad had been here since seven this morning and it was nice being able to spend time with him working on the house. Growing up, he hadn't been around much as he'd worked two weeks on, one week off, but he didn't come home every week that he had off, so sometimes I wouldn't see him for six to eight weeks.

I didn't blame my mom for eventually leaving him. I think she didn't know who he was anymore after so much time apart. Once I went to college, they officially separated.

My phone vibrated in my back pocket and a parade of goosebumps popped. I snorted and placed the sandpaper on the stair and took it out of my back pocket. 'Kendra Calling' lit across the screen.

I tapped answer. "Hey, you."

"Are you at the new house?" she asked, her tone higher than normal and bubbling with excitement.

"Yeah," I said.

"Okay, good. I'm five minutes away and have coffee. Is your dad there?"

"Yeah," I replied.

"Hmm, okay. I better pick up donuts, too."

I laughed. Ally and me met Kendra at the gym in college five years ago. She was taking journalism courses. She hated the gym just as much as we did, and we ended up bailing on spin class and hitting the pub instead. We'd been friends ever since.

"Everything okay?" I asked.

"I can't tell you over the phone," she said. "See you soon."

Ten minutes later, she flew into the house like a whirlwind, carrying three steaming coffees and a box with colorful pictures of donuts all over it. Her cheeks were flushed and her eyes were bright and beaming.

She hugged me, then called to my dad at the top of the stairs who was plastering a crack in the drywall. "Hi, Doug. Coffee and donuts have arrived."

He waved with a smile. "Kendra. Good to see you. How's the sports world?"

My dad was into hockey, and since Kendra was a sports reporter, they always had lots to chat about. She was still working her way up the ladder, but she was determined to be one of the best female sports reporters on the air.

They chatted a few minutes about the possibilities for next season, but I could tell from her fast speech and the fact that she was virtually dancing on her tiptoes, that she itched to tell me something.

"You girls go out back and chat. I'm going to finish up here. We really need to get those pipes done, Eva," my dad said. "And pick out a fridge."

I smiled. "I know, Dad. But the excavators are booked for months." They were scheduled to dig up my front yard to get to the lead pipes that had to be replaced. "And I'll get a fridge soon."

He made a gruff, grunting sound and went back to plastering.

I grabbed a coffee and a sugar twist donut, Kendra just a coffee, and we walked outside onto the wraparound front porch to the two-seat swing—so far, the only thing in this house that didn't need repairing.

I sat and sipped the coffee. Kendra leaned against the railing, her hands wrapped around the coffee. She was like a loaded spring, ready to be sprung at any moment.

"Guess what happened?" she said.

I squished my lips together. "Well, it's something good."

She nodded with a broad smile.

"So, it's either you met someone or you were promoted."

She nodded again, smile broadening and showing off her perfect white teeth. Kendra was exceptional on camera, relaxed, and her natural beauty was soaked up by the lens.

I set my coffee on the porch. "And since you can't contain yourself, I'm guessing you got promoted?" Because Kendra had guys asking her out all the time and even if she'd met a famous hockey player, she'd rather interview him than date him or have sex with him.

Her motto was "a player on the field was a player off the field" and that included the ice rink. Kendra had no interest in a player unless it involved a camera and a microphone.

"I got promoted," she squealed, and jumped up and down, her chin-length, blonde hair bouncing with her.

Yes.

I let out a loud woot and leapt to my feet, yanking her into a bear hug. "Oh my God, that's amazing. I'm so proud of you. Wow."

We separated, and she picked up her coffee and leaned against the railing while she told me all about it. From the moment her boss called her into his office to when she ran to the roof of the building and screamed "I got the job" as loud as she could.

The job was for interviewing hockey players in the NHL, and it meant she was going to travel with them, too, so she could get the scoop at their away games, as well.

"You have to tell my dad," I said.

She nodded. "Yeah. I wanted to tell you first."

"Do Ally and Charlotte know yet?" Charlotte was Kendra's sister who lived outside of the city. She's sweet and cute, but that sweet and cute evaporates when it comes to defending abused animals, which had landed her in handcuffs numerous times when she was younger. Not so much since she had her beautiful little girl, Maddie, who was now five. The father wasn't in the picture, and she had yet to share who the father was. She had an animal sanctuary that sat on twenty acres and was why she rarely had time to meet up with us. But next month, the three of us were spending the weekend there.

"I'll tell her later. She's knee deep in manure at this time of day."

We sat on my porch swing and I curled my legs underneath me as I ate my donut, white powder speckling my top.

We chatted for another ten minutes and I was going to tell her about Deaglan, but we were talking about her job and I didn't want to take away from that.

So, I didn't.

And it may have been a mistake when the silver Audi with tinted windows drove up and parked on the street where it distinctly said no parking.

Of course, I knew the car. I'd ridden in it twice now and knew who was in the car. How did he find out I owned this house? I hadn't told him about it, but I shouldn't be surprised, since he'd found out everything else about me.

Deaglan slid out of his car. His head turned in our direction as he peered over at us.

Oh boy.

How do you tell your friend in five seconds about Deaglan Kane? You do it fast and to the point.

"We had sex. When I left his place, I was mugged. He thinks it wasn't a mugging and has something to do with the not-so-nice people he deals with. So he had someone install an alarm system in my rental house. We are not a thing. And neither of us wants to be a thing."

Kendra stared open-mouthed at me, then at Deaglan, then back at me, then back at Deaglan, who walked across the front lawn with his usual, mouth-watering swagger, wearing jeans and a grey tee.

"Not sure where to go with all that," Kendra murmured. "A little speechless here, Eva."

And Kendra was rarely speechless.

"Yeah, I was going to tell you, but I didn't want to take away from your big news."

She frowned. "You having a one-night stand is big news. You getting mugged is vital news, Eva. Were you hurt? He didn't—"

I cut her off. "No. Just a few bruises."

Deaglan's boots thumped up the three front steps. And despite the overhang on the porch shadowing us, he kept his mirrored, gold-rimmed sunglasses on. That wasn't to my benefit because I couldn't tell his mood from his expression.

Kendra stood. "Hi. I'm Kendra." She offered her hand and he shook it.

"Deaglan." He shifted his attention to me. "Your house."

Definitely not a question. "Yeah. But I don't live here." Of course, he knew that. "I will, though. Soon-ish. I hope to open a women's center here."

There was hammering. Shit, my dad was inside. I didn't want him seeing Deaglan and asking questions.

Dad was protective of me after what happened with Curran, and I had a feeling Deaglan wouldn't be received very well with his ba-dass-ness, tattoos, and take-no-shit attitude.

"Are you going to invite me in?" he asked.

"No," I said, standing, so I could attempt to usher him off my front porch and back into his car.

Kendra coughed to hide her choked laugh. "I have to run. I need to get uptown before traffic." She touched my forearm. "Call me later." She turned to Deaglan. "Nice to meet you."

"Same," he replied.

"Thanks for the coffee and donuts," I called after her. She waved as she hopped in her car.

Deaglan leaned his shoulder against the pillar.

I shifted a few feet away from him. "I never paid your friend for

58

the alarm installation? Should I pay you?"

The corner of his mouth drew up. "No."

"Is there a company I pay?"

"No."

Hmmm. I chewed my lower lip and his eyes flicked to my mouth. Shit. "I'm not going to ask how you found out I own this place. I'm getting that you are pretty good at finding out whatever you want. But if you're not here for the money, then why are you here?"

He pushed off the pillar and stalked toward me. I had nowhere to run as the back of my knees hit the seat of the swing.

Deaglan Kane was intense and sexy. Both of which set my body on fire, especially since I knew exactly what it was like being naked beneath this man.

I knew the sound of his groans right before he came.

The sound of his raspy voice saying my name when he did come.

The hard thrust of his hips as his hair fell in front of his eyes and fingers dug into my hip.

I swallowed as he halted inches away.

"My dad's inside," I blurted, hoping it would deter him from standing so close. It didn't.

"Good. I don't like you being alone here."

Oh. The armor cracked and I sagged a bit. "Did you find the guy? Is that why you're here?"

"No."

"Oh."

His jaw clenched. "You want to explain to me why you never mentioned having an ex-boyfriend named Curran Carrick who spent time in jail for assault, Eva."

Oh, shit.

Eva

THE ANSWER WAS NO. I DIDN'T WANT TO EXPLAIN CURRAN CARRICK, and luckily, I didn't have to when my dad came outside.

The screen door bounced closed behind him.

Deaglan didn't step away from me. He also didn't flinch or look at all uncomfortable with the fact that he was about to meet my dad.

But then why should he? We weren't a thing and never intended to be. But it left me in the awkward position of explaining him to my dad. And no matter how old I was, telling him I had a one-night stand wasn't an option.

"Dad, hey." Good start. "This is Deaglan Kane. Deaglan, my dad, Doug Tatum."

Deaglan nodded and they shook hands.

"Irish name," my dad said.

"Yeah, I grew up in Dublin," Deaglan replied.

Dad's brows lifted. "Play any rugby?"

"Yeah."

Oh, no. Dad loved rugby. Said it was real man's football. I said it was an organized demolition derby without the cars. Those guys were fearless and it totally fit that Deaglan played rugby. "Until I was seventeen. Thought about going on, but things didn't align."

Dad nodded. "Yeah, I get that. Thought I'd play hockey, ended up on an oil rig." Dad had been an incredible hockey player. My mom met him at one of his games. They were seventeen. When she got pregnant with me, he gave up the idea of making it big playing hockey. He now played hockey with a bunch of guys every Saturday night at a local ice rink.

"How do you know my Eva?"

I jumped in. "He had an alarm installed in my place. The rental place. Not this house." I nervously laughed. "Of course, you know not this house. His friend did it, actually, but Deaglan organized it. So, it's done. And in. And working."

And I was babbling.

Dad looked from me to Deaglan. "She's jabbering. So she's either nervous or drunk."

I dropped my chin. Oh God.

Dad continued. "I've never been comfortable with her living in that place, but Eva can be stubborn. I was hoping to get this house finished so she could move in sooner rather than later. Turns out there's more work to be done than building a damn house."

I held my breath waiting for Deaglan's response and praying he didn't mention the mugging. I hadn't told my dad and had no intention to because that would lead the question of what was I doing in an alley at six in the morning.

"Care to come in for a beer?" my dad asked. I gaped. "They're in a cooler and not ice-cold anymore, but cold enough on a hot day. No fridge yet. Eva can't make up her mind on which one." He shook his head with a grin. "She has at least twenty, shiny-ass fridge brochures, all with yellow Post-it notes with each of their pros and cons. They all look the same to me. I say go with the one that works when you plug it in."

Deaglan chuckled.

I inhaled a deep breath and considered putting my head in the garbage can. "Dad, it takes time, and I've been busy."

His brows lifted. "It's been six months, sweetie. You need to make a decision."

"I'm waiting for a sale." Which was true; however, he was right about the brochures and the sticky notes. I'd read a million reviews and buyers' reports, and whenever I thought I knew which fridge to buy, I read something else and changed my mind. It was just a fridge, but it was the biggest appliance in the kitchen.

"You wait too long, the sale price will be the regular price," my dad said.

I rolled my eyes.

"We'll go pick out a fridge," Deaglan said, and headed down the steps. "Be back in an hour and I'll take you up on that beer, Doug."

I jolted. Huh? Deaglan wanted to help pick out a fridge for my house? Right now?

My dad laughed. "Might be longer than an hour with Eva. But the beer will be waitin'."

"Don't you have to *work* or something," I said to Deaglan.

"No," he replied, standing on the pathway waiting for me. "Did that."

I know what the "did that" referred to. He found out about Curran, although I wasn't sure how yet or if he knew what Curran's assault charge had been from.

"I can't just go pick out a fridge," I stammered. "I don't have the brochures or any of my notes." They were in my kitchen drawer at the other house.

"Sweetie, go with your friend if you'd like. I'll finish up sanding the bannister," he said, opening the screen door.

Crap.

It looked like I was going fridge shopping.

"And this one has the ice maker on the inside with the freezer on the bottom," the salesman said as he opened the drawer.

Deaglan had yet to mention Curran again, but it was only a matter of time before he did, so I was on edge and couldn't concentrate on the fridge-making decision. It didn't help that Deaglan's hand rested on the small of my back as we followed the salesman up and down the aisles, looking at different models and makes.

Why was he suddenly so quiet? When we walked into the appliance store, Deaglan found a salesman, asked him to show us every fridge they had. The salesman's eyes bulged with the prospect of a sale and he quickly directed us to the back of the store.

Did he have to stand so close? Every inhale contained Deaglan's scent, and my body reacted with quivers each time. I was so heated by the time we reached the tenth fridge that I considered climbing inside, and I would've if they would have been plugged in.

"And that's the last one," the salesman said, his round face a little flushed after spending the last hour giving the spiel on each one. "Any particular one you like?"

"Give us a few minutes," Deaglan said. The first thing he'd said since asking the salesman to show us the fridges.

"Of course. Of course." He wandered away.

I placed the pile of new brochures on top of one of the washing machines behind me and spread them out to flip through them.

"Eva," Deaglan said, the pressure of his hand on the small of my back increasing. "Pick a fridge."

"I'm looking," I replied.

"You're looking at advertising. They all get cold when plugged in. Which one do you like?"

I shook my head, sifting through the glossy images. "I'm not sure. It's hard to decide. I like the features of this one." I pointed to a brochure. "But the drawer on the bottom is cool on that one." I pointed to another. "But this digital display is neat. And this has a great review so—"

"That's it," Deaglan said.

My head snapped around to look at him, but it was too late to consider possible escape routes as he flipped me around so my butt was against the washer and his arms landed on either side of me.

"What's going on?" he said in a low voice.

"What do you mean?"

"This isn't about a fuckin' fridge. What's going on?"

I swallowed and licked my lips. "We're looking at fridges. Of course, it's about fridges, and I can't decide. It's a huge purchase."

"A house is a huge purchase. This is not." His tone lowered. "Why aren't you making a decision, Eva?"

"There are too many fridges and…" My voice trailed off when he scowled. "I don't want to pick the wrong one."

"You don't like it, you return it." His voice softened, but he pushed. "What's going on?"

I shrugged. "You use a fridge a hundred times a day and…." I clamped my mouth shut when his scowl intensified. God, he was stubborn.

"Fine. I'm scared. Okay? I don't know what I'm doing. I know nothing about renovating a house or opening a women's center. I'm a nurse. Not a social worker. What if I hire the wrong people? Or if a woman gets beaten or killed by her husband or boyfriend because someone at my center gave her the wrong advice? What if I can't get her the help she needs? Or I say the wrong thing."

His brows lifted as if he was surprised by something. "A place for abused women?"

I nodded.

His head dipped and his hand slid up my back to my neck where his fingers curled. He was quiet a minute before he raised his head and met my eyes. "You're giving women a place to find their voice. A place where they don't feel alone. That's what matters, Eva."

Tears pooled in my eyes. Goddamn tears over a stupid fridge. But we both knew this had nothing to do with a fridge.

Deaglan didn't know why this was so important to me. Why this really mattered. Why this scared the hell out of me, and yet somehow I needed to do this for other women as much as for myself.

And yeah, I was afraid of the tight little ball in the back of my head unraveling. Of talking about my own experience, but how could I ask them to if I couldn't?

"What if they go back, Deaglan? What if they go back and I can't help them?" I said.

"You can't stop people from making their own choices. Whether it's the right ones or not." His finger twitched at the back of my neck, sending a swarm of goosebumps down my spine. "Sometimes people need to take the wrong path in order to lead them to the right one."

There's something in his voice that made me wonder if he'd been on that path. Had he once took the wrong path? Did he make the wrong choice?

He sighed when I remained silent. "Eva, no matter what happens, it sure as hell won't be over a fridge."

He was right. Of course, he was right. I was procrastinating because I was scared.

He shoved away from me. "Pick a fridge, baby."

I scanned the row of fridges and pointed to the one I'd seen six months ago and liked because it had the freezer on the bottom, a water and ice dispenser, and a cool digital display. "That one."

Deaglan nodded to the salesman hovering fifty-feet away and he hurried over. Deaglan told him which fridge.

"Do you need an oven?" Deaglan asked.

I nodded.

"Okay." He turned to the salesman. "She needs an oven, too."

Nine

Eva

"ARE YOU GOING TO ASK ME ABOUT CURRAN?"

We were in the car and almost at my house after buying a fridge and an oven. Deaglan had yet to mention Curran again.

He glanced over at me. He was wearing his sunglasses and I couldn't see his eyes. There was no question he could pull off gold-rimmed, aviator sunglasses especially considering his sexiness meter was off the charts.

"Yes, but I'm giving you time."

I frowned. "For what?"

"To process."

"Process what?"

"You've been delaying shit on the house for months. Now that is over and you're going to get shit done. You need time to process that."

"So, we're not going to talk about Curran?" I asked, hopeful.

He snorted. "Yeah, babe. We're talking about him. And just so you can process this, too, know that I'm pissed you failed to mention him. But first I'll have a beer with your dad, then we'll talk."

I stayed silent. He obviously didn't know the person Curran

assaulted had been me; otherwise, he'd have said that.

I considered telling him I was busy later and couldn't talk, but then I'd have the impending conversation looming over me. Tomorrow I had a twelve-hour shift at the hospital and needed a clear head, which meant sleeping tonight. But he was right to be angry. I should've mentioned Curran. I didn't, and now I had to explain him.

"You have a name for this women's center?" he asked.

I laughed. "Deaglan, I couldn't pick out a fridge. Picking out a name pretty much solidifies it's happening."

There was an upward tug at the corner of his mouth. "It's happening, Eva."

I smiled. "Yeah." It was. And instead of feeling more stress, some of the weight had lifted. I was doing this. I was going to help other women.

There was silence for a minute before I said, "Vic isn't very cheerful, is he?"

He laughed, and we chatted about Vic, which didn't take long because apparently Vic is super private and has no family except his *brothers* in the military with him. He worked for VUR, Vault's Unyielding Riot, which was owned by Deck, with Kai and Connor as partners.

Deck, Vic, Tyler, and Connor had been in the Special Forces and Kai had "other experience," which Connor had been involved with, too, at one point. When I asked what that meant, he said it was better I didn't know.

"And you work for them, too?"

"No. I work for myself, but I help them out, and they do in return. Owe a lifetime marker to Deck."

"Marker?"

"Debt."

Before I could ask what debt he owed to an ex-Special Forces guy, Deaglan pulled into the driveway and shut off the car. I reached over and touched his arm before he got out.

"Please don't mention the mugging to my dad," I said.

He scowled. "It wasn't a mugging. You need to get that through your head, baby."

I hesitated. "I get it. I just don't want to get it." Because it was a lot easier thinking it was a random mugging rather than a dangerous guy with a knife who wanted to find out who I was because I'd been with Deaglan.

"And your dad should know what's going on," he said. "But it's not my place to tell him, unless things change. Then I will, Eva." He opened the door and got out.

My dad went home after having a beer with Deaglan on the front porch, chatting about rugby while I sat on the porch swing, knees bent with my arms curled around them.

Deaglan sat beside me and why I was curled up in a ball at the far end of the swing because his thighs were parted and relaxed, arm lying casually on the back of the swing, and a beer in his other hand perched on his thigh.

After my dad left, I headed into the kitchen with the empty beer bottles. "I'm going to lock up and head home," I called to Deaglan.

I bent and dropped the bottles in the blue bin at the back door. I'd decided I'd rather have a restless sleep with a looming Curran conversation than talk about it now.

When I straightened, Deaglan was right behind me. His hands settled on my hips and my pulse zipped into a frenzy. "What are you doing?"

My belly felt as if it were bursting with colorful, sweet, candy-coated chocolates as my ass pressed against his hardness and his warm breath wafted across my ear.

"The conversation needs to happen, Eva."

Deaglan was good at herding, I decided. Because he turned me around and herded me into the spot where the new fridge was going to go. He was slow and gentle about it, though, almost cautious.

My spine hit the wall.

Having Deaglan against me gave me mind-mush and I couldn't think about anything except his mouth on mine.

Damn it, I wanted him to kiss me.

"I thought we were talking about my ex," I managed to say.

"We are, except I've been thinking about fucking you all damn day, Eva."

"But you're only with a girl once," I said.

"You mean fuck a girl?" he drawled.

"Yeah," I said in a breathless whisper.

His head tilted, mouth inches from mine. "You're a girl to break rules for."

My chest tightened.

Push him away before he crushes the last fragment of resistance. Remember the feeling when he kicked you out of his place, Eva.

"Curran and I dated for a couple years," I blurted, hoping to get him to back away.

"A couple years," he said. "That's more than dating."

"We lived together a few months." Five months and four days. "How did you find out about him?" Even if he managed to get into any of my social media, he'd never find a picture of me and Curran because Curran refused to have any pictures of himself on social media. He said it invaded his privacy.

"Evan," he said.

I frowned. "Evan? You talked to Evan? Bartender Evan." Evan knew about Curran because I'd freaked out in self-defense class when he came up behind me and put his hand on my shoulder.

"Yes. I asked him if he'd seen anyone suspicious watching you over the last week. He told me to ask you about your ex, Curran Carrick. I did some research. There is nothing on your ex before he moved to town and bought a shipping company seven years ago. Two years ago he gets charged with assault and thrown in jail for a year. No one has heard from him since he was released." He placed his finger under my chin and tipped my head up. "Why did Evan tell me to look into him, Eva?"

I bit my lower lip. "He was in jail because of me," I whispered. "When I moved out of his place, he didn't like it. I ended up in the hospital and he ended up in jail."

I'd blamed myself for a long time afterward. I was a nurse and I'd seen abuse victims. I treated women who had been abused, held them while they cried and I led them to the right people to help them.

But I'd stayed with Curran. At least, for a while. I kept thinking the little things weren't anything. Until the little things became big things and it was too late. At least, I felt as if it was too late.

Deaglan's expression turned volatile. Anger rippled off him in waves and every muscle flexed with tension. His eyes were like a violent thunderstorm of greens, yellows, and specks of black, all crashing into one another.

A tremor went through me and it wasn't a good tremor.

"Christ, Eva." He shoved away from me, spun on his heel and stormed out of the kitchen. I heard his booted feet on the hardwood floors until the front door slammed.

Deaglan reacted badly when he'd found out about my mugging, so I expected a similar reaction because I was getting that this was the type of guy he was. But it felt more than that. As if he took it personally.

I pushed off the wall and walked out onto the porch. Deaglan had his phone to his ear as he paced the front lawn with long, stiff strides. The casual swagger had vanished.

I sat on the swing, curling my legs underneath me and tightening the ball that was threatening to rip wide open.

"I want all of it," he growled into the phone. "Fuck yeah. Those, too." Pause. "Don't care, Deck. Unseal it. I need to see it. Photos. Reports. Everything." Another pause and he ran his hand through his hair. "He is mine, Deck. I need the bastard found." He said something else I couldn't hear, then shoved his phone into his back pocket and faced me.

Our eyes met across the yard and locked for a few seconds. Then he made his way toward me.

Up the three steps, then across the wooden porch to the swing.

He stopped in front of me and I had to crank my neck in order to keep eye contact. "The scar on the back of your head?"

My breath hitched. "Yeah," I replied in a barely audible sound. I didn't think he'd noticed that. It wasn't noticeable to see, but you could feel the scar where the six sutures had been. "He... uh, struck me and I fell. My head hit the corner of the granite countertop on the way down."

He inhaled a ragged breath before running his fingers through his hair again. "Fuck."

I thought he might walk away, but Deaglan lowered onto the swing beside me.

He leaned forward so his forearms rested on his thighs, hands clasped, head bent. "Why didn't you tell me?"

I sighed. "Deaglan, it's not something to bring up in idle conversation with a guy you slept with once."

"I didn't think we just had idle conversations, Eva." He kept his voice soft.

I guess we hadn't, but still, it wasn't easy to talk about with anyone, let alone a guy I barely knew. "It's been two years since I've seen or heard from him. It's a part of my life I'm not proud of and he's out of my life."

His hands clasped and unclasped, head still bent, eyes on the porch planks. "The women's center."

I nodded.

He lifted his head and leaned back in the swing. His weight shifted and sent the swing into a soft lull back and forth.

He was silent and so was I for several minutes, and then, "Tomorrow, we'll install an alarm here, too. I need to make sure you're safe, Eva."

I didn't argue. I just accepted it, and besides, after Vic installed the other alarm, I felt safer, and feeling safe was huge.

"I need to know all of it." His hands rubbed up and down his thighs. "I don't like being in the dark, but I don't expect you to tell me. So I'm not going to ask that of you. But I have to know what he did and I asked Deck to get that for me."

"Why? Why do you need to know, Deaglan?" I wasn't comfortable with him seeing photos of what Curran had done to me. Maybe it was embarrassment or that I didn't want him to see me weak and broken.

He remained silent. Then his feet flattened on the porch as he steadied the swing and peered at me. "Do I scare you, Eva?"

My breath hitched. "No." And I meant it. Deaglan may be scary, but never once had I been scared that he'd physically harm me. Even when he was angry when I told him about Curran, he walked out of the kitchen. God, he'd found me at the hospital as soon as he saw the security footage of me being mugged.

"I'd never hurt you. I know you might not get that yet, but hurting a woman...." He ran his fingers through his hair and inhaled a ragged breath. "Babe, if you're ever scared of me, I need you to tell me."

I nodded. "Okay."

He cupped my chin, thumb lightly grazing my lower lip. "Fuckin' rare."

The swing swayed back and forth again, and I leaned against the backrest. The sun was setting behind the large oak tree in the front yard and it cast an orangey haze over the sky.

We sat next to one another without touching and watched the sun go down in silence. Just the creak of the swing as it rocked and the rustle of the leaves in the trees filling the air around us.

There was comfort in the silence. Comfort in that he was here with me.

And I wanted this moment to last a really, really long time.

Ten

Eva

"HE HELPED YOU PICK OUT A FRIDGE?" ALLY SAID, TWO DAYS later after work while we were in the locker room. "And an oven."

"Fuck me. I've been trying to get you to buy appliances for months. Did he fuck you in the showroom? Was that his strategy?"

I laughed. "God, no. We're not sleeping together." My phone vibrated and I glanced at the screen.

Deaglan: Tyler is in the drop off zone.

I hit the smiley face with the tongue out, and hit Send.

Deaglan was in super overprotective mode since he found out about Curran. Especially since no one had heard from or seen Curran Carrick since he got out of jail. But according to Deaglan, he still owned the shipping company.

Ally slammed her locker shut. "What did your dad say when he met him? What did you tell him? I bet he liked him."

"Why do you say that?"

She shrugged, sitting on the bench while waiting for me to finish dressing. "No-bullshit type of guy. Tells it like it is. Complete oppo-site of Curran." My dad and Curran didn't have anything in common, and the two times they met, it was awkward. Dad thought Curran was too reserved and hiding something. Turns out he was. His personality. "Plus, he helped you pick out a fridge, and even if your dad didn't like him before, he would after that."

I shut my locker, grabbed my purse with the pearl beads on the front, and we headed out of the hospital. I told her about sitting on the porch having a beer, chatting about rugby, then bit the bullet and told her about Deaglan finding out about Curran.

"I don't know why you didn't tell him in the first place."

"I slept with him and he kicked me out. I didn't feel like spilling my guts about an asshole boyfriend I haven't heard from in two years."

"Does he still think the mugger isn't a mugger?"

I nodded. "I have no clue how he'll find him, though. And since he now knows about Curran, he's sending someone to pick me up and drive me home. It's silly when I'm literally a five-minute walk, but the guy is overly cautious. As soon as he tracks down Curran and this mug-ger guy, he'll let it go."

"And let you go?" Ally said. "I don't know, Eva. Guys don't go fridge shopping, install alarms, and have a beer with a girl's dad when they aren't interested. And he's trying to keep you safe, so that's good, too."

I shrugged. I couldn't figure Deaglan out, and it was probably bet-ter not to try because it made me think about him more, and thinking about him more made me like him more. And Deaglan Kane was off limits for more reasons than the fact that he lived in another country and didn't do relationships.

"Eva?" I stopped at the automatic sliding doors as Greta hurried toward me. "A gentleman was looking for you earlier. Said he was a friend of yours."

"Oh." Who would be looking for me? Did one of Deaglan's friends come by to check on me? Shit. It was probably that bodyguard,

Luke, he wanted me to meet. "Did you get his name?"

She shook her head. "No, sorry. I asked, but then the phone rang and he left before I got the chance."

I put my hand on her forearm. "Don't worry about it. If he's a friend, he'll call or drop in again."

"He was a nice-looking man, not as nice as the other one, though. The one with the tattoos and the faded, snug jeans." She winked then turned back to the nurses' station.

Ally smacked my arm. "Greta has the hots for your man."

I lifted my eyes heavenward. "He's not my man."

"He's totally into you. He showed up at a pub to take you home because he was worried about your safety. And he stayed the night on your couch. Your lumpy-as-shit couch that you need to dump and not take to your new house. He installed an alarm. And he's looking into your shit-hole ex. Totally into you."

We walked through the automatic sliding doors of the Emergency Room and Ally nudged me with her elbow as we both staggered to a stop.

"Tyler?" Ally whispered.

"My guess."

But it wasn't a guess, because Tyler looked every bit the commando guy as he stood leaning up against the front of a kickass, souped-up SUV, with his muscled, tattooed arms crossed over his chest clad in a navy T-shirt.

He wore jeans with a black leather belt, and combat boots. Unlike Deaglan, though, Tyler was blond, and when he lifted his head to look at us, he grinned, and it was friendly.

"Eva. Hey." He pushed off the vehicle and walked toward us. Swagger check. Confidence check. Dangerous, not sure yet.

"Does he have any non-hot friends?" Ally leaned into me whispering, as she stared at the sexy commando.

So far no. "Maybe it's a prerequisite to being his friend."

Ally giggled.

Tyler held out his hand. "Tyler," he said.

I shook his hand, and Ally did, too, while introducing herself. After a few niceties, Ally said goodbye and headed to the parking lot.

Tyler opened the door for me, and I slid into the seat. He jogged around the front and folded in.

"I guess you know where I live," I said as he put the SUV in gear.

"Yeah. All the guys do."

I frowned. "All the guys?"

"Yeah, who work at VUR."

Right. "And what exactly does VUR do?"

He turned out of the hospital parking lot, then glanced at me grinning. "Hunt down the worst motherfuckers in the world."

My eyes widened. "Oh." I knew they did security of some kind, but I hadn't expected that. "And how long have you and Deaglan been friends?"

"I don't know about calling us friends. Fuckin' guy can't stay in one country long enough to be considered a friend. But we've known one another six, seven years. I know his cousin, who is a good friend of Deck's."

He turned onto my street because that's how close I was to the hospital.

He glanced at me and smirked. "Whatever Deaglan had to do must have been important, otherwise he'd never let me pick you up."

I frowned. "Why not?"

He grinned. "Because you're smokin' hot."

I half-laughed. "Ah, thanks?"

He pulled into my driveway and shut off the car. "I'll check out your place before I go," Tyler said.

I shrugged. "Sure. But the alarm never went off. It would've said on my phone app." And Deaglan's.

He grinned. "Babe, an alarm is only as good as a man with skills. I have skills, and as good as I am, I know there are a few other guys in this world who also have skills. But I say a few, babe. Not many.

Because I'm fuckin' good at what I do."

I laughed and got out of the car.

Tyler was playful and casual, but there was no question he had that same awareness about him as Deaglan. He didn't just walk up to the door with me. He kept me shielded with his body as he scanned the area.

I unlocked the door and the beeping immediately sounded. I quickly punched in the code and the beeping stopped.

"Have at it." I gestured to the tiny bungalow.

Tyler walked through the house, checking all the rooms and closets, before coming back out to the living room. "All clear," he said. "Do you plan on going out? I can stay—"

I shook my head. "No. I just pulled a twelve-hour shift. Shower and then sleep for the next eight hours."

He nodded and opened the front door. "Lock and load." I raised my brows and he chuckled. "Lock the door and code in the alarm."

I smiled. "Got it."

When Tyler left, I locked the door, slid the chain across, and set the alarm. I showered, ate a grilled cheese and tomato sandwich, and then crawled into bed.

The tantalizing scent of Deaglan filtered into me and I thought I was imagining him until the mattress dipped and an arm slid around my waist from behind.

I jerked upright. "Deaglan?"

"Shh, go back to sleep, baby," he drawled, and with one firm tug, he pulled me into his body so his length spooned mine. He wasn't under the covers, except for his arm that was slung over my waist.

Deaglan was here. Not on the couch, but in my bed and holding me to him. God, it felt good. He felt good. More so because I'd woken up three times already with Curran's image popping into my head like a freakin' jack-in-the-box.

Talking about him two days ago with Deaglan had rolled that ball to the forefront of my mind.

I'd stayed with Ally for a month after I'd been released from the hospital with a broken arm, a concussion with sutures in my scalp, and my right eye swollen shut.

"You're thinking," Deaglan murmured.

"Yeah." I thought I was strong, but recently I felt like a piece of tissue paper.

"He won't get near you again, Eva."

"Yeah," I whispered. But it was hard to believe him when the police told me that, too. When the restraining order did nothing to keep him from nearly killing me.

I shifted on to my back and tilted my head so I could see him. He was up on his elbow leaning over me, his fingers gently playing with strands of my hair.

"Thanks for picking out the fridge with me. And an oven."

The corners of his lips tugged upward, and I felt the tension in his body ease. "You're welcome."

The arm slung over my waist moved and his palm slid across my belly, one fingertip grazing my bare skin because my camisole had lifted when I flipped onto my back.

My lips parted as desire spread across my skin like a speckling of embers. "And also having a beer with my dad. That was nice, too. You didn't have to do either of those things."

His hand stopped playing with my hair and his brows lowered. "The fridge was important, and if I didn't want to drink a beer and shoot the shit with your dad, I wouldn't have. I didn't do it to be nice, Eva. I don't work that way. I did it because I wanted to."

Velvet daisy petals lifted in my belly and twirled. "Oh."

God, I liked this guy. I didn't want to like him as much as I did, but I couldn't stop it, especially when he said stuff like that. Maybe I'd managed to snuff it out temporarily by the morning-after incident, but the embers still burned, and they were burning hotter.

His fingers slid under the edge of my camisole and lightly traced across my belly.

My breath locked in my throat and goosebumps rose.

I swallowed, unable to move or look away from his heated eyes. There was no question I wanted him. My body screamed for him, even when my mind fought the idea.

But I didn't want to fight whatever this was. Not tonight.

His palm flattened on my belly, only his thumb slowly rubbing back and forth. "Go to sleep, Eva."

"I'm not tired." I ran my tongue over my lower lip and his eyes flicked to my mouth.

He stilled. Fingers in my hair motionless. But his eyes weren't. Even in the dark, I saw his sun-streaked, ocean eyes swirl and intensify with a kaleidoscope of colors.

My heart skipped a beat.

Deaglan was like jumping off a cliff. Knowing the end was going to hurt, but leaping anyway because everything before the landing was worth it.

With his eyes locked on me, his palm slid up under my camisole where his fingers traced underneath one breast and then the other. "You thinking about my cock inside you or my mouth on your pussy?"

Jesus. "Yeah," I managed to whisper.

"Yeah, what?"

"Yeah to both."

"Fuck," he muttered as he leaned over me, his mouth a breath away from mine.

Deaglan Kane was on his way to being way more, and I didn't know what to do about that yet, it didn't matter. Not tonight.

I chewed my lip, half-smiling. "You're breaking your rule."

"Baby, I broke every fuckin' rule in my book the second I walked up to you. Did it anyway."

My heart lodged in my throat and feathered quivers tickled my skin.

"Every rule, Eva."

He lowered and his mouth crushed mine. My belly twirled with a rabble of butterflies in a heated coil.

Rough. Penetrating. Consuming.

It was Curran being wiped away.

It was leaping off that cliff.

It was falling with your arms out into a bed of dandelion puffs.

His groan vibrated against my lips.

"Fuck, baby. I can't stop wanting you," he said as he trailed kisses down my neck.

He pinched my nipple and I gasped, arching my back. He soothed the pain with a soft touch before he flicked it with his thumb then did the same to the other nipple.

He shoved down the duvet that separated us, then kicked it aside with his feet. I reached up and slid my hand up his chest to the back of his neck and tried to drag him down to me. But he resisted.

"Top, baby," he murmured as he lifted my camisole.

I ducked my head so he could pull it off. He tossed it to the end of the bed before his hand ran between my breasts, down my belly, to the drawstring of my pajama pants.

He slowly pulled the string, his eyes locked with mine. I felt the bow release and the band around my waist loosen.

With his palm flat, he skimmed his hand into my pants and my breath hitched. "Open your legs."

"I want you naked," I said.

"You'll get that. But not yet. Open, baby."

I parted my thighs and closed my eyes, arching my neck as the heat of his hand cupped me between the legs.

"Fuck," he groaned. "You're soaked."

If there was a word for more than soaked, I was pretty sure that's what I was because my body was so spun in a tornado of desire that I could barely contain myself.

He shifted to lean over me while his fingers played and teased.

His mouth was an inch from mine, but he hesitated, and I held my breath, waiting for him to kiss me. Instead, he lowered and nibbled my neck, his scruff rubbing against my skin like sandpaper and sending tingles shooting through me.

His fingers circled my entrance, before moving away, only to do it again. And again. And again.

"Deaglan. Please," I begged as his fingers tormented me. He drew my nipple into his mouth then flicked it with his tongue.

Then he slid lower, a trail of kisses following.

His hands curled around the band of my pajamas, and he tugged as I lifted my butt.

Those were tossed aside, too, although I didn't know where because all I could think about was his mouth on me.

"Bend your knees for me," he said in a deep, raspy voice.

I did.

His hands on my thighs, he eased them open wider and settled between them. I reached for him, my fingers weaving into his strands of hair and tightening the second I felt his mouth between my legs.

"Oh my God," I said between ragged breaths, my head sinking into the pillow as I closed my eyes and my other hand curled into the bed sheet.

He sucked. He played. His tongue danced and he rubbed his harsh stubble over the most sensitive spots.

I writhed and panted.

"Easy," he purred. "Not yet."

He parted my lips and sucked deeper.

"Deaglan. I can't."

His head lifted, but he didn't stop touching me as he pushed two fingers inside me and I gasped. "Fuck, you're beautiful. If I could fuckin' keep you like this, on edge and panting with my fingers inside you, I would."

NASHODA ROSE

I shook my head, biting my lower lip while I tugged on his hair. "I need to come."

He slowly pulled his fingers out of me; they glistened with wetness. He placed them to my mouth. "Open," he urged.

I opened and tasted myself on his fingers as I sucked.

"Jesus." He growled as he watched me, eyes raging with desire.

Seeing the undeniable raw hunger on his face, rose a greater urgency in my core.

God, I wanted the weight of his body on top of me, the fullness of his cock pushing deep inside me.

"Deaglan, I want you naked." I pulled at his shirt. He ducked his head and I yanked it off. My hands slid over his shoulders and down his arms, the heat of his skin against mine sending new waves of desire through me.

He grabbed my hips as he stared at me. "Tonight is only about you. I'm erasing bad fuckin' dreams, Eva."

My belly flipped and I nodded. "Okay."

His head dipped between my legs again.

And when I screamed his name, body shuddering against his mouth, I knew Deaglan was capable of erasing more than just the bad dreams from tonight, but the bad dreams from always.

82

Eleven

Eva

I HAD TO PEE AND DEAGLAN HAD ME TRAPPED. ONE THIGH WAS SLUNG over mine, and his tattooed arm was locked across my chest. His front was to my back with his chin perched on my head, so every time he exhaled, my hair rustled.

And despite wanting to stay snuggled in his arms, my bladder was having none of it.

"Deaglan?" I whispered, my hand rubbing up and down his forearm that lightly pressed against my breasts. "Deaglan?" I wiggled to try and escape and he groaned.

"Babe," he rasped, his leg clamping down on me.

"Deaglan!" I trashed the idea of waking him quietly. "I have to get up."

A subtle snort as he jerked awake. "Eva? You good?" he said in a sexy, sleepy voice that made me want to turn over and kiss him.

Unfortunately, there was no time for that. "Well, sort of. I have to pee," I said.

"Okay, go pee, babe," he said, kissing the top of my head.

"Your leg?" I wiggled again to try and get from under it.

He lifted his leg and I scrambled out from under him as he

chuckled. "Not funny," I said, and leapt out of bed.

When I came back, Deaglan looked like he was asleep again, so I sat on the edge of the bed and checked my phone. It was seven-twelve and I'd slept through the rest of the night, a good six or so hours. I scrolled through my e-mails, one from the bank, five spams, two book club notices, and one from my mom complaining I hadn't called her. Shit. I hadn't talked to her in three days.

I began to type a quick message back that I'd call her tonight when an arm hooked my waist and yanked me back.

My phone landed somewhere on the bed and my body landed on my back with Deaglan straddling me, and his hands locking my arms to the mattress on either side of my head.

His gaze roamed over my face and settled on my parted lips. "Jesus," he murmured just before his mouth took mine.

It wasn't soft and gentle; this was crushing and bruising.

Raw. Carnal. Starved.

He held me pinned beneath him, and I wanted more of him. I craved all of him.

God, I was drowning in this guy.

He released one of my hands as he shifted to the side to play with my nipples and he continued to kiss me. I ran my hand down his chest to his abdomen and his muscles flexed beneath my touch.

My fingers slipped under the band of his boxers.

His groan vibrated against my mouth and he tensed as my hand wrapped around his throbbing cock.

I broke from his kiss. "I want this inside of me."

He stared at me, eyes flaring with desire. "You'll get that."

I moved my hand up and down his shaft, slow and gentle, then hard and fast.

His jaw clenched. "Your hand on me... Jesus."

He inhaled a sharp breath as I slid my finger along the ridge of his shaft and head then gently squeezed.

He growled. "Fuck, enough." He grabbed my hand and pulled it away from his cock. "I'm not spilling my load in my fuckin' briefs like a teenager."

I smiled. He didn't.

Deaglan shoved off his boxer briefs before he reached over the side of the bed. I heard rustling denim before he rolled back with a gold package.

He ripped it open with his teeth and rolled the condom on with one hand before he ran his fingers across my belly to between my legs.

I gasped, closing my eyes and arching as he pushed two fingers inside me. His thumb rubbed my clit in slow, circular motions.

"Deaglan," I breathed. "I want you inside me."

"So fuckin' wet for me, Eva." He grabbed his cock and rubbed it up and down my wetness before settling at my entrance. I lifted my butt off the mattress to get him to push inside, but he pushed me back down. "Open your eyes."

I opened them.

Deaglan hovered over me, eyes piercing and heated. His chest rose and fell as he breathed hard, matching my own.

"I can't make promises, Eva."

I curled my hand around the back of his neck. "I know."

"Jesus." His mouth crushed mine at the same time as he shoved inside me, my gasp swallowed by his kiss.

We rolled and the sheets tangled in our legs. We rolled back and he thrust harder. We gripped one another like it was the last time. There were no rules. No inhibitions. No quietness about it.

His fingers bunched in my hair and he tilted my head back as he kissed me, his body smacking mine.

"Oh God," I cried against his mouth. "Deaglan." My body spun on its axis as the pressure peaked inside me and my entire body stiffened.

He broke the kiss, grabbed my hands from around his neck and shoved them above my head, interlocking our fingers.

Then he drove deep. Hips rocking. Jaw clenched.

My body tensed. "Oh God. Oh God." I fell over the peak, hard, and my inner core shuddered in pure ecstasy with wave after wave.

"Fuckin' Christ," he growled.

I quivered again as I watched him. He threw his head back as his body tensed and his thrusts eased.

Neither of us moved. Deaglan kept his eyes closed as he hung his head, hair falling in front of his face. His hands locked in mine above my head. His cock still inside me, pulsing.

I lowered my legs that were hitched on his hips and Deaglan squeezed my hands before he rolled off me.

I perched up on my side, head resting in my palm, body tingling.

I watched him remove the condom and walk across the room to the bathroom to dispose of it. He walked back, immodest by his nakedness, and I loved that about him. So self-assured in his own skin.

He tagged his phone off the nightstand and frowned as he tapped on it. I sat up, taking the sheet with me.

He tossed his phone on the bed and I tensed, waiting for it. The quick departure.

I was okay with it. I mean, I'd be okay with it. I just had to get used to it.

His eyes roamed over my face. "I have to head out, but I need a shower first. You good with that?"

I nodded. "Sure. Yeah." I was totally fine with it. He'd just given me an orgasm that I'd feel for a week. And he'd stayed. All night.

"Do you want coffee to go?" I asked, still holding the sheet while I reached for my camisole at the end of the bed.

He leaned over and snagged the camisole from my hands, tossing it aside.

I frowned. "What are you doing?"

"Eva, if I want coffee to go, I'll stop at a fuckin' coffee shop. You don't make me coffee to go." He yanked the sheet I held up to my chest out of my hands and I lie naked in front of him. "What I want is you in the shower with me so I can take you up against the wall and have your body shuddering in my arms. And then I'm going to wash every inch of you."

Oh boy. My eyes widened and between my legs throbbed.

He smirked. "Then we'll have coffee sitting at your kitchen table."

Oh.

His brows lifted. "I'm giving you two seconds to move that sweet, luscious body before I toss you over my shoulder," he said.

I knew from experience that Deaglan followed through with his threats, so I scrambled from the bed and ran into the washroom.

He followed and the door clicked shut behind him.

Twelve

Eva

"I CAN'T BELIEVE HE GOT US TICKETS TO SEE STRIKEBACK," ALLY SAID, bouncing on her toes to peer over the crowd. "It's impossible to get tickets at Avalanche when a big band is playing. Can I just say, I love your new man."

I snorted as we weaved through the crowd toward the bar. "He's not *my* anything." But it was beginning to feel like it, especially when for the last two weeks he'd slid into bed with me. Sometimes, he just curled me into his arms, and other times he stripped me naked and kissed every inch of my body before making me arch and scream beneath him.

Yesterday, I woke to find him making scrambled eggs and toast... in his jeans with the top button undone and no shirt. When I came up behind him and kissed the back of his shoulder, he picked me up and placed me on the kitchen counter where he had me naked again in five seconds.

The toast burnt and the eggs turned to rubber.

"Over there." Kendra pointed to an empty booth near the stage with a reserved sign. God, Deaglan must be really good friends with the owner to get us a booth that close to stage.

I was getting that Deaglan was thoughtful, as well as demanding and stubborn, but he actually bought me a new can opener. I didn't know he had until I found it in the kitchen drawer when I went to open a can of tuna for Mr. Cavendish's cat. It was just a can opener, but he'd bought it because I needed it, placed it in the drawer and never told me.

"Whoa, you see the hottie bartender?" Ally said as we slid into the booth. The band hadn't started playing yet, but the music was loud and the place was packed, so she'd virtually yelled the words.

I glanced at the bar and saw a tall, lean, tatted guy wearing a snug black tee. As if sensing eyes on him, he lifted his head and peered over at us. He chin lifted then went back to serving the blonde girl who was obviously trying to get his attention with leaning over the bar with her over-sized boobs.

"How old do you think he is?" Ally asked. "Thirty?"

"He's thirty-four," a girl said, appearing beside our booth wearing a short black apron over her jeans and a white tee.

"Is he single?" Ally asked.

Kendra and I rolled our eyes.

The waitress laughed. "Don't worry, I get asked all the time. Recently single. But Matt's only relationship is with this bar."

"Matt?" I asked. Deaglan had said the owner of Avalanche was a guy named Matt. "Is he the owner?"

She nodded with a smile. "Yeah. Which of you is Deaglan's girl?"

Ally pointed at me. "She is."

The young waitress smiled. "Well, drinks are on Deaglan tonight and he said don't argue," she said with a smile. "So, what can I get you?"

Ally ordered three shots of tequila and a pitcher of beer for the table.

The waitress tucked a few stray strands of her long, dirty blonde hair behind her ear. "I'll be right back with your drinks."

It was an hour later, while listening to Strikeback on stage and drinking our second tequila shot and laughing over the piece of toilet paper stuck to Kendra's heel when she came back from the washroom, that a shadow cast over our table.

"Phone's for you," the very masculine voice said.

I glanced up to see the bar owner, Matt, holding out a cell phone. "Me?" I asked.

He nodded. "Your man."

"My...." Oh my God. Deaglan. That's the third time tonight someone said he's my man. "He's not my..." my voice trailed off as he slid the cell on the table and walked away.

Ally gaped, her eyes following Matt as he strode toward the bar. "Now, that is a sweet, tight ass."

I placed the cell to my ear. "Deaglan?"

"Babe, where's your cell?" Deaglan said, his voice abrupt.

I was learning that Deaglan was to the point and there wasn't a lot of fluff in his texts or his calls. I no longer took it personally, especially since he was calling or texting because he was checking to see if I was okay.

"It's in my purse." I rummaged through my purse and took out my cell. Six missed calls. All Deaglan. Not good. "What's wrong? Why are you calling the bar?"

"I'm on my way."

"Girls' night means no men allowed, and you need to stop saying I'm your girl. I'm not your girl." But even as I said the words, there were parts of me that liked that he said that.

"We need to talk, Eva," he said quietly.

Okay. That sounded serious. "But Strikeback is playing."

Kendra watched me, frowning, her disapproval of my "fling" evident on her face. She thought I was going to get hurt. She was probably right, but going two years without sex, then having amazing sex with a man who had alarms installed which made me feel safe, and helped me get unstuck with plans for the house, it topped the heart getting hurt part.

Silence, then, "It's important."

Okay, he was worried, which made me worried, and the hairs on the back of my neck rose. "Umm, yeah, okay."

"I'm on my way. Be there in ten."

He was gone before I had the chance to say goodbye. I slid the cell on the table and glanced at Ally and Kendra, who both watched me. "Deaglan is picking me up."

Kendra shook her head, lips pursed. "I'm not sure about him, Eva."

"He had alarms installed. And took her fridge shopping," Ally said. "Most married men don't do that."

The waitress appeared. "You done with Matt's phone? I'll give it back to him," she said with a sweet smile, revealing her perfect white teeth.

"Oh, yeah, thanks," I replied, passing her the phone.

She smiled. "No problem."

Kendra poured more beer in her glass. "What happens when he goes back to Ireland?"

"He goes back to Ireland. We're not in a relationship," I replied.

"Exactly," Kendra said. "You need someone who is going to be there for you. And lives in the same country. What about Bob? He's sweet, super hot, and has money. And he's looking for a relationship."

I laughed. "You mean Boring Bob?"

She snorted. "Why do you guys call him that?" Because he's boring and his name is Bob. "He's not boring. He's settled."

"He's boring as fuck," Ally blurted.

Kendra rolled her eyes, but a smile toyed at the corners of her mouth. She damn well knew Boring Bob was boring. But I knew she was concerned about me and didn't want me to get hurt again.

"Why is he picking you up?" Ally asked,

I shrugged while sipping my beer. "He won't say."

"Maybe he found the mugger?" Kendra suggested.

Maybe.

"Or Curran. You said he was trying to locate the asshole," Ally said.

Or he'd seen the sealed police report on the assault. Deaglan had said he needed to know what Curran had done to me.

But I didn't want him to see the photos. I knew logically what happened wasn't my fault, but that wasn't always easy to believe.

Ally leaned back on the seat and slowly turned her beer bottle. "He's so going to kill Curran when he sees what he did to you. He was scary mad when he saw those bruises on you after only knowing you for one night. Now he's fucked you a lot and he's going to freak."

I huffed. "He is not going to freak. Deaglan doesn't freak." He gets scary and quiet, but freaking out he doesn't do.

Ally lifted her brows and shook her head. "He's going to go postal when he sees the police photos, Eva."

"The police don't release evidence to the public, Ally." But as confident as I sounded, I wasn't, because I was learning Deaglan was capable of getting his hands on anything he wanted. Including the evidence that had put Curran away for a year.

It wasn't ten minutes later, it was five minutes when I saw Deaglan walk up to the bar. He and Matt shook hands and chatted for a second before both sets of eyes landed on me.

Firecrackers set off inside me and my belly flip flopped.

He said something else to Matt, then made his way toward me. I couldn't help but notice the women gawking at him as he passed.

Even if you weren't into that type of guy, you'd still look because Deaglan demanded attention. But he either didn't notice or didn't care that twenty-plus women stared at him because his eyes were on me, and I liked that. A lot.

I swallowed as he approached the booth. "Ladies," he said with a nod to Kendra and Ally.

"Hey, Deaglan," Ally said, smiling, her cheeks flushed from drinking and singing to Strikeback's 'Only Once'.

"Sorry for interrupting your night, but I need to steal your girl."

Kendra didn't say anything and it was because she was glaring at Deaglan.

Deaglan's gaze met hers. "You have issues with me."

Oh, shit. "We should go." I slid out of the booth, and Deaglan's hand settled on my lower back as if an automatic gesture.

Kendra raised her chin and met his eyes. "I don't want to see Eva get hurt. So, yeah, I do." Kendra interviewed some of the cockiest and most confident men in sports, so she wasn't afraid of meeting Deaglan head on. Which was exactly what I was afraid of.

Deaglan's expression softened. "I'm good with that, it means you're looking out for Eva. You'll get over it."

My eyes snapped to his face. *You'll get over it?* What did that mean?

Ally giggled. Kendra huffed.

I said goodbye and Deaglan kept me glued to his side as we weaved through the crowd and out to his car that he'd parked in front of Avalanche where it said no parking.

"Are you going to tell me what's so important that you needed to drag me away from watching Strikeback?" I asked as he opened the door for me.

"We're meeting the guys at VUR."

I frowned. "Now? It's after nine on Saturday night."

"It's important." He met my eyes and my heart skipped a beat, but it wasn't a good skip because he looked serious. "My warehouse blew up and the guy who attacked you is dead."

Thirteen

Eva

MY STOMACH LANDED SOMEWHERE BACK ON THE PAVEMENT AS MY mind spun because I wasn't sure what to grasp first: they found the guy who mugged me, him being dead, or that Deaglan's place blew up.

"Eva, you're chewing your lip."

I released my lip. "I'm processing."

"Not a lot to process."

"Umm, yeah, there is. Your place blew up, Deaglan." I inhaled a shaky breath because saying the words made it so much more real. "You could've been in it. You could've been there and…" Words locked in my throat and I swallowed several times. "Was that the plan? Was someone trying to kill you? God, why would someone want to kill you?"

He turned right onto the ramp and merged onto the highway. "My guess, I pissed them off somehow."

A snort-huff escaped. "If I piss someone off, they give me the finger, not blow up my house."

He made a gruff sound. "I've made a few enemies over the years."

"What kind of enemies?"

I knew whatever he did for a living was dangerous and involved security of some kind, and hunting bad guys, but he hadn't been exactly the sharing type of guy and I hadn't pushed because we weren't in a relationship.

"Babe, nothing is touching you."

But the truth was, I hadn't even thought about what this had to do with me. I was thinking about Deaglan. "Was it the guy who mugged me who blew up your place?"

"No. His body washed up on shore. A man walking his dog found the body two days ago. It's why it took us so long to find him."

"Oh." My fingers fiddled with the hem of my little black dress. "How did he die?"

"Overdose."

"So, he did mug me for money to buy drugs, and it has nothing to do with you?" Does that mean Deaglan will stop coming over at night? Will he go back to Ireland?

He pulled off at the next exit. "There were no needle marks in his arms, but there were signs on his wrists that he'd been restrained. Ernie, a retired Navy SEAL who works for Kai, has spent some time with the homeless, so he asked around. None of them have ever seen him. Meaning he wasn't homeless and likely wasn't a drug user." He glanced in his rearview mirror, then changed lanes. "The police know it's homicide, but they can't prove it yet, so for now it's ruled as an accidental overdose."

"Someone killed him," I said quietly.

"Deck wants you to look at a photo. Confirm it's the guy."

"I didn't get a good look at his face. I don't think I'll recognize him."

"We need you to take a look anyway, babe," he said. "Confirm it's the same tattoo on the back of his right hand."

"Oh."

He pulled up in front of a modern, four-story office building and parked.

"Eva." He dangled one arm over the top of the steering wheel as he turned to face me. "I don't know if Deck called her in tonight, but I don't want you walking in there blind to the fact that VUR's secretary and I were together. Once. Before she worked here. She'll make it clear that we were a thing, but that thing was one night."

I was well aware of the fact that Deaglan had been with other women and didn't do relationships. I opened my door and said over my shoulder. "I'm sure she won't be the first girl I meet who has sucked your cock."

He snorted. "Jesus, babe."

Deaglan opened the frosted glass door for me, his hand on the small of my back. There was a silver plaque on the door that said, VUR by Appointment Only. If you didn't know VUR, you would have no idea what it stood for or that these guys hunted bad guys. Or as Tyler said, "the worst motherfuckers in the world."

The place was classy, yet minimal with hardwood floors, a black bench in the foyer and straight ahead an oak desk where a twenty-something-year-old woman wearing bright cherry-pink lipstick typed on a computer.

I wasn't exactly thrilled meeting a woman he'd slept with, but I was fully aware of Deaglan being sexually active without strings. This was bound to happen if we spent any time together outside of my bedroom.

She didn't look at me. She looked at Deaglan, her brown eyes dancing and her tongue gliding across her plush lower lip.

She squeaked and jumped from her chair. "Deaglan. Why didn't you call me? I didn't know you were back in Toronto."

I rolled my eyes and leaned into Deaglan, whispering, "Did she squeak like that while you were—"

"Eva," he growled, arm sliding around my waist and fingers digging into my hip.

God, she was nothing like me. Nothing.

She pranced around the side of the desk wearing spiked, red heels, and a tight, mid-thigh-length red dress. It looked like she'd been out at a club when she'd been called in to work.

"Claire," Deaglan said. "Are Deck and the others here yet?"

Her hips swayed and large, gold-hooped earrings dangled as she approached. Her gaze flicked to me then to Deaglan's arm loosely hooked around my waist.

She stopped in front of us and I gagged on her pungent, flowery perfume.

"When the guys asked me to come in tonight, I didn't know it had to do with you. Are you okay?" she purred, with her painted pink lips squished into a pout. She placed her hand on his chest, matching pink fingernails grazing his shirt.

Deaglan's fingers twitched on my hip. "Deck?" he repeated.

Her sweetness catapulted to venom as she glared at me like it was my fault she was being rejected.

"Boardroom." She spun on her heel and walked back to her desk and sat. "Connor, Tyler, and Vic are here, too. Kai is on his…." She glanced past us to the door. "Just pulling in."

I shifted to look through the glass doors and saw a tall, lean man wearing a tailored suit climb out of a classy charcoal-gray sports car.

He strode into the building. Sunglasses, expensive. Shoes, expensive. And suit, expensive.

Not a commando guy. But from his confident stride, he looked just as foreboding.

"Deaglan Kane," he said in a husky voice with a hint of humor, but it wasn't exactly friendly.

"Kai," Deaglan said, and they shook hands. "Been a while. How's that figurine collection coming along?"

Not a chance did this man have a figurine collection.

Kai chuckled and the sound was like smooth, fine brandy. "How is your Crown collection?"

Your Crown collection? My eyes darted to Deaglan. What were they talking about?

Deaglan tensed and his fingers tightened on my hip. "They aren't mine, as you're well aware."

Kai's brows lifted, but he didn't say anything. He removed his sunglasses and turned to me. I was met with hard, piercing green eyes that were definitely assessing, as if he were trying to figure out if I was worthy of his attention. If you could get past his intensity and scariness, he was absolutely beautiful and had a magnetic quality about him.

"Kai." He offered his hand and I shook it.

"Eva," I said.

The hardness evaporated from his eyes. "The nurse from St. Micks Hospital. You met my wife London at the Treasured Children's charity."

Oh wow. This was Kai. London's husband, Kai, the mysterious, wealthy, sex god who worshipped the ground she walked on.

Everyone in the medical field knew of London and her work in finding a cure for cancer. She'd written several research papers and owned a laboratory north of the city.

We'd spoken for several minutes at the charity event before her little girl, Hope, dragged her away to go see the horses.

"Yeah, that's me."

Deaglan urged me forward down the hall. "Deck's waiting."

Kai didn't follow as he stopped to speak to Claire.

The door was open into the boardroom and there was a twelve-person, glass table and twelve, black leather chairs. Along the far side of the room were tinted floor-to-ceiling windows with the blinds pulled a quarter of the way down.

There was also a small, stainless steel fridge in the far corner beside a filing cabinet.

The men were standing around the table, leaning over and sifting through a bunch of photos and papers.

Vic, Tyler, Connor, and Deck straightened as we walked in. All wore cargo pants, some black, others khaki, and every one of them was muscled and tall. Deck was the broadest and scariest, well, besides Vic, but I didn't count him because I was pretty sure Vic wasn't human.

"Eva," Deck said, nodding.

"Hey." I half waved.

"You met Connor O'Neill at the charity event, Georgie's brother," Deaglan said.

"Yeah, hi, again," I said.

Connor offered a grin and his eyes were friendly, but there was a hidden seam behind that friendly. Something dark and painful that I hadn't noticed the first time we'd met, but then I had been focused on Deaglan. But I shouldn't be surprised as I imagined all these men had experienced the unimaginable being in the military.

Connor had his tattooed, sculpted arms crossed. He wore a black T-shirt with a holster that contained a gun in full view, which in Canada was highly illegal.

Deaglan gestured to Tyler, who flipped a pen between his fingers as he perched one foot on a chair and leaned his forearm on his thigh. "You know that asshole. And Vic."

I smiled at Tyler who winked at me. I half smiled at Vic on the other side of the table, who didn't do anything but briefly glance my way.

Kai walked in. "Gentleman," he said as he pulled out a chair and sat.

Everyone else did, too, with Deck at the far end, Tyler on one side, Vic on the other, and Connor beside him.

With his hand on the small of my back, Deaglan directed me to the seat beside Tyler, who already had pulled it out for me.

"We were just going over the police file," Deck said.

He sifted through a few of the photos before handing one to me. "Frank Davidson, the man we believe attacked you. Forty-two, military for two years before he was discharged for assault. Numerous charges since. Most minor and given a slap on the wrist. He's a known lackey in the underground, does shit jobs for shit money. Video footage at Deaglan's reveals a man we think is Davidson was in the alley seven times. And that's what we can confirm. He knew to keep out of view of the cameras. We assume he was there more often and likely doing surveillance. First time we saw him was the day Deaglan arrived here from Ireland."

He nodded to me. "Is that the tattoo?"

I studied the photo. The man looked ten years older than Deck said he was. My eyes trailed down to the hand in the photo and my heart skipped a beat. "That looks like it. The spider. It had long legs and the eyes. The eyes were red like that. But it happened so fast and… I can't be sure."

"And he only wanted your purse?" Deck said.

I swallowed. "Yeah."

"No chance Frank Davidson was after a few dollars," Connor said.

"Staged as a mugging," Deaglan said. "It might have worked if he'd avoided the cameras when he chased her with a fuckin' seven-inch, serrated blade."

Deck nodded.

Connor, Vic, and Kai sifted through the other photos on the table.

Tyler picked up the written report. "He was known to do jobs for Seth Garrett." He lowered the piece of paper. "Didn't that asshole die?"

"He went off the grid years ago," Connor said. "Word spread that he was dead. But I did a search on the dark web and he's back in business," Connor said. "Didn't you have a situation with him, Deaglan?"

Deaglan nodded. "Yeah. Seven years ago."

Kai let one of the photos slip from his hand and it fluttered to the table. "Don't know him. What was he into?"

"He's an exporter," Deck said.

"Of what?" Kai asked.

Deaglan, Deck, Connor, and Vic visibly tensed, and I didn't know what was going on, but it was obvious they didn't want to say anything with me in the room.

"I'm not twelve," I blurted. "You can say it in front of me. I won't freak out." Deaglan's hand lowered onto my thigh and I turned to him. "I work in a busy downtown hospital. I've heard and seen everything."

Deck looked at Deaglan who nodded. Oh my God, such commando men.

"Human trafficking," Deck said.

I stiffened, my stomach rolling. Yeah, that wasn't what I expected and I was silently freaking out. This wasn't just a not-so-nice guy; this was a disgusting, malicious person with no conscience.

Deck continued, "Seth Garrett won't be easy to find. No one knows what he looks like, except Deaglan." My eyes shot to Deaglan, but he was looking at Deck. "There are no pictures of him on the web and we suspect he doesn't use his real name. He's been laying low for years, and anyone who works for him is too scared to betray him. Word is he won't just kill you, he'll make your life hell for a fuck of a long time then sell your body parts. And that's if you're lucky." He addressed Connor. "Any dark web chatter on his location?"

Connor shook his head. "Nothing."

Deck turned to Kai. "Vault contacts."

"I'll ask around," Kai said.

I silently freaked while the men chatted about where to find this Seth guy and who might be working for him. Deaglan said something about Ireland, but I wasn't really listening any longer.

This wasn't about a mugger. This wasn't about a low life with a grudge against Deaglan for some hit and run. This was about one of the worst motherfuckers in the world.

How did this happen? And why would Deaglan know a man like that?

Deaglan's hand lightly squeezed my thigh. "I want more eyes on Eva. I can't be there all the time," Deaglan said.

Tyler toyed with the pen between his fingers. "I'm available.

Twenty-four-seven."

Deaglan snorted. "She's with me."

"Like *with* with? Or temporarily with?" Tyler asked, and it was obvious he was trying to get a rise out of Deaglan... and it worked, because Deaglan's jaw ticked and his back stiffened.

Vic made a gruff snort and Kai chuckled. Connor watched me with curious eyes. I wasn't sure what it was about, but it wasn't hostile.

Kai glanced at his phone as it vibrated on the boardroom table. "London needs me home. Hope wants to show me her ballet routine before bed," Kai said.

"Hope's in ballet?" Tyler asked. "Thought she'd be at the gun range by now."

"She's fuckin' four," he replied.

Tyler grinned. "Weren't you killing people by the age of four?"

My eyes darted to Kai. His brows lowered over his piercing green eyes and I thought he'd punch Tyler or pull out the knife I'd glimpsed under his suit jacket.

Instead, Kai smirked. "My daughter won't use a gun to protect herself. It's for pussies like you. She'll use a knife." He rose and headed for the door.

Tyler dropped the pen and called, "Or piano wire?"

Kai snorted and vanished around the corner.

Deck shifted his attention to Deaglan. "I'll ask my buddies at the police station to keep an eye on Eva's places." He stood and slid photos and reports into a folder. "Okay. Let's find Seth Garrett."

Connor, Vic, and Tyler stood, but Deaglan didn't. "Anything on the police report?" Deaglan asked.

I tensed and cold shivers pierced my skin like ice picks.

Deck shook his head. "No. But I'll deal with Curran. You're too close to it."

"Can't do that, Deck," he said quietly.

Close to it? Because we were sleeping together? Or was it something else?

Deck's lips pressed together and his brows lowered, but he didn't say anything. It was obvious he wasn't happy about Deaglan wanting the police report on Curran.

And neither was I.

I swung my gaze to Deck. "I don't want anyone to see the police report."

Deaglan tensed beside me, his palm resting on the table, curling into a fist.

Tyler cleared his throat and Connor shifted his weight.

Deck dropped the file folder on the table. "You need to talk to Deaglan about this, Eva."

I pushed my chair back and stood. "Curran beat me. He beat me so bad, it put me in the hospital and he went to jail. He's gone and I want it to stay that way. There's nothing else any of you need to know." I raised my chin and looked at Deaglan. "Nothing."

"We'll talk about it," Deaglan said.

I shook my head. "Just like we talk about everything else? Like why you're too close to it, Deaglan? Or why you were involved with a human trafficker? Or should we start with something simpler like how old you are?"

The room was quiet and the tension so thick I felt as if I was suffocating in it.

I had to get out of here. I couldn't breathe, damn it.

Deaglan stood and reached for my hand. I ripped from his grasp and rushed by him.

I heard him swear and come after me, but I didn't stop.

I had to get out of here.

Everything was crashing down around me.

I pushed through the doors and the cool evening breeze wafted into my heated cheeks. I placed my hand on the brick wall and inhaled several deep, ragged breaths.

My emotions were like a live wire as they ping-ponged inside me. God, what the hell was I doing with a guy like Deaglan? Who was he?

What had he been involved with to know a man like Seth Garrett? Why was he so intent on finding Curran and unearthing something I'd buried?

"Eva," Deaglan said, coming up behind me.

I closed my eyes as the heat of his body seeped into mine.

And at that moment I knew why this mattered. Because I liked him more than I should. Because I wanted him. Because this was temporary and yet it felt as if I was slowly being tied to him and the knot was tightening.

Deaglan was too close to the situation with Curran, but I was too close to him. "Why is it so important to see the police report?"

His fingers settled on my hip and it was like a bolt of electricity charged through me. "I want him found, Eva."

I jerked from his touch and spun around to face him. "That's not what I asked you."

"We'll talk about it."

I huffed. "Just take me home, Deaglan." I brushed past him and walked to the car.

He opened the car door for me and I slid inside, my hands shaking as I did up my seatbelt.

We drove in silence, and even though I was desperate for answers, I needed the quiet. My head was a runaway train with so many doubts and questions about what was happening. How I felt about him. How this was no longer a fling. This was more and all of it mattered.

"I can't do this anymore, Deaglan." My throat tightened as if threatening to cut off my words. "I know we're temporary and you're leaving and you don't do relationships but…." But it felt like a hell of a lot more. "I don't want you staying with me. Frank Davidson is dead, and Deck said he'll have the police watch my place, and I have the alarm."

His brows lifted as he glanced at me. "You're freaked. I get that, Eva. And I'll let you have that tonight. But tomorrow morning I'm here and we're having coffee and we'll talk about it."

Crap. My determination to end this would be in the gutter by morning because I'd be tossing and turning all night thinking about him not being in my bed. "I don't need to talk about it."

"Too bad."

"You've had lots of time to talk, Deaglan. It's too late."

He pulled up to my rental house, shut off the engine and turned to look at me. "I'm not leaving you, Eva."

But the truth was you can't leave someone you've never really been with.

I unclicked my seat belt and opened the car door.

I got out and walked up the pathway. I heard his door open and his booted feet behind me.

I swallowed back the tears and searched through my purse for my keys, but my hand shook so badly I couldn't find them. "Damn it, Deaglan, just go," I blurted.

He gently pried my purse from my hands, took out my keys, and unlocked the door. The alarm beeped and he urged me inside with his hand on my back. He plugged in the code and handed me my purse.

I tossed it on the couch and walked toward my bedroom.

"I'm thirty-two," he said.

My step faltered, but I kept walking. It wasn't enough.

"I'll be outside," he said.

My shoulders sagged, and the parts of me that I couldn't keep from wanting Deaglan, cracked. Because that hope that he'd maybe give me more slipped away.

Fourteen

Eva

WE DIDN'T TALK IN THE MORNING OR FOR THE NEXT FIVE DAYS because Deaglan was gone, although I didn't know where.

He'd left me with an extra appendage, Luke, my new bodyguard who looked like a freight train. At night, Luke left as soon as the police car parked across the street from my house.

I was a taut thread ready to snap and it had nothing to do with the fact that I had a bodyguard and the police watching me. It was that I missed him. I missed him in my bed. I missed talking to him. And, yeah, I was worried about him.

At work today, I had to ask Ally to draw my patient's blood because my hands shook so badly. The shaking was because I hadn't slept in five days.

I walked through the sliding doors of the hospital after my shift and was surprised to see Vic's Range Rover idling instead of Luke's black BMW.

I opened the door and climbed in. "Where's Luke?"

"Emergency with a client." He put the car in gear and pulled out.

I bit my lip and neither of us said anything for a minute, but I couldn't take it. I had to ask. "Where is Deaglan?"

Vic glanced at me with a scowl. "He had to deal with some shit."

I wanted to ask what shit he was referring to, but talking with Vic was hard to do because Vic was uncommunicative and brooding and pretty much what you'd imagine a scary commando guy in a fast-paced, action-packed movie to be like—where one guy goes around pretty much saving everyone in the entire city. Or maybe he's the guy who single-handily kills everyone. The judgment was still out on that.

"Is he okay?"

He shrugged. "He's supposed to be back tonight."

"Back?"

"Flew to Ireland four days ago."

My heart stopped and it was as if the crushed pieces snapped into tiny fragments and scattered like a box of thumbtacks. He left? Deaglan went home and he didn't tell me?

Vic pulled into the driveway and shut off the engine. I went to get out of the car and he grabbed my forearm. "Don't judge him before you hear his reasons."

My breath hitched. "What?"

"You heard me."

I had, but I didn't understand why he'd tell me that. "Reasons for what?"

His fingers twitched on my arm before he released me. "Police car is here."

I glanced over my shoulder and saw it sitting at the end of my driveway. I threw open my door and got out. Vic followed until I was safely inside, then he left and I sat on the couch with my phone in my hand staring at Deaglan's text from five days ago.

I wanted to call him. Text him. Find out if he was okay. Why he went to Ireland. And most importantly, if he was coming back.

I must have picked up my phone a zillion times throughout the evening to call him, but I couldn't. He'd left and I was the one who drove him to flee.

I always knew he'd leave. He'd been clear in the beginning we were temporary.

And this is what I wanted. But it was for different reasons. I wanted more than temporary. I wanted what he couldn't give me—him.

I curled up on the couch and mindlessly watched TV, attempting to forget him and doing a piss-poor job of it. And when my cell rang just after ten, I fell off the couch trying to get to it thinking it might be Deaglan, which was silly, but that's where my head was at.

It was my mom whom I hadn't spoken to in a week because I knew my dad told her about Deaglan and she'd jump to conclusions.

"Hey, Mom," I said.

"Eva, dear, how come I had to hear from your father about the young man you're dating?" I inwardly moaned. "Why didn't you mention you were seeing someone? I want to hear all about him. What's he do for a living? Is he a doctor at the hospital? You really should date a nice young doctor."

"We're not dating, Mom." Even when he'd been in my bed every night, it hadn't been dating.

"He met your father and helped you pick out a fridge. Your dad said he was also at your house when the deliverymen arrived so he could install the appliances. That was nice, sweetie. Oh, and he's Irish? Is he going to move..." Mom went on, and I leaned my head back on the couch and closed my eyes.

I loved her more than anything and respected her for raising me on her own because Dad was gone most of the time. She probably would've divorced my dad years prior if it hadn't been for me. So I was glad she had found a man and lived down south and was happy playing golf with her friends.

We chatted for a while, thankfully no longer about Deaglan, but golf, and it kept my mind off the fact that I hadn't heard from Deaglan.

I crawled into bed after midnight and tried to sleep. Tried being the optimal word because I tossed and turned and punched my pillow more times than I could count. Several times I got out of bed and looked out the window, for what, I didn't know because Deaglan was thousands of miles away across an ocean.

I must have dozed off because I woke to the piercing sound of the alarm.

My heart sprang into my throat and sent me over the edge of the bed in a tangle of sheets.

Shit.

I kicked the sheets aside and dove for my phone on the nightstand. I quickly scrolled to the app and checked the alarm.

Back door open.

Holy Christ, someone's in the house.

Or maybe the back door flew open in the wind? Was it windy? Did I forget to lock it before bed? It was a shitty door, so there was a good possibility.

I didn't care. I wasn't being the stupid girl who gets blown up because she thought it was the wind and not an intruder planting a bomb.

"9-1-1, what's your emergency?"

"My alarm is going off and the app says the back door is open and I may have left it unlocked and the wind blew it open, but I don't want to go check because if it's not then—"

"Slow down, ma'am. What's your address so we can confirm and get someone there right away?"

I gave her my address while I scanned my bedroom for a weapon.

Lamp. I tore the plug out of the socket and grabbed the lamp around the neck, tore off the shade, and held it above my head as I walked to my bedroom door.

"Ma'am, officers are on their way. Can you lock yourself in a room until they get there?"

"Yeah, but there's a cop right outside." At least, there had been. Why wasn't he busting through the door to see if I was okay?

My phone beeped, and Deaglan's name flashed on the screen. A tidal wave of relief swept over me and I quickly tapped the phone to switch calls.

"Deaglan." My hand shook, and I gripped the phone tighter as I slid to the floor, my back against my bedroom door.

"Eva. What's going on?"

I shook my head as a tear trailed down my cheek. I wasn't sure if it was from hearing his voice after five days or the fact that someone could be in my house. Maybe both. "I was asleep and the alarm went off. I called 9-1-1."

He swore beneath his breath. "Vic's close. Sixty seconds out. Is the cop with you?"

"I'm in the bedroom," I said. "I don't know where the cop is."

"Okay. Stay on the phone with me until Vic gets there."

I nodded even though he couldn't see me. "Okay."

"Eva. We're going to talk. I'm on my—"

Bang.

I dropped the phone at what sounded like someone kicking in the front door. I gripped the lamp with both hands.

Was it this Seth guy? Was someone planting a bomb like they did at Deaglan's?

"Eva!" I heard the muffled sound of Deaglan's voice in the phone.

The alarm silenced.

Footsteps thumped.

"Eva, pick up the phone."

I held my breath and tightened my hold on the lamp.

The floorboards creaked.

The hairs on the back of my neck quivered, and my heart pounded so hard I swear the intruder could hear it.

"Eva?" A low rumbling voice sounded on the other side of the door.

"Vic?" I said and scrambled to my feet, moving away from the door to open it.

Vic stood in front of me with a gun drawn, and it was the best sight, second to seeing Deaglan, I'd ever seen.

He shoved the gun in a holster strapped to his thigh. "Lamp," he said and slowly reached for me, eyes on me not the lamp.

Right. I still had the lamp up above my head. I lowered it and handed it to him.

He set it on the floor and picked up my phone. "Deaglan. She's safe." He didn't wait for a response as he pressed End and handed the phone to me.

But I didn't take it. Instead, I threw my arms around his neck and pressed my cheek to his chest. "Thank you." Vic's arms remained at his side, his body tense and unmoving as I hugged him.

No comforting arms. No light touch of reassurance. Nothing. Vic was cold as ice, and yet, I still had never been so glad to see him.

Vic's hands peeled my arms from around his neck and I let him go, stepping back.

His jaw was rigid and his eyes were dark and swirling with... I didn't know what it was. Maybe pain? Or anger?

"Your phone," he said, placing it into my hand. "Get dressed and come out to the kitchen." He walked out of my bedroom.

I grabbed an over-sized sweatshirt from my dresser and yanked it over my head and quickly changed my pajama pants to a pair of yoga pants before walking out to the kitchen to see Deck and three police officers along with Vic.

"Eva. You okay?" Deck asked, coming toward me.

I nodded. "Yeah. Yeah. I'm okay. What was it? Do you know why the alarm went off?"

"Someone jimmied the door open. They ran when the alarm sounded. The cop chased on foot, but lost him."

Someone broke in while I was sleeping. God, if I didn't have the alarm, I wouldn't have known.

"Sit, Eva," Deck urged.

"I'll, uh, talk to the police. They'll want to know what happened." Although I didn't have much to tell them other than the alarm went off.

Deck moved in and softly cupped my chin. "Eva, you don't deal with this. We deal with this. Sit before you land on your ass."

His hand dropped and he urged me to a chair at the kitchen table. "Vic will stay with you."

"I'm okay, really."

He didn't say anything as he moved away and spoke quietly to the three officers. They peered at me a second before walking out of the kitchen and outside to the front porch steps.

Vic stayed, leaning against the counter with his arms crossed and his dark eyes unreadable as usual.

"Eva," Tyler said, walking through the open front door. "Fuck, man, you didn't get her a drink. The woman needs a drink. And Skittles." He tossed a bag of Skittles on the table and winked at me.

I half-smiled and some of the tension eased.

Tyler pulled out the chair next to me and sat. "You okay?"

"Yeah. I'm fine." Sort of fine. I was getting to fine.

A glass of water plopped in front of me. It was Vic. "Thanks."

He nodded and went back to his position leaning against the counter.

"I said a drink, not fuckin' sewer water," Tyler said. He glanced at me. "You have scotch? Or rum? Vodka will do in a pinch, but it's not the same when it's clear and looks like water. You want the dark stuff when shit like this happens."

"Beer or wine. That's it." The wine was mine and the beer for my dad if he popped in. The only time I'd seen Deaglan drink was that beer with my dad.

Tyler grabbed the bag of Skittles and ripped them open. "Wine doesn't set your throat on fire, sweetcakes. You need kick. A drink that makes you want to slam your fist into something." He grinned. "Like Vic. He's up for it. I always feel better after a shot of the good stuff and a few shots at Vic."

I smiled and he passed me a few Skittles, and I placed one in my mouth. Tyler popped a handful into his.

Tyler winked. "Nothing like a burst of flavor in your mouth when you're coiled up tight."

But that coiled up sprang when Deaglan strode into the house. He didn't stop to talk to Deck or the officers, he came straight for me.

I heard Tyler mumble something, but I couldn't tell what because I was focused on Deaglan. Five days. Five days I hadn't seen him and yet it felt like a lifetime. God, how did this happen?

I rose just before he reached me. His eyes roamed the length of me. It wasn't sexual; it was as if he was making certain I wasn't hurt.

He pulled me into his arms. "Eva," he said in a ragged voice. "Jesus." He kissed the top of my head. "You okay?"

I peered up at him. "Yeah. I'm okay." I attempted a smile, but failed miserably. "The idea of blowing up... I freaked a bit when I saw Vic."

Tension riddled his body as he held me close, one hand at the back of my head as I curled into him. "I told you. I won't let that happen."

He had. Numerous times. "Vic said you were in Ireland."

"Yeah. Just flew in. Came straight from the airport." His fingers tucked a few strands behind my ear. "I had to deal with shit back home, Eva. Shit, we'll talk about. But we're not doing that tonight."

I nodded.

He pulled back, but only enough so he could look at me. "I'm getting you out of here. The guys can look after this. We'll go to my hotel."

"You have a hotel room? But you just flew in."

"Baby, I've had a hotel room ever since my place blew up."

I hadn't thought about it because he'd been staying with me up until five days ago. And I assumed he'd stay with Deck or Tyler if he needed a place.

He glanced over my head at Tyler and Vic. "Call me if you have anything."

Deaglan released me, but only enough to slip his hand in mine as he led me past the commotion. Shielding me from it. Like he always did.

Fifteen

Eva

DEAGLAN TOOK ME TO HIS HOTEL ROOM, WHICH TURNED OUT TO BE in a five-star hotel. And the suite didn't have basic essentials. It had elaborate essentials.

A king-size bed sat opposite the floor-to-ceiling windows with a beautiful gray velvet bolster. Two gold-wrapped chocolates lay on the pillows and two swan-folded bath towels at the foot of the bed. There was a living space, with a couch and two chairs and glass coffee table, and everything was done in soft beiges with splashes of red.

Deaglan ordered room service despite telling him I wasn't hungry, but he seemed to think I'd be hungry after the adrenaline wore off.

I decided to have a quick shower before the food came and changed into one of the white fluffy robes. When I came out of the washroom, Deaglan was out on the balcony chatting on the phone. His voice was low, but the French doors were open so I heard his conversation.

I sat on the edge of the bed and watched him half-bent, forearms resting on the balcony railing, one leg slightly cocked.

"Don't be a fuckin' dick," he said with a hint of humor in his voice. "I'm not telling you shit." Pause. "Yeah. And stay clear of my place, Ronan. I told my guys to kick your ass if they see you." Pause. "I'll be back in a few weeks." Another pause and he straightened, turned and leaned against the railing. His eyes landed on me and instantly heated with desire as they roamed up my naked legs to where the robe parted.

I swallowed, and my girl parts tingled and clenched.

"Have to go. Talk soon." He lowered the phone and walked into the room, tossing it on one of the two beige chairs seated around the small, round coffee table.

He stalked toward me.

Our eyes remained locked, even when he towered over me and I had to crank my neck to look up at him. "Is everything okay?"

His hand cupped the side of my head and my chest rose and fell rapidly.

His eyes flashed amusement. "I didn't have time to see my brother when I was in Ireland and he's pissed. But, yeah, he's fine."

"Your brother?" I whispered.

"My half-brother Ronan. We have the same father." Deaglan tipped into me. "Eva, I should've been with you." His thumb slid across my lower lip. "I shouldn't have left."

"I'm the one who told you to leave, Deaglan."

His lips hovered over mine. "I didn't leave because you told me to, Eva."

"Oh," I whispered.

My breath stilled. My heart raced and my blood rushed through my veins like a raging river.

"I never want to leave you, Eva."

He kissed me. I expected fierce and bruising, which I loved. But what I got was passionate, intense, and slow.

He held my head between his hands, as his mouth roamed over mine in deep exploration.

It wasn't a fling kiss. This was penetrating and consuming.

It was more.

And it meant something. I wasn't sure what yet, but it was more than I thought either of us expected.

He groaned and released me. "I kiss you any longer, we won't be eating anything but each other."

I smiled. "I'm good with that." God, I liked this guy too much.

The tension in him eased as he chuckled, then released me to walk into the washroom.

A knock sounded on the door, and I crawled off the bed to answer it when Deaglan intercepted and corralled me against the wall.

"You don't get the door, Eva."

"It's just the food," I said and tried to duck under his arm.

He blocked me with his forearm and his fingers curled into my hip. "This is about keeping you safe." Scowling, his eyes roamed the length of me. "And you're not answering the door dressed like that."

I frowned. "No one knows we're here, and what's wrong with this? I'm wearing a bathrobe. It's practically a snowsuit."

Another knock and a man's voice, "Room service."

His eyes flicked to the crevice between my breasts where the robe parted and lower to my naked legs. "He's not looking at you in that," he said, jaw clenched, lips firm and his eyes unyielding.

I'd never seen him like this, but I had no energy to fight the issue, and it was silly anyway. So I let him have it and Deaglan opened the door while I sat cross-legged on the bed.

I saw the waiter attempt to wheel the cart in, but Deaglan stopped it with his foot. He shoved a bill in the waiter's hand and wheeled the cart in himself. I was uncertain whether that was a safety issue or because I sat on the bed in a bathrobe.

Deaglan placed the tray of food on the bed, and I scuttled up to the top and leaned against the velvet-padded headboard.

Deaglan's brows rose. "You're hungry."

I nodded smiling. "Starved."

"Here." He passed me a white napkin before picking up a large tiger shrimp with his fingers and holding it out to me. I bit into it and he popped the rest of it in his mouth.

"Mmm. Delicious," I said.

He sat beside me, legs outstretched, a bowl of linguine on his lap that he currently spiraled with his fork. With one hand cupped under the fork, he held it out to me. I opened, and he slid it into my mouth. His heated eyes remained on me as he watched me chew.

I swallowed. "Does linguine turn you on?"

"You turn me on," he replied. "Everything you do makes me rock-hard, baby. When your tongue licks your lower lip when you chew, barely visible, but enough to wet the surface. And when you like what you're eating, your eyes soften, and you slow your chewing as you savor every bite." He paused, twirling the fork in the pasta again. "It's the same look when your mouth is around my cock." He lifted the fork and ate a mouthful of pasta.

"Because I love the taste of your cock and I want to savor it."

He finished chewing and swallowed. "You don't need to savor it. You can have as much of it as you want."

I laughed.

And that was how it went. We talked, and he fed me linguine and shrimp while sitting in bed, and when we were done, he stripped off my clothes, then his, before he teased my nipples with chocolate ice cream, then proceeded to suck on my ice-cream-covered nipples.

We showered, and he washed every inch of my body before he kissed every inch, then fucked me against the foggy glass with my legs around his waist and his hands on my ass.

He toweled me off himself, and as he did it, his tongue captured pearls of water clinging to my skin. I ended up sitting on the bathroom counter with his mouth between my legs and my body shuddering.

When he was done, he swept me up in his arms and carried me to bed where he wrapped me against his warm, hard body.

Then we slept.

When I woke, Deaglan wasn't in bed and I sat up holding the sheet to my naked chest as I looked around the room for him.

A breeze wafted into the room and the sheer white curtains billowed before settling back in place. The balcony doors were open and Deaglan stood in his jeans, while leaning his forearms on the railing.

At first, I thought he was watching the sunrise, but his head was tilted down and his hair fell forward in front of his face. I reached for my panties and over-sized sweatshirt at the foot of the bed, slipped them on and climbed out of bed.

Padding across the room, I walked out onto the balcony. I didn't say anything, and neither did he.

I came up behind him and slid my arms around his waist, pressing my body into him and resting my cheek on his naked back. He didn't move, but his shoulders slumped and his head dipped lower.

We stood like that for a while. Neither of us saying anything as the sun rose and the city awoke below us.

His hand slid down my forearm and rested on top of mine for a second before he moved.

He straightened, and my arms fell from around his waist, but not for long as he faced me and drew me into him again. This time, my cheek rested on his chest as he towered over me, arms holding me to him.

He kissed the top of my head. "Morning."

"Morning," I whispered in a sleepy voice.

Something had shifted last night, mostly with him, but me, too, because when he kissed me, when he thrust inside me, it wasn't fucking. It was more. It was him. All of him.

"How long did he hit you for?"

I tensed and tried to pull back, but he tightened his arms and I relaxed against him again. "A few months." The physical. The emotional was a lot longer. It was as if he was preparing me for when he finally did hit me. Making certain I was worn down enough, so when his slapped me the first time, I questioned myself, not him.

His chest rose as he inhaled a ragged breath. His hand cupped the back of my head and his thumb lightly brushed over the scar. "It wasn't your fault, Eva."

I tried not to stiffen, but I did and his arms tightened. "I know."

He gently kissed the scar on my head. "Do you?"

I swallowed. "Logically, I do."

"A man like that is a coward. He tries to crush a woman, break her down to make himself feel powerful and in control. But he's fuckin' scum."

He had crushed me. He invaded and made me feel powerless. Alone. I'd felt really alone and maybe that was the biggest reason I wanted to open the center for women in similar situations. So, they didn't feel like they were alone. They had others to fight for them. With them.

After a minute, I whispered, "Why is this personal to you, Deaglan?"

He was silent a minute and I didn't think he'd answer me when he said, "My mom. She was abused for years." My chest clenched and stomach coiled. "I was too young to do anything about it."

That was why he was so protective. He'd been unable to protect his mom from the abuse he'd witnessed as a child.

"She tried to hide it from me, but even being so young, I knew. Maybe not exactly what was happening, but I knew it was wrong. I knew the man was a bad guy." He paused. "She'd hide me in a trunk under the window when she knew it was going to be bad. I'd wear these big earmuffs that she'd decorated with all these fake gems to make it look like a crown. She tried to make it a game and told me I was the king and the trunk was my private throne room where I was protected and nothing could touch me.

But covering my ears wasn't enough. I heard her screams. Her crying. But worse was the sound of her body hitting the floor. That thump. Fuck, I hated that thump. I think I was scared she'd never get up again. That one day she'd stay on the floor."

My throat tightened and tears pooled in my eyes and slipped over the rims. What he must have witnessed as a child hearing his mother being abused. It explained a lot as to why Deaglan was the man he is today. Why he was adamant about protecting me after I was mugged. The relentless need to find who was responsible. Why he was so angry when he found out about Curran.

I pulled back to look up at him and his eyes were dark and riddled with emotion. "Was he your father?"

He shook his head. "No. I didn't meet my real father until I was twelve and went to live with him when the bastard finally went too far and killed her."

Oh God. "That's why you want to find Curran."

He placed his finger under my chin and tilted my head as he bowed over me. "My mom escaped him, Eva. But she lived for years looking over her shoulder with the constant fear he'd find her. And he did. One day, the bastard did." He tightened his hold. "I won't let that happen to you, Eva."

Sixteen

Eva

"CHEERS," ALLY SAID, RAISING HER MINT AND LIME TEQUILA refresher. "To Kendra landing the man of her... I mean, job of her dreams."

It had been four days since the false alarm, the hotel, and Deaglan telling me about his mom. I suspected there was more, but I didn't ask. I knew it had been hard for him to share what he had about his mom.

We stayed at the hotel because he didn't want me living at the rental, and when I wasn't working, he was also with me, which meant he helped me paint the foyer in the new house and hang the chandelier.

And tonight, he was meeting me at the bar to celebrate Kendra's promotion. I thought it was to make sure I was safe even if I had Luke, but he'd said it was because Kendra was important to me.

"You look amazing." Charlotte said. Kendra's sister was twenty-five, single, and had a five-year-old little girl, Maddie.

I glanced down at my sexy little black dress that was snug, mid-thigh and had a low V-neck. I wore my black, two-inch pumps with the turquoise soles and angel hair straps that circled my ankles. "Thanks."

"Does it have anything to do with that Irish stud in your bed every night?"

I smiled, "Maybe. He's coming tonight."

Her thin arched brows lifted as she chewed on her straw. "Really? Kendra told me he only shows up at night for sex and leaves in the morning."

I raised my eyes heavenward. "Your sister doesn't approve of casual sex. Even if it's amazing casual sex." And feels more than casual.

"My sister is so focused on her career, she's forgotten what it's like to have a man between her legs." She sipped her drink. "Hey, when are you coming up to the farm? Maddie is dying to see you."

"I'm not sure. There's a lot going on right now." I'd have to talk to Deaglan about it, but maybe getting out of the city was a good idea. "How's Maddie? Is she staying at your parents' tonight?" Maddie was five and fearless. She was also inquisitive, and like her mom, loved animals.

They lived three hours north on twenty-five acres in an old three-story farmhouse with a wraparound porch. She'd bought it for cheap, but there were reasons it was cheap, one of them being the entire house had to be rewired. The other was one of the barns was collapsing and unusable. So, Charlotte knew exactly what I was going through with my house.

She pushed her shoulder-length, thick brown hair behind her slim shoulders. "My parents came to the farm because Maddie didn't want to leave the piglets."

"Piglets? You have piglets?"

She laughed. "A pig I rescued last week was pregnant. She just gave birth, and Maddie saw it happen. Now she's obsessed with them. Mom and Dad will have a hard time getting her to sleep in her own bed tonight. She wants to sleep with the pigs. But, then last month, it was the calf Dory. If I'd let her, she'd set up her bedroom in the barn."

I laughed. We talked about Maddie and the animals for a while longer, then she told me about a corporation she was currently fighting with about the inhumane treatment at their factory farms.

Charlotte nudged me with her shoulder and nodded to Bob. "He's eyeing you up. I bet my sister told him you're available." I groaned. Charlotte laughed.

Boring Bob smiled at me.

He was handsome with defined features, soft, coffee-colored eyes and a cute smile. He looked good in in a crisp, white, button-down shirt with dark gray slacks.

But he wasn't Deaglan.

When he shook my hand, it had been weak as if I were shaking hands with a dead fish. One of the first things I'd noticed when Deaglan introduced himself to me was his firm handshake. Not crushing or overbearing, but strong and with conviction. Like he meant it.

My phone vibrated in my purse and I pulled it out, glancing at the screen.

Deaglan: Be there in ten.

I smiled and my belly flipped.

"Deaglan?" Charlotte asked.

I nodded. "Yeah."

"Wow, you really like him."

I did. I really liked Deaglan. I had reservations, of course, and I only had one foot off the cliff, but I was teetering on the edge of falling completely.

"I think it's great and can't wait to meet him," Charlotte said, and set her glass on the table. "I'm hitting the little girls' room. Want me to grab you another drink?" Charlotte said, rising.

"I'm good, thanks," I replied. It was only a minute later when Bob made his way around the table toward me. Shit.

"Hey, Eva. Mind if I sit?" he asked.

He stood with a beer in hand. Not in the bottle, but in a long-stemmed glass with the little white napkin stuck to the bottom.

I glanced toward the entrance of the bar for Deaglan but couldn't see him yet. My watchdog Luke sat at the bar with a glass of sparkling water in hand, his eyes on me.

"Oh, yeah. Sure," I said, offering a smile.

Bob sat, and Kendra, who sat across the table, caught my eye and winked. I rolled my eyes.

I had no interest in Bob. I had no interest in anyone except Deaglan.

That was dangerous, but I wasn't fighting it any longer. He'd given a piece of himself and I knew how hard that had been when he was closed off about his past.

I lifted my drink and sipped while Bob chatted about... well, I didn't know what exactly because Bob's voice was monotone and why he was nicknamed Boring Bob.

The hairs on the back of my neck quivered and my breath caught in my throat.

I didn't have to look to know Deaglan was here. I felt him.

My body awakened and everything shifted from gray to Technicolor.

Seventeen

Eva

I TURNED IN MY CHAIR, SEARCHING THROUGH THE CROWD FOR HIM. MY gaze bounced from person to person, but I couldn't see him.

Until I did.

And then my heart slammed into my ribcage and heat spread from the top of my head right down to the tips of my toes.

Bob was still talking, but his words faded into the background as Deaglan strode toward me.

Women stared, men did, too, and everyone moved out of his way. He didn't have to slide between groups of people or ask them to move; they got out of his way.

He drew attention everywhere he went, but especially in a bar full of suits with fancy drinks while he wore snug jeans, low on his hips with a black leather belt. He had on a fitted charcoal-gray shirt, long-sleeved, but he had them pushed up a bit so you could see the tattoos on his forearms.

I bit my lip, chest tightening as I stared at him. I couldn't believe I got to be with this man. There was so much more I wanted to know about him, but I didn't know if I'd get that chance.

I smiled as he drew closer. His gaze slid over me and his lip twitched.

Warmth covered my hand on the table and I jerked, stiffening as my eyes darted to Bob's hand settled over mine. "Eva?" he said. "Did you hear me?"

I yanked my hand out from under his and my heart slammed into my chest.

Bob frowned with concern. "What's wrong?"

My gaze jumped to Deaglan.

The muscles in his arms flexed and his jaw tightened as he glared at Bob.

The sounds in the bar merged into low hums. Music and voices undecipherable to the skulk of warning that blanketed me.

Deaglan stopped beside me and placed his hand on my left shoulder.

He squeezed.

I couldn't tell if it was gentle or bruising. Because the memory sucked me under the suffocating depths of its sludge.

My body weighed a thousand pounds as everything inside me pinballed with red flashing warning bells.

I wanted to scream. To run. But my lungs were frozen. My limbs caked in heavy wet mud.

"Deaglan," Ally called from across the table. "You made it."

"Ladies," he said with a nod. "Congratulations, Kendra."

Everyone at the table spoke and yet, I couldn't focus on the words.

"And beside Eva is Bob, my boss," Kendra said.

I lowered my head and placed my hands on my thighs. Squeezing. Squeezing.

Warning.

He's warning me with his hand.

My stomach cramped and bile rose in my throat.

"Hey." Bob said, offering his hand, but Deaglan ignored it as his eyes were on me. At least, I felt like they were. Burning. Watching. Warning. "Are you a friend of Kendra's?" Bob asked.

"Eva," Deaglan said quietly. Was it a warning? Was he angry?

No. No. I swore I'd never let this happen again.

Curran wasn't here. Deaglan. This was Deaglan.

He crouched beside me. "Eva, baby. Look at me." I slowly raised my head and looked at him. "Fuck," he growled. I inhaled a deep breath. "Let's get you out of here." He held out his hand.

I stared at it for a second. He didn't force me to take his hand. Or grab me and yank me to my feet. He patiently waited for me to decide.

My mind scrambled to shove the dark pieces back in the crevices.

This was Deaglan. Deaglan. He'd never hurt me. He'd done everything to protect me.

I met his eyes as I put my hand in his and stood. Deaglan drew me in close and kissed the top of my head.

"You okay, Eva?" Ally asked from across the table. I hesitated, looking over at her and she frowned. "Shit, you're not okay." She shoved her chair back and stood. "Let's go to the restroom. Kendra?"

"I'll look after her," Deaglan said.

Kendra rose. "Eva?"

"I, uh…" I gazed up at Deaglan. This was my battle. These were my demons. I wasn't that girl anymore. "Yeah. I'm okay. Really." Ally and Kendra looked at one another, then their gazes shifted back to me. "I swear. We'll be back in a minute."

Deaglan's hand lightly squeezed mine and we moved through the crowd. He led me across the bar and down a hallway where the music wasn't as loud. Three girls passed us who had come out of the restroom laughing.

He stopped at the emergency exit and released my hand. I sagged up against the door.

Deaglan's head dipped as he turned and walked away two strides. He stopped and jerked his fingers through his hair.

I crossed my arms over my chest as a shield, but it wasn't against him. It was to try and stop the trembling.

Deaglan inhaled a ragged breath before slowly shifting to face me. He raised his head and our eyes locked.

Oh boy. Brows furrowed. Lips firm. Jaw rigid.

But it was his eyes that contradicted the anger. A worried and concerned quietness lingered in the depths.

"I'm trying not be angry here, Eva." His hand went to the back of his neck as he paused. "He put that there. That piece of shit put that fear in you." He swore beneath his breath as he lowered his head again as if he needed a minute to control his fury. "You were shaking. No, fuck. You were trembling. Jesus."

I gnawed my lower lip. I had been. It had been the succession of moments that triggered the reaction in me. Bob sitting beside me. His hand touching mine. Deaglan approaching and his gaze shifting to Bob. The final straw was his hand on my shoulder and the squeeze.

I touched my hand to my shoulder. There was no pain. But I knew that already. It had been gentle. Reassuring. Not bruising with warning like Curran.

His booted feet thumped as he moved toward me. "Baby." His arm bridged my head as he leaned in, but he didn't look at me. Not right away.

His chin was dipped as he inhaled a deep breath again. "He doesn't deserve to breathe for what he did to you."

I placed my palm on his chest and his muscles tensed as his eyes met mine. "I wasn't scared of you, Deaglan. It wasn't you."

His jaw clenched. "That bastard put that there. I saw it in my mom, too. The triggers that set the fear off in her."

Deaglan closed his eyes, and when he opened them again I saw so much sorrow in the dark depths that it crushed me. This was a lot more than the fear he'd seen in me. This had to do with him seeing that in his mom and being unable to stop it.

I reached up and cupped his cheek. "Stop blaming yourself. You would've helped her if you could've, Deaglan. She knew that. And I have no doubt you're the reason she finally found the courage to leave. She knew you would've tried to stop him. You would've protected her. And he'd have hurt you, or worse, killed you for it. None of it was your fault."

Just like it wasn't mine. And for the first time, I really believed it.

With his head dipped and his eyes on the floor, he said, "Caitlyn. Her name was Caitlyn MacKenna." He raised his head and our eyes locked. "She'd have loved you, Eva. Fuckin' strong, and determined, but still vulnerable and kind. She'd have seen how rare you were like I did the second I met you. Confirmed it after we spent the night together. Solidified it that day we picked out a fridge and I had a beer with your dad. I saw more of you and I liked what I saw." My heart double-dutch skipped. "I never expected you and I wasn't prepared. It took time to wrap my head around the possibility of more with you." He lowered his head and his hand found mine, fingers entwining, and my heart squeezed. "I still don't know if I'll get the chance of more."

Oh. My. God. My body quivered and my belly was a hurricane of swirling butterflies.

He cupped my chin, his thumb grazing my lower lip. "But whatever you'll give me, I'll treasure."

My chest tightened and my insides lit up like the Fourth of July. I could love this man. And maybe I did already.

But loving Deaglan would be crushing.

Destructive.

Ruining.

Because you'd never walk away from loving a man like Deaglan whole. He'd keep pieces of you. The important pieces you'd never get back because they belonged to him.

Deaglan protected and he did it with everything he was.

And if he loved, I had no doubt it would be consuming.

Time. The word echoed in my head as if I was in a cistern. But I wouldn't ruin what we had now with what hung over both of us. I wasn't going to live diminished. I was going to live.

I smiled. "I hope we have lots of time, Deaglan. I want lots of time."

"Baby," he said in a raspy voice and drew me into his arms.

His mouth pressed against the top of my head and goosebumps popped across my skin. He pulled back and I rose on my tiptoes to meet his lips.

His mouth settled over mine like it was the only place it was meant to be.

His kiss wasn't bruising or crushing.

It was devastating.

His touch. His subtle groan against my lips. His ability to make me forget everything except him.

His mouth softened, and he kissed me lazily as his fingers slid from my chin to my neck where he curled them. Not tight, but firm as he kissed me a while longer.

He pulled back. "Thirty minutes long enough with your friends?" he asked.

My lips tingled. I licked them, tasting Deaglan. "Yeah," I whispered.

He kissed me again briefly. "I don't think I can wait any longer than that before taking you home and having you ride my cock."

A flare between my legs. "Okay."

He smirked. "I have my bike. Are you good on it, baby?"

My eyes widened. "Your bike? I thought it was in your place when it was destroyed."

He slipped his hand in mine. "It was. I bought a new one."

I shook my head. "You just went out and bought another bike? But you don't even live here."

He smirked. "We'll see."

He led me back to the table with his hands on my hips, body shielding me from being bumped by the crowd. And then Deaglan pulled out a chair for me, then he sat in the chair next to it, but I didn't sit.

I looped my arm around his neck and settled in his lap.

Then I kissed him. It was brief and quick, but I heard his low groan rumble in his chest.

For the next half hour or so, Deaglan chatted with my friends and it was nice. Really nice. Charlotte told him about when she was seventeen and spent a few weeks in Ireland and how much she loved it. She also told him about the girls' weekend at her farm when we played Truth or Dare and I had to pretend to pole dance for five minutes with my underwear on my head.

Deaglan laughed at that, then kissed me and whispered, "Fuck, my girl drunk and pole dancing without me to fuck her afterward."

I scrunched my nose. "You don't fuck a girl if she's drunk."

"If she's my girl and she knows she's mine, then I do."

"Oh," I replied, liking that.

Deaglan ordered me another drink, and I sipped on it while he had sparkling water.

I liked Deaglan with my friends. A lot. He chatted effortlessly with everyone, although I noticed he kept the conversation about them.

When Kendra got up to walk to the bar, Deaglan kissed my neck and lifted me off his lap. "Back in a sec."

"Okay. I'm almost done. Then we can go," I said.

He nodded and stood.

I watched him walk across the bar and move in beside Kendra.

Ally and Charlotte watched them.

Kendra was important to me, and I knew she was being protective of me. But I also knew she loved me enough to listen to Deaglan, especially since him showing up tonight said something more than us being a fling.

My chest tightened as I watched. His forearm was perched on the bar top and one leg half-cocked, casual and relaxed. His hair fell across the side of his face, which meant I couldn't see his expression or attempt at reading his lips. Not that I could, but I'd certainly try.

Whatever he was saying to Kendra was likely non-confrontational because her shoulders sagged a bit and she nodded. Okay, that was good.

They talked another minute before Deaglan and Kendra made their way back to the table, she with a fresh drink. Deaglan winked at me before walking around the table to talk to Ally.

Kendra leaned into me and whispered, "I know I'm an overprotective pain in the ass, but after Curran, I need to be for myself as much as for you, Eva." I smiled. "I saw the look in your eyes earlier. The fear. It was Curran, wasn't it?"

I nodded.

She peered over at Deaglan. "He erased it. He put that beautiful smile and light back in your eyes," She kissed my cheek. "I hope he stays. I hope he's the one to erase all the bad." She smiled broad. "Oh, and he's getting me an interview with his brother, Ronan."

I frowned. "Ronan? Really?"

She nodded enthusiastically. "Yeah, he told me who his brother is and I nearly peed my pants. Ronan Kane is big. He plays football for Ireland and the guy never does interviews."

"But you don't interview football players."

She shrugged. "It's an exclusive. Bob is going to totally freak when he finds out." Kendra walked away, grinning ear to ear.

Deaglan came up behind me and I placed my half-full glass on the table then stood. "You didn't tell me your brother is a famous soccer, or rather football, player?"

He smirked. "Yeah. He's a cocky shit disturber, but he's one fuck of a football player."

"You're going to arrange an interview for him with Kendra?"

He shrugged. "I need points."

I huffed. "Trust me, you have the points without the interview."

"Doesn't hurt to have extra."

"Do you have any other famous brothers I should know about?"

He chuckled. "Cousin, Kite. He's in the band Tear Asunder."

"What?" I choked out. "Holy shit, Kite. The drummer. His last name is Kane."

His arm hooked my waist and he tugged me into him. "He's taken, baby. And you're mine."

I was his. And even when he went home, there would always be a part of me that was his. I stood on my tiptoes and nipped his lower lip. "Kite is sexy as hell and in a rock band."

He grunted. "But I can rock your fuckin' world, baby."

A rabble of butterflies fluttered and between my legs throbbed. Because he could. He did. "We should go."

"Mmm," he murmured.

We quickly said goodbye, and with his hand in mine, he led me outside to his bike. That was illegally parked. "Do you have an issue with legal parking spaces?"

He laughed. "I believe in getting to you as fast as I can."

I snorted. "That's bullshit, but a good answer."

He plopped a helmet on my head and adjusted the chin strap so it was snug. "Good?" he asked.

"Yeah." I was getting on a motorcycle and it was probably a stupid thing to do because I knew the danger of motorcycles. But Deaglan was Deaglan and he was super protective. He also had confidence in spades, which meant he didn't need to show off.

He undid a satchel on the side of his bike and pulled out a black leather jacket. "I don't have anything for your legs, but this will help."

He helped me tug on the leather jacket, and it was obviously too big, but it covered my bare arms and offered padding and warmth for my upper body. He zipped it up.

"Sexy as hell in my leather and helmet, Eva."

I laughed. "I feel like I have a bowling ball on my head."

He grinned. "If you like riding with me, I'll get you a helmet."

My breath stilled because his words were as if he'd be here longer.

He put on his helmet, then threw a leg over the seat and started the engine. It rumbled to life and settled into a deep purr.

I was nervous, but it was overridden by excitement.

He patted the seat behind him. "Hop on, baby."

I climbed on behind him and he pressed his hand to the small of my back, sliding me closer to him, so my pelvis was snug to his ass.

Okay, I really liked being on a bike with him.

And I felt as if I was tossing aside my safety net as the thrill of danger rose.

I was so not a thrill-seeking person, but I could see why people did things that scared them. Why they pushed their boundaries. It was blood pumping and belly flipping.

He showed me where to put my feet, and once my arms were tight around his waist, he eased onto the road.

And Deaglan rode just as I expected him to, carefully. He was cautious taking the corners, and when we stopped at red lights, he put his hand on my thigh and checked in on me.

It was sweet, and I loved that he did that.

And I loved the vibration of the bike underneath me. The feel of the wind against my skin. The freedom of nothing between me and the road. Me and him.

The bike slowed and he stopped. I glanced up at my house.

He shut off the bike and I climbed off. "Why are we here?" I asked, frowning.

He snagged my hand and drew me close to him, then he undid the chin strap of my helmet. "Eva, you own a house you don't live in. And you love this house." I did. I totally loved this house. "I saw it when you sat on your porch swing, pink and yellow pillows with little-beaded shit all over them surrounding you."

I scrunched my nose. "I love those pillows."

He chuckled. "I know you do. They're all over your bed, too." Deaglan gently removed my helmet and hung it on the handlebars. "That day I drove up here, you sat in that swing looking comfortable, proud and protective as hell about your territory."

I laughed. "You can't be protective of a house."

"It means something to you. Your dad knows it, too." He cupped my chin. "It's more than a house, Eva. You're building something. Every repair you make. Every new light that's hung or damn fridge that's installed, it's you. You're repairing, baby. You're building you. And one day, you'll help other women find the strength to build what's in them."

I melted into a liquid pool of goo at his feet. Tears pooled in the rims of my eyes and my throat tightened. He was right. I didn't know it until he said the words, but I felt it. When the fridge arrived. When the toilet was installed. When I finished sanding the bannister and painted the foyer.

They were all building blocks to repairing myself. To finding my strength again.

He lightly kissed my quivering lips. "I want to be part of that, Eva. And it's time to get out of that shit rental. Your landlord is a fuckin' dick."

My eyes widened. "You talked to my landlord?"

"Yeah. Didn't want you to deal with that asshole. And he's an asshole, babe."

"I can't stay here without running water, Deaglan. The pipes are old and made of lead so they all need replacing."

His warm hand linked with mine as he led me up the path to the door. The cobblestone path was the second feature that made me fall in love with this house. It meandered. It was wide in places, narrow in others. It was the imperfect perfection. And I couldn't wait to plant pink and yellow tulip bulbs in the fall and watch them bloom next spring.

"Keys?" he asked, holding out his hand.

I dug through my purse and found the keys and handed them to Deaglan. He opened the door and the alarm Vic installed beeped. Deaglan pressed the four-digit code and the sound stopped.

I lifted my brows because I had no idea he knew the code of this house, too. "I've decided Vic isn't good at keeping secrets."

He smirked. "Your dad either."

My jaw dropped. "My dad? My dad told you the code?" I jolted. "Wait, you spoke to my dad? You have his phone number? You talk?"

He didn't say anything as he closed and locked the door, then reset the perimeter alarm.

I tossed my purse on the floor in the foyer and he flicked on the light.

"Do you want something to drink?" I asked, stepping toward the kitchen. "I have a fridge now."

Deaglan laughed as he snagged my hand and I yo-yoed backward into him. "Upstairs, baby."

"Upstairs? I don't have anything up there yet." He didn't say anything as he herded me up the stairs in front of him.

"Have you seen the showerhead? It's really cool. Well, it will be when it's working."

His arm hooked my waist and he leaned in, kissing my neck. "I'd love to see your showerhead, Eva."

Why that sounded sexual, I had no idea why, but it did, and my body quivered.

"Okay," I said.

He trailed a path of kisses up my neck to my ear where he nibbled on the lobe.

Tingles. Shudders. Goosebumps. Everywhere.

At the top of the landing, I pointed to the right. "There are two bedrooms down there. And a washroom, but the washroom doesn't look like one right now because there is nothing in it. I think it used to be a nursery, but I'm turning it into another bathroom for when guests stay over."

He didn't say anything and I turned left toward my bedroom. The oak floors were worn, scraped and creaked, but I liked them that way because worn, scraped, and creaked said they were old, and had a story. It was one of the reasons I fell in love with this house.

"My bedroom is in here—"

My heart hit the roof of my mouth and my belly landed smack on the floor as I stared at my bedroom.

"I... how...? Deaglan."

Eighteen

Eva

WORDS LODGED IN MY THROAT AS I STARED AT MY FURNISHED bedroom.

My king-size bed sat near the window dressed with the green comforter and all my throw pillows from my bedroom at the other house.

My antique dresser with the oval mirror stood across from it and there was a gray, fake fur rug on the floor at the end of the bed that I'd never seen before, but loved immediately.

"I don't understand." I peered at Deaglan. "How... did you...? Oh my God, did you do this?"

"I spoke to your dad. He met me here. The excavators and plumbers met us here, too. Vic and Tyler brought your bed and dresser over. Barstools are downstairs too for something to sit on until you get the movers organized. Ally swung by to put all that frilly shit on your bed, because as much as it's you and I like that you love it, I can't put that shit on the bed how you like it."

Tears filled the rims of my eyes. "You spoke to my dad," I repeated in a barely audible whisper as my eyes swung back to my bed. "Ally came by. Vic and Tyler." Then, "That's why you arrived late tonight?"

A tear escaped and slid down my cheek. "You did this," I whispered.

He tucked strands of hair behind my ear. "I can't give you all of me, Eva. But I'll give you the best pieces I have."

My breath caught in my throat and another tear fell. He wiped that one away, too, before he bent and his lips claimed mine. It was gentle and sweet, but still, Deaglan in that moment when he kissed me, he kissed all of me.

He trailed kisses down my neck and I ran my hands up his corded back, fingers weaving into his hair.

"We can stay here? There's running water?"

He nibbled on my chin with a low, "Mmm."

"But they couldn't replace the pipes for weeks."

He kissed either side of my mouth. "I'm persuasive, babe."

He did this. I couldn't believe he did this, and my dad and Ally knew. Ally knew tonight when I saw her, and she never said anything.

I looked up at Deaglan and I finally stepped off the cliff.

I had no idea where it led, or when I'd land, but right now it was in the arms of Deaglan Kane.

His hands cupped my butt as he picked me up off the floor and I wrapped my legs around his waist. We crashed into the wall, mouths starved as we entwined in a frenzy of need.

Rough. Heated. Abandoned.

His hand skimmed up my back and his fingers bunched in my hair, gripping tight as he kissed me.

His groan vibrated against my mouth. "Eva. Christ. I can't give you up."

My lips tingled and face burned from his stubble as I panted in his arms. "I don't want you to, Deaglan."

"My past isn't pretty, baby."

"But it made you into the man standing in front of me. And that's the man I want."

"Fuck," he rasped, before his mouth claimed mine again. "You on anything?"

"Yeah." I'd been on the pill since I was nineteen to control ovulation cramps.

"You good with my bare cock inside you?"

I nodded. "Yeah."

"I'm fucking you in every single room in this house, so our story is engraved in the walls."

Oh God.

"But first, I'm going to take my sweet ass time and fuck you in your kickass bed with the frilly pink pillows under your ass."

"Okay."

He grinned before he picked me up in his arms and walked across the room to the bed. "Keep the heels on Eva."

I licked my lips as he lowered us. "Okay," I whispered.

He tossed me on the bed and I bounced twice before his hands were on me and my little black dress was off and on the floor. He stood at the end of the bed, and my heart fluttered.

"Un-fuckin'-expected," he said in a low raspy voice as he stared at me.

But it was Deaglan Kane who was unexpected. And I was going to hold onto the unexpected for as long as we had together.

Nineteen

Deaglan

I STOOD IN THE WOODEN BOX STARING AT THE ROARING CROWD ALL AROUND ME. *The smell of cigarette smoke and whiskey pungent in the air.*

I'd learned to block out the sounds.

The slap of skin meeting skin. The crushing blow of bone and the spray of blood.

The thump.

That fuckin' thump of a body hitting the floor.

The cries. The screams. They were silenced here.

"Okay, kid. You're next." A slap on the back. A kid? Was I a kid anymore? I didn't know. I couldn't see myself. I didn't know who I was.

The lid opened. The fake gems scattered to the cement floor and the crowd cheered and roared.

I stared at the cage. My opponent salivating like a rabid dog as he waited for me.

Blood dripped from his fists as his eyes gleamed with excitement.

Hatred blurred survival. Survival crushed morals. Morals suffocated under revenge.

I climbed out of the trunk and into the cage.

They chanted my name. "Crown. Crown. Crown."

I stepped into the cage and the door clanged shut behind me.

My eyes flew open. It took a second before the nightmare I'd had for years slowly faded into the dark corners of my mind.

I tightened my hold on the soft warm body that was curled into me.

Eva. I gazed down at her and the tension slowly eased from my body.

This woman. Fuck. I didn't deserve her. My past was stained with so much hatred and filth. And yet I couldn't let her go.

This wasn't about just protecting her and it hadn't been for a long time. Fuck, maybe I knew before I took her back to my place the first time. No, not maybe. I knew Eva was more and I took her anyway.

She sighed in her sleep, her full lips parting slightly.

I'd never had a relationship. Never wanted to settle with anyone. But more than that, I never wanted the attachment. To need anyone and yet, Eva… fuck. I had no choice in her. She was the hinge that opened the trunk and let me breathe.

But my past was filled with more than a little boy wearing a crown hiding in a trunk. It was the boy seeking revenge. It was the teenager fighting to destroy. It was the man unable to find the silence.

I carefully unwound my arms so as not to wake her and slid from bed. I snagged my jeans off the floor and tugged them on before padding barefoot across the room to the dresser. I grabbed my cell and quietly left the room.

As I walked downstairs, I tapped on my phone then placed it to my ear. It rang five times before I heard it click and Ronan's heavy breathing. "Fuck, bro, this better be good."

No doubt, he was with a chick. Cocky. Confident. And a famous football player was a lure for girls, and my brother took full advantage. "Need a favour."

"Shit," he grumbled. "I hate your favours."

I put the phone on speaker and tossed it on the counter as I filled the coffee carafe with water. "I've never asked you for a favour, asshole."

NASHODA ROSE

"Yeah, that's why I know I'm going to hate it," he replied.

Smartass. Ronan had been two when I moved in with the Kane's. I was an angry, sarcastic and seriously fucked-up twelve-year-old. The kid immediately clung to me like a soothing blanket and I tried to push him away like I did everyone else, but it didn't do any good. Ronan was a badger. Even when I came home bloody and bruised from fighting, he wasn't scared of me.

Instead, Ronan barreled right through my cement walls. It may have taken years, but he was the reason pieces of me remained intact and I was able to fight the path of destruction I'd been on.

"I need you to do an interview," I said.

"Jesus Christ." I heard the phone crackle as if he was pulling a shirt over his head. "Why the hell would you ask me to do that? You know I hate talking to the fuckin' media whores."

I snorted. I didn't know Eva's friend Kendra very well, but I knew enough that she'd sock him one if she'd heard him say that and he'd deserve it. "And I need you to do it over here."

"You're kidding. You want me to do an interview and fly there? No chance."

"Those charges were dropped," I said. The charges that would've landed him in juvie and gotten him expelled from school, which would've ended his chances to make it in football. I called in a favor, or some might call it blackmail, with a dirty politician and the charges dropped.

Silence then, "You're really going there."

I scooped coffee granules into the basket. "Yeah. I am."

"It's for her. This chick you're fucking."

I didn't like his word choice, but I didn't call him out on it. "Yeah." Kendra had every intention of flying to Ireland for the exclusive, but I wanted Ronan here so he could meet Eva.

"Shit." There was a bang like a door slamming, then a steady stream as if he was taking a piss, which no doubt he was. "My fist is in his face if he asks me about the charges."

142

I heard Eva walking down the stairs and picked up the phone taking it off speaker. "I'll tell her it's off limits."

"What? Her? It's a fuckin' chick? This better not be for some women's magazine."

"Need to go. I'll let you know when." I pressed END.

I peered over my shoulder at Eva as she padded into the kitchen looking cute as fuck wearing my gray shirt hanging mid-thigh, sleeves pushed up to the crook in her elbows.

"Morning," she said in a husky, sleepy voice.

"Morning, babe."

She nodded to the new coffee maker. "You bought a new one?"

I poured coffee into the two mugs I'd bought, along with the coffee maker, and then scooped half sugar into hers. The china sugar jar was the one from her rental house. I thought it meant something because she kept it, despite the chip in the lid, so I packed it with her frilly pillows.

"Selfish reasons. I knew we'd want coffee and I didn't want to go pick up coffee."

"My coffee maker at the rental works."

"Your coffee maker sucks, Eva. Half the time there are granules floating in the coffee. Its next stop is the bin."

When she reached me, she slid her arms around my waist from behind and tugged me in close, her cheek pressed against my back.

My cock jerked. Fuck, I loved that she did that.

It had been a long time since I allowed anyone besides Ronan to get close and I forgot what it felt like. I forgot how consuming it was. And, yeah, I sure as fuck forgot how dangerous, especially when I had my past knocking at my door and it put Eva at risk.

She squeezed me. "Thank you. For everything last night."

I slowly turned in her arms and her hands settled on my chest. "Your mouth around my cock wearing those heels was fuckin' perfection, babe."

But the truth was, all I needed was to see the expression on her face when she saw her bedroom.

To see the spark in her eyes.

And, yeah, to erase that fear I'd seen on her face last night.

With my finger under her chin, I tilted her head. "Eva," I whispered before I kissed her.

She sagged in my arms as my mouth roamed over hers. I tasted the mint of her toothpaste as her velvet lips melded under mine. I groaned when her body quivered and I deepened the kiss.

When we broke apart, her cheeks were flushed and her eyes soft and gentle. I loved her stubborn and sass, but her soft and gentle undid me.

"You found the toothbrush," I murmured.

She smiled. "You remembered everything."

I kissed her again, loving how her mouth surrendered to mine.

Last night, we'd fucked hard then gentle, and when she woke in the middle of the night and kissed me, I fucked her lazy from behind while spooning, both of us half asleep. I'd never done that before and I liked that it was a first with her. Fuck, everything felt like a first with Eva.

I knew the night I met her she was more. Confirmed it in the morning, and why I and kicked her out so abruptly. But Eva wasn't a woman to fuck and forget. She invaded. Not full force, but soft and quiet with a bit of sass that worked its way through the cracks in my armor.

I knew in the beginning that protecting Eva was in some way trying to repair where I failed my mom. But it wasn't possible to fix something broken when all the pieces weren't there. Particles of me existed, floating around in the darkness. I'd never tried to find my way out. Never cared.

Until now.

"You sleep okay?" She picked up her mug, curled both hands around it and sipped.

"You have a great bed," I replied. "Too many pillows."

She laughed, and the sound filtered into me. "I like the pillows."

"I like the pillows under your ass when I fuck you," I teased.

She licked her lower lip and her cheeks flushed. Christ, I liked that, too. "I might have to pick up bigger ones," she said.

I chuckled then leaned into her and kissed her again.

Christ, I was falling hard for this woman.

Eva truly was rare. She was determined. Stubborn, but still vulnerable. Sweet and compassionate, but strong.

But Eva didn't know about Crown. The person or the place. She didn't know what my mom had been. What I'd done for years after she was brutally beaten. My mom's death had been the stepping-stone that led me down the wrong path. A catalyst into the darkness. Because the underworld sucked me in and I'd become someone the immoral respected. Fuckin' coveted.

It was Deck who dragged my ass out of the death cages. He locked me in a room and refused to let me out until I found some sort of sanity and civility.

It was opening Crown and finding purpose in hunting criminals that in some way offered me a path to personal redemption, even though that redemption would never be found. The particles were lost in a sea of wrongs and I'd done more wrongs then I cared to admit.

Even now, I skirted the law when I dealt with the scum of the Earth.

There wasn't a place I called home. I never settled in one place long enough to make it a place to call home. Even Ireland. Finding scum took me all over the world, sometimes for months.

Eva's hand touched my forearm. "You okay?"

I forced a half grin. "Yeah. I want coffee with you on your swing." *Everyfuckin'day.*

"I want you to fuck me on that swing," she said, sliding her teeth over her lower lip. "Not now because it's light out and I don't want to scare my new neighbors by having sex on the front porch on my swing. But I'll be on top so your feet can keep the swing steady." She squished her lips. "Or not. Maybe it will be good swinging. I'm not sure yet."

Jesus, Eva dragging her teeth over her lip, saying fuck and discussing her swing and the two of us fucking on it, was like a hit to the solar plexus.

I raised my brows. "You've thought about this a lot, I take it. We may have to test it out a few times."

She laughed. "Yeah."

I picked up my mug and slid my fingers between hers as I led her out to the front porch swing. The sun rose over the horizon and offered a yellow glow across the yard and the summer breeze carried the scent of freshly cut lawns.

I held Eva's mug and waited until she settled on the swing with her legs curled to the side of her, then I passed her the coffee. I lowered into the swing beside her and placed my hand on her naked thigh, thumb slowly stroking back and forth.

I didn't know where this would go or end up. A long-distance relationship was impossible, and her coming to Ireland was out of the question with Crown and the darkness that surrounded me there. And whatever was happening with Seth Garrett in Toronto was a consequence of that. After seven years, I'd somehow become a threat to him, and I didn't know why. The problem was, the guy was like a shadow and impossible to find.

I'd left Eva those five days to ask my old contacts in Ireland about Seth Garrett. Then I asked the girls at Crown. Information was worth money and they listened. I didn't like it, but what they did wasn't up to me. My name gave them the protection they needed and if anyone fucked with that, they'd end up in a body bag.

Eva rested her hand in mine and lightly squeezed. "I like you here, Deaglan."

It was a simple gesture, but my insides warmed and my heart skipped a beat. Fuck. I wanted all of her, but I'd never get that without giving her all of me. Who I'd been. What I'd done. About Crown. I wasn't ready to give her all the ugly. Not yet.

I inhaled a ragged breath. "There are things I haven't told you, Eva."

"I know," she said quietly. "Don't just leave. Don't leave without saying goodbye."

Jesus. I put my arm around her shoulders and pulled her into me. "I wouldn't do that to you, baby."

But we both knew it was a lot more complicated than leaving without a goodbye.

Twenty

Eva

"NOW, THIS IS A BIG BOY BURGER, PRINCESS," TYLER SAID TO Vic as he piled his burger high with every single condiment laid out on the patio table, including condiments that weren't meant to be condiments, meaning ketchup-flavored potato chips. "No wonder why you're so feeble, eating beans and shit." Vic had a plate full of bean pasta salad.

I bit my lip to keep from laughing aloud. Tyler was looking to get his ass kicked, but he didn't seem too concerned about it. And by Vic's stone expression, he was used to Tyler's banter.

We were at Kai and London's house in their backyard after their daughter's Muay Thai exam. They lived near Casa Loma, a famous old castle that the neighborhood was named after. Their massive, stone house backed up to a ravine and had a salt-water pool.

Last night, while Deaglan had me naked on the marble kitchen island, he'd asked if I'd come with him today. Of course, I would've said yes either way, but I hemmed and hawed about it until Deaglan sank deep inside me and told me to answer the question.

I was living at my new house full time, albeit with no furniture except the bed, barstools, and the porch swing. The moving company was coming Tuesday because I had to work tomorrow and Monday. But the phone company came yesterday and hooked up the cable and Internet and two unlisted phone lines for the women's center. I also had workmen there, workmen Deaglan checked into thoroughly, who were putting in a separate entrance on the side of the house where I'd have an office.

I felt unstuck and even though it was scary as hell to face my demons, the idea of helping other women who were going through what I did gave me the will to push forward. Deaglan gave me the will to push forward.

He also didn't let me think too long about decisions that needed to be made. But he let me make them, just on a shorter time frame.

But over the last few days, Deaglan had been tense and didn't crawl into bed with me until near morning. I knew he and the guys from VUR were searching for Seth Garrett and Curran, although not much was said about it.

I understood why Deaglan had to find Curran. He'd never forgive himself if anything happened to me. Just like I suspected he never forgave himself for being unable to protect his mother.

But he'd been twelve years old. A kid. How was he supposed to protect her against a man like that?

Today he was relaxed.

Today I was with his friends, whom I really liked.

Hope was adorable, showing off her kicks and punches. And even cuter when her eyes looked to her father, Kai, for approval. But pride was all over his face and I had no doubt, he'd be proud no matter what she did.

It was later into the evening, when everyone was getting ready to leave, that I glanced over at Deaglan. Hope was in his arms while he chatted with Connor. Her head lay on his chest, and her palm on his forearm where she traced the tattoos with her finger.

He laughed at something Connor said and the sound filtered into me. He was completely at ease with the little girl in his arms.

My heart swelled and tears filled my eyes as I watched him.

He was beautiful. Every part of him.

The way he was with me, knowing when to push and when to let me do my thing. How he did things for me without any expectations in return. His protectiveness. His support and patience when I got stuck.

And then there was this side of him, like when we met. Relaxed and casual with his friends. His playfulness and overabundance of cockiness. Earlier he'd tossed Connor into the pool, and when I laughed, he slung me over his shoulder like a sack of potatoes and threatened to jump in.

I laughed and screamed and he ended up carrying me into the bathroom where he kissed me until my lips were swollen.

Right then it was as if a mallet slammed in to my stomach and left me breathless.

I loved him. I loved Deaglan Kane.

Completely and totally.

There was no denying it. And maybe I had been trying to deny it for a while. But there was no pretending that this was temporary, because it wasn't. There was nothing temporary about how I felt. It was consuming, just like I knew it would be.

And it was too late to stop what I felt for him. I wasn't sure when it happened exactly, but it crept up on me. Not the attraction to him. That had been like hitting a cement wall the moment I saw him. This was deeper. This was him.

The problem was I didn't have enough of him. Even though he shared a piece of himself, there was still a wall around him that I couldn't penetrate. Hidden parts.

But the love I felt at this moment for Deaglan was like being swept up in a tidal wave. It had the power to take me wherever it chose to, and there was no fighting it. I could ride the wave or drown in the destruction of its force.

Deaglan kissed the top of the little girl's head, then put her down.

He said something to Connor and they shook hands before he made his way toward me.

My heart burst with love, but also with heartache because it was going to hurt like hell when the wave crashed into shore and it ended.

Kendra was right. He was going to break my heart. We were on different paths and it was impossible for them to intersect even if we both wanted them to.

When we arrived at my place, Deaglan unlocked the door, turned off the alarm then grabbed me by the hips and shoved me against the wall.

His mouth collided with mine and I sagged in his arms. Teeth jarred. Mouths fused. Tongues danced.

It was desperation. Need. Urgency. And for me, it was love for this man.

I raked my fingers through his hair and moaned beneath his bruising assault.

"Baby," he murmured, as he trailed nips across my chin and down my neck. "Fuck, you're easy," he said.

"Easy?" I smacked his chest and tugged on his hair to pull him away. "I'm not easy, asshole."

He nipped my neck. "Shut up, Eva. That's not what I'm saying." He stopped kissing me and cupped my chin as our eyes locked. "Easy to be with. It's effortless. And today... Eva, you mingle. You laugh. You're comfortable with my friends and easily get along."

My heart thumped. "It's easy when the people are great and really nice."

He chuckled. "I wouldn't call Kai or Vic nice in front of them. They'd take offense."

I slid my hands over his shoulders and down his chest, my palm settling over his heart.

God, I never want him to leave.

He ran his finger down the side of my face, then tucked my hair behind my ear. "Baby, I spoke to Deck tonight about staying."

My breath stilled and my fingers tightened on his shirt. "You did?"

He nodded and a few strands of hair fell in front of his face. I brushed them back with the tips of my fingers. "I can stay here on a work visa, but the processing takes time. Reckon Deck can pull some strings, though."

"A work visa," I murmured as if the words weren't real.

"Deck said he'll hire me as a VUR specialist."

My heart slammed into my ribcage and skipped beats all over the place. Deaglan was trying to stay. He might not return to Ireland. Well, he would in that he'd visit his brother, but he would stay here. Live here.

"With me?" I asked, still trying to grasp that this was happening.

He smirked. "Yeah, Eva. With you. You good with that?"

"Does that mean you're still going to hunt the worst motherfuckers in the world."

He nodded. "Baby, I already do that, but now I'll be part of Deck's team." He tilted my head so I was forced to look at him. "This is what I do, and I need to do it."

"Yeah." I knew he did. That was part of what made him Deaglan. I stood on my tiptoes and kissed him. "I know."

"We have a lead on Seth. We need to jump on it tonight."

"Oh," I said. "So, you're sure it's him? The man who is after you?"

He nodded. "Seth disappeared seven years ago. It was after we had issues, Eva. Suddenly there's movement and it's against me." He smoothed his hand over my head. "The police are outside and I have Kai's man Ernie watching the house. Luke will be here in the morning if I'm not back."

I nodded. "Okay."

He lowered his head and kissed me.

And in that kiss it was all of him. All of us.

He pulled back and I caressed his jaw with my finger before meeting his eyes. "Be safe, Deaglan."

He tightened his hold and whispered, "Eva, I've never wanted to live as much as I do knowing I have you."

Twenty-One

Eva

I WOKE TO MY PHONE VIBRATING.

Rolling over, I snagged it off the nightstand and with one eye squinting open, I pressed answer and placed it to my ear.

"Eva?"

I bolted upright the instant I heard the tremor in Ally's voice.

"What's wrong?"

I reached for Deaglan to wake him, but his side of the bed was cold. Right, he'd gone hunting bad guys.

"Don't freak," Ally said.

"You saying don't freak doesn't help, Ally." I threw my legs over the side of the bed. "What's wrong?" I pulled my phone away from my ear and glanced at the time. It was five in the morning.

"Is Deaglan with you?"

"No. He's with Deck. Or, I think Deck, he didn't really say. He could be with Vic or Tyler. Maybe all of them."

"Oh," Ally said.

"What's oh?" I tugged on panties and jeans with my phone pressed between my shoulder and my ear. "Ally Schmidt, tell me right now."

"The rental house blew up."

I froze. My heart stopped pumping and my stomach dropped out and landed on the floor flopping around like a fish out of water.

Shit, breathe. *Breathe, Eva.*

"No one was in it," she blurted. "At least, they don't think so because you're not there."

"My house blew up," I repeated. "My house blew up?"

"I saw it on the news," Ally said. "Your neighbors were being interviewed."

Holy crap. My house blew up. Like Deaglan's warehouse blew up. Deaglan. *Please, Deaglan, be okay.*

"I'm coming over," Ally said.

My phone beeped and I pulled it away from my ear to look at the screen. Deaglan calling flashed across the screen. A wave of relief poured over me.

"Ally, Deaglan's calling. I'll call you back, okay?"

"Okay. But swear you'll call?"

"Yeah."

I switched to the other line, and before I could say anything, Deaglan spoke. "Eva. We're five minutes out. Do you have medical supplies there?"

My breath hitched. "What's wrong?"

"Eva. Do you have shit there to deal with a gunshot wound? Deck's guy is out of town." Deaglan ground out as if he were in pain.

Gunshot? Deck's guy?

"Eva," he barked.

I inhaled a ragged breath. "Yeah. Yeah. In my car I have a first aid kit, but the hospital is—"

"Baby, we don't need questions."

Shit. Doctors were required by law to contact the police if a victim came to the hospital with a gunshot wound.

I swallowed and tried to calm my racing heart and the nerves that cannonballed through my body. "Were you shot?" *Please say no.*

"It's minor. Four minutes out."

The line went dead. He was gone.

I stood frozen for a minute, my mind scrambling to catch up to everything that was happening. My house blew up and Deaglan had been shot.

What the hell was happening?

I ran into the kitchen and shoved everything off the island for a place to treat the wound. God, I had no idea how much blood he'd lost.

If he lost too much, he'd have to be taken to the hospital. I wasn't risking Deaglan's life because of questions being asked.

I pressed in the alarm code and ran to my car and yanked the first aid kit out of the trunk. I saw Kai's guy, Ernie, on his cell across the street, his eyes on me. Luke was with him.

I ran back inside and opened my bag on the kitchen counter and took out what I thought I'd need. I was a goddamn nurse, not a doctor. I couldn't do surgery. Shit, did he expect me to do surgery?

There were no tires squealing or loud announcements they were here. The VUR boys were calm and cool as Deck walked in first, then Vic, Tyler, and finally Deaglan.

Deaglan who was walking. Okay, walking was good. But his left shoulder was soaked with blood.

"Deaglan," I said, rushing to him, my eyes darting to his hand covered in blood that was pressed to the wound. "How long ago were you shot? Do you feel lightheaded? Dizzy?" I needed to know how much blood he'd lost.

"Seven minutes," Deck offered as we walked into the kitchen.

"Lie on the island," I directed Deaglan.

"Eva, I'm not lying on the fuckin' island," he said, and instead sat on a barstool. "And I'm not dizzy. I've been shot before and this isn't serious."

I ignored the part where he'd been shot before. I couldn't think about that right now. "Any bullet in the body is serious, Deaglan."

He smirked, but there was a hint of pain in his eyes as he did it. "I like it that you're worried about me."

I narrowed my eyes. "I'm a nurse. Of course, I'm worried about you." But he was right. I was worried because I loved him. And right now, I had to keep that pushed back to the far corners of my mind and focus on what I had to do.

I grabbed the scissors from the first aid kit and stood between his thighs as I cut his shirt off and peeled the blood-soaked material away from the wound.

Immediately the bleeding intensified and I pressed a wad of gauze over the wound. "Hold it there. Hard," I instructed.

I peered at Deck who leaned against the counter. "He needs a doctor."

Deck's eyes shifted to Deaglan. "Your call."

He shook his head. "It's a through and through. She can do it."

"Deaglan. I'm not a doctor and this is a first aid kit. I don't have any antibiotics. You need antibiotics."

"No bullet to extract. Disinfect it and bandage it up, baby."

Jesus. Stubborn bastard.

Vic stood with his arms crossed leaning against the fridge while Tyler pulled out a barstool and sat on it backward, leaning his arms on the backrest.

"Fine. But I don't have lidocaine and this is going to hurt," I told him as I grabbed the bottle of disinfectant. "It would be better if you lie down. If you pass out from the pain, I can't catch you."

Tyler burst out laughing. Deck chuckled. Vic didn't do or say anything.

Deaglan lifted his brows with a grin. "I'm not going to pass out."

"Vic, maybe you can hold him just in case." This time Vic did something. He grunted. But he made no move to hold Deaglan in case he passed out.

I frowned. "God, you guys are such… men. Why do you have to act so tough?" I glared at Deaglan. "Can't you drop the hard-ass attitude for ten minutes?"

Deaglan's voice softened as his fingers curled around my wrist holding the disinfectant. "Eva, I'm good."

I raised my chin and met his eyes. "Remove the gauze, tough guy," I said.

Deaglan chuckled, which was sharply cut off when I poured disinfectant into the wound.

He swore beneath his breath, but didn't move.

I glanced at the exit wound on the back of his shoulder. The bullet had ripped through his flesh leaving it tattered. "This should be debrided then stitched." Then I added. "By a doctor."

The guys remained silent.

Shit.

I cleaned the wound as best I could with what I had and grabbed the sterile bandage material from my kit.

I paused, looking at Deaglan who had his eyes on me. "Does you getting shot have anything to do with my rental house blowing up?"

No one said anything.

I glanced at each one of them before my eyes settled on Deaglan again. "I'm treating your bullet wound in my kitchen. I have the right to know."

"Yes," Deaglan said. "We were there."

Oh God, they were there.

"A fuckin' mad minute," Tyler said, and Deck shook his head while Deaglan swore under his breath.

I frowned. "What? What's a mad minute?" I asked, looking at Deaglan, but it was Tyler who answered.

"A firestorm of bullets," Tyler said.

Deaglan scowled at Tyler.

Tyler shrugged. "What? She asked."

"Anyone on the other end of this mad minute get hurt?" I asked.

Tyler chuckled. "We were aiming, sweetcakes, so, yeah."

Oh my God.

I got it. I mean, I kind of did. These guys had been in the military. They were Special Forces, except Deaglan, but he obviously had experience of some kind, too. They'd been in dangerous situations and killed people. So, it was not a big deal to them. But it was a big deal to me.

I finished bandaging Deaglan's shoulder. "Will the police be knocking on my door?"

"No," Deaglan said. "We'll deal with them. Deck has already put a call in about the bodies."

I jerked my eyes to Deaglan. "Bodies. What bodies?"

"Only two," Tyler offered, like that was going to make me feel better. "Really, it wouldn't have been our first option, to leave them in the house, but the fuckin' alarm was going when we arrived and the police were on their way. Shit went down fast."

"You blew up my house to hide bodies?" I said, mouth agape.

"Fuck no," Tyler said. "Bad guys set the bomb, sweetcakes."

I didn't know what to say to that.

Tyler continued, "No way would we blow up all your shit. Do you have contents insurance?" Tyler asked. Before I had a chance to respond, he continued. "If you don't, Deaglan has a shitload of money. Can't say if it's legally obtained money, but he can help out. You two are moving in together anyway, right?"

"Jesus, Tyler." Deaglan shook his head.

I backed away from Deaglan and turned, placing my palms on the edge of the counter. The reality of what just happened with Deaglan and the house penetrated and the steadiness slowly faded.

Shit. *Keep it together, Eva.*

"She's losing it," Tyler stated.

"Eva," Deaglan said, and his footsteps approached.

Yeah, I'm losing it.

My hands trembled. My knees, too. And my heart raced. It was like the balloon popped and my body was slowly losing air as I inhaled deep breaths.

Because Deaglan had been shot tonight.

Because there'd been a mad minute.

Because these men, one whom I loved, the others whom I really liked and who had great families, were in a house just before it blew up. And there were bodies, plural.

"Eva," Deaglan came up behind me. "Sit, baby."

I shook my head. "I'm fine. I just need a sec."

Deaglan slowly turned me around and cupped my cheek, his thumb stroking back and forth. "Eva, look at me."

I closed my eyes for a second.

"Eva?"

He could've been killed, damn it. Someone wanted him dead. And it was too late to turn back from loving a man like Deaglan.

"Look at me, Eva," he said in a firmer tone. He waited until my eyes met his. "Nothing is going to touch you."

But it already had—Deaglan. And this had nothing to do with me. I was worried about losing him.

His good arm hooked my waist and he dragged me into him. He kissed the top of my head. I wanted to sag into his arms, but I couldn't because that would lead to falling apart and I couldn't do that. I didn't want to fall apart.

I pulled from his hold and glared at him. "Don't get shot again." It was stupid to say, because he hadn't intended to, but I was trying to keep my shit together.

He smirked. "I'll tell the bad guys I'm off limits."

I huffed. God, I couldn't believe I was even asking this. "Who were the men who were killed?"

"We were following a lead on Seth Garrett's men. We were hoping they'd lead us to Seth. They led us to your house," Deaglan said.

I swallowed, hard. "Were they trying to kill me?"

"Likely, it was a warning," Deaglan said. "I want you out of town until we find Seth, Eva."

"Deaglan, I can't just leave town."

"There's no discussion on this," he said firmly.

I yanked from his hold, but he snagged my waist before I could walk away. It was his good arm, but he must have wrenched his bad shoulder because a gruff grunt emerged.

I frowned. "If that starts bleeding again, Vic can bandage you up and I'm pretty sure Vic won't be as gentle as me."

I'd never seen Vic grin, and it wasn't exactly a grin... it was more like a flash of light in his eyes.

"Eva." His fingers curled around the back of my neck and he tugged me into him. "I'd never order you to do something unless your life was at risk. We're close and he knows it. That was a warning. Next time it won't be. You're leaving town until this is over."

I pulled from his arms and walked out of the kitchen before the tears spilled over the rims of my eyes. Because the words trapped in my throat were that next time, he might end up dead.

Twenty-Two

Eva

"THANK YOU SO MUCH. I'LL BE IN TOUCH WITH A LIST OF contents." I hung up with the insurance company.

I was leaving town, but Ally was coming with me and we were going to Charlotte's farm three hours north. Deaglan was sending Vic with us to make sure we weren't followed. The hospital let me take some last-minute vacation time and I called my dad to let him know I was going to Charlotte's. I didn't tell him about Deaglan being shot or my rental blowing up, though.

"Eva." I lifted my head as Nurse Greta spoke from behind the desk. "That's the man who was looking for you last month."

I glanced in the direction she was looking, assuming it was Luke.

My cell slipped from my hand and bounced off the floor.

It was like being catapulted into a sealed cistern.

Lungs screaming for air as I suffocated in the darkness.

I tasted metallic on my tongue. But I didn't know if it was now or then. Real or imagined.

My scream echoed in my head. Memories of the sting as his hand struck me across the face and sent me crashing into the granite counter assaulted me.

The pain.

The fear that sucked the air from my lungs.

Cold. His eyes had been so cold and unemotional as his fist came toward me.

Crushing agony.

Then his face as he picked me up off the floor by my hair was all I could see.

His words echoed in my head like fingernails scraping a chalkboard. "You think you can walk away from me. Leave me, Evangeline. No one walks away from me. No one."

"Eva?" Nurse Greta's voice penetrated the horror but didn't stop it.

Because he was here.

Striding toward me.

Curran Carrick.

He had an imposing attractiveness and an heir of royalty about him. Untouchable. As if a tornado would change paths just to avoid him.

I'd been attracted to his confidence. To his politeness. To his charm. But I didn't see any of that now. All I saw was a cold, callous monster.

"Eva? Are you okay?" Nurse Greta asked, her hand reaching out to rest on my forearm.

He can't hurt me anymore. He can't touch me.

And all it took was one phone call and he'd end up back in jail.

I crouched and picked up my phone, ready to call the police.

His penetrating black eyes drilled into me as he stopped in front of me. "Evangeline."

Cold shivers jarred my body at the sound of my full name on his deep, smooth voice.

He can't touch me. He can't hurt me anymore.

I lifted my chin and met his stare. "Are you looking to wear an orange jumpsuit again, Curran? Because if you don't turn around and walk back out those doors, I will call the police and you'll be back with your friends."

His eyes briefly flicked to my cell in my hand before they steadied on me again. "I'm not here to harm you, Evangeline. What I did was unconscionable and I'll never forgive myself for destroying what we had. For hurting you."

I crossed my arms, then uncrossed them again because it appeared weak, and I never wanted to appear weak in front of this monster again. "Hurting me? You nearly killed me, asshole." I heard Greta's sharp intake of breath. "And I want nothing to do with you. Leave before I call the police."

His jaw clenched, but his eyes contradicted the action as they filled with what looked like regret. But I didn't believe for a second he regretted what he did to me. He was only capable of regretting being caught.

Curran Carrick hid behind a red velvet curtain of deception. But slowly the curtain was peeled open and the monster emerged.

"Can we speak in private, Evangeline?"

The ever-polite Curran. Guess a year in prison hadn't changed him much. I used to like that he was polite and courteous to people, but now I knew it was condescending and everything about him was a lie.

It was ironic that Deaglan once stood here asking the same thing, and yet there was nothing similar about these two men. Nothing.

"Your fists spoke a lifetime of words, Curran. And I don't have to listen to you anymore."

He shifted slightly. "I'd never expect you to forgive the unforgivable, Evangeline."

My phone vibrated in my hand and my heart leapt as I glanced at the screen. Deaglan.

Do I answer it? Tell him that Curran was standing in front of me?

Deaglan would kill him. What happened to his mother rooted deep and if he walked in here right now and saw Curran, he'd never let him walk out alive. Not that I cared if Curran died, but I cared a hell of a lot if Deaglan went to jail for murder.

I pressed End and the vibrating stopped.

"Your boyfriend?"

I failed to hide the gasp that escaped my throat. "How do you know I'm seeing anyone? Did you forget the restraining order includes stalking?"

His brows lifted. "You're stronger than you used to be." He glanced at Nurse Greta behind the desk and lowered his voice. "I'm not often surprised, but learning you're with a man like him was rather shocking, Evangeline."

"You know nothing about him. Go back to whatever hole you've been hiding in for the last year, Curran. That's where you belong." My phone vibrated with a text.

His thin lips curled up. "But I do know him, Evangeline. And I know about his girls in Ireland. The question is, do you?"

I jolted, and he noticed because a satisfied gleam hit his eyes. Girls in Ireland? What the hell was he talking about?

Don't believe anything he says. He lies. He's lying.

"Fuck you." I raised my phone to call the police when I saw Deaglan's text.

**Deaglan: I need to see you. Do not leave.
I'm on my way. Two minutes.**

I froze.

Shit.

Deaglan was coming here.

And as much as I hated Curran, I didn't want Deaglan to end up in prison. And he wouldn't last a half second in the same room with Curran without going right for him.

My eyes flew to Curran's face, then to the hospital doors. "I suggest you leave before you end up in a body bag."

He stiffened, eyes narrowing. "Is Deaglan Kane coming to protect one of his girls?"

NASHODA ROSE

I didn't know what to grasp first. The 'one of his girls' part or that he knew Deaglan's name. Had he been stalking me? But Deaglan would've known. He'd know if I was being stalked.

"You know nothing about Deaglan."

Curran smirked and my heart skipped a beat. "Oh, but I do know Deaglan Kane, my love. Or should I call him Crown, that's what they chanted in the cages when he fought." What was he talking about? Cages? "That's what he named his... what should we call it? Establishment? Or would whorehouse be more accurate?"

It was as if he'd slapped me and I staggered back, shaking my head. No. That wasn't true. "You're lying. I don't believe you."

He grinned and a spark gleamed in his eyes. "He never told you about his fighting? His famous Crown? I can't say I'm surprised."

Crown? Like the crown his mother called the earmuffs when he hid in the trunk to block out the sounds. Kai... he'd mentioned something about his Crown collection. Could that mean...

Bile rose in my throat.

Curran continued, "Deaglan Kane's house of sluts, as I like to call it. Beautiful women who are well looked after, but then he has the funds to do that."

No. Please, no.

He's lying. It's what he did. He knew how to change the truth to whatever he wanted the truth to be. My fingers curled around the counter as my knees shook. No, my entire body shook. "You're lying."

Why? Why would Curran risk coming here to tell me this? Why would he lie?

His brows lifted as he offered a subtle grin. "Ask him. Ask him about the girls he has living in his house. Ask him about the cage fighting. How many men he killed with his bare hands."

I struggled to find something to cling to. But my head spun with his words.

Deaglan. Crown. The girls. Cages.

They were lies, except I knew... I knew they couldn't all be lies.

166

I had to leave. I couldn't be here. I had to get out of here. The shock of his words was like a leech slowly sucking the blood from my veins and coldness penetrated.

I grasped the last morsel of sanity as I turned to Greta. "Call security. Have this man removed from the premises."

I shoved past Curran and ran down the corridor. I didn't know where I was going. I just needed to escape.

I stumbled as my legs nearly gave out. I placed my hand on the wall for support and stopped, inhaling several deep breaths.

"Whoa, Eva. What's wrong?"

Ally. Ally was here. *I can't breathe.*

I was suffocating under the weight of the lies. Or were they truths? God, I didn't know. I didn't know what to believe.

She hooked her arm in mine. "Shit, what the hell happened? What's wrong?"

I let Curran get to me. Why would I believe anything he said? Why did I let him get to me? Because he knew Deaglan. Because he called it Crown and it had meaning. Because Deaglan didn't talk about his past. About his life.

My phone vibrated in my hand again.

Ally spoke, but I didn't hear her, all I heard were Curran's words replaying over and over in my head.

My phone stopped and started again. I yanked from her grip and staggered back two steps. "I have to go. I need to get out of here."

Ally nodded. "Okay. Okay. Let's grab our stuff and we'll go to the farm right now."

I didn't wait for her as I rushed toward the locker room to grab my things. My phone continued to vibrate and I knew it was Deaglan.

But I couldn't talk to him right now. I couldn't talk to anyone.

I was in a daze, unable to comprehend what was happening around me.

There were sounds. Lots of sounds whirling in a hurricane of thoughts and emotions. I couldn't grasp just one because they were moving too fast.

I pushed open the door into the change room, Ally right behind me.

My phone vibrated again.

The screen flashed Deaglan Calling. I pressed Decline and shoved it in my pocket.

My mind was a chaotic scramble of words and thoughts.

It was as if I was in the middle of the ocean, treading water in the darkness.

Slowly sinking while the sharks circled.

Crown. House of sluts. We've met.

Oh God, I was going to be sick. I half-tilted with one hand on the lockers for support.

Keep it together.

Ally put her hand on the small of my back. "Do you want me to call Deaglan?"

I jerked upright, shaking my head. "No. I… I can't see him right now." I undid my lock, but it took five tries because my hand was trembling.

"Okay. I'll text Vic to see if he can meet us out front."

"I can't wait for him, Ally. I can't," I hitched my bag over my shoulder and tagged my purse off the bench.

I pretty much jogged out of the hospital with Ally on my heels. Within minutes, we were in her car and on the road.

The friction inside me was agonizing as Curran's words and my love and trust in Deaglan were constantly at war with one another.

"Eva, what's going on? Shit, you're shaking like a leaf."

I undid the window and closed my eyes as the breeze wafted across my face. "Curran. He was there," I said.

The car jerked to the right as her head snapped to look at me. "Jesus Christ. He was there? In the hospital?" I swallowed, nodding. "Jesus, are you okay? No. Shit, you're not okay. Did he touch you?" I shook my head. "Was it by accident? I mean, was he hurt or something and that's why he was there? Does Deaglan know?"

I inhaled a ragged breath, trying to calm the catastrophic storm twisting inside me. "He came to see me and told me... he told me stuff about Deaglan. God, I don't know what to believe right now, Ally."

She reached across and squeezed my hand in my lap. "Don't believe anything he says, Eva. He will say or do anything to get what he wants."

I nodded. "I know." And I did know, but it was hard not to have doubts when it made sense. I didn't want it to make sense. I wanted it to be lies and I needed Deaglan to tell me it wasn't true.

I took out my phone, ignoring Deaglan's numerous texts messages, as I typed.

Eva: What's Crown?

My phone immediately rang and my finger hovered over the decline button, but I needed to hear it from Deaglan. I needed to hear the truth.

I didn't give him a chance to say anything as I blurted, "What's Crown?"

"Where are you? We need to talk about—"

"What's Crown?" I shouted, my stomach snaking into a tightly coiled ball.

Deaglan swore beneath his breath. "Eva, damn it. Tell me where you are. We'll talk about it. I'll explain everything."

No. No. It can't be true. "What the fuck is Crown?"

"I'm not doing this over the phone, baby. We'll talk about—"

I threw my cell out the window.

The phone shattered when it hit the shoulder, bits and pieces flying into the ditch.

Bits and pieces of me right along with it.

Twenty-Three

Eva

THE TIRES CRUNCHED THE GRAVEL AS WE DROVE UP CHARLOTTE'S driveway three hours later.

After I told her everything Curran said about Deaglan, Ally called Charlotte and Kendra to let her know what happened.

Vic called Ally and he did not sugarcoat how pissed he was we left town without him. She gave him the address, not that he wasn't capable of getting it, and he hung up on her.

And Deaglan… he called Ally's cell numerous times, but those calls she did not pick up.

Ally shut off the engine and placed her hand on my thigh. "It'll be okay."

"Yeah." One day. One day it would be okay.

I climbed out of the car and inhaled a deep, quivering breath.

The screen door squeaked on its hinges and Charlotte ran out with her two large dogs prancing at her side. She didn't stop until her arms were wrapped around me.

"That piece of cow manure Curran. Are you okay? He didn't hurt you?" she asked.

"I'm okay." But I wasn't okay. I was angry and hurt, and yeah, there was a quiver of fear that hovered. But the fear had nothing to do with Curran. It was the fear of losing Deaglan.

She pulled back. "I know you might not want to hear this, but Deaglan called, wondering if you arrived yet." I should've known he'd get Charlotte's number, "He said he couldn't reach you, so I told him your phone ran out of juice. I don't think he believed me."

A wet nose nudged my hand and I ruffled the mastiff's large square head. "I'll talk to him later." Much later when my throat didn't feel like it had rope burn and my stomach wasn't swimming with drowning butterflies.

Charlotte looped her arm around my waist, and I lay my head on her shoulder as we walked up the house. "Let's get you a drink."

"I'll be there in a sec," Ally called as we stepped onto the porch. "Kendra's calling."

Charlotte ushered me inside. The dogs followed and took up their spots in cushy dog beds in the living room. "Sugar with scotch. You need a Mary Poppins evening."

Scotch being the medicine with the bowls of sugar extravaganza on the coffee table.

"Be right back. I need to check on Maddie. You know where everything is." She ran up the narrow steps and I went into the kitchen.

I reached up into the cupboard and took out three glasses and poured scotch into each of them. But I didn't wait for either of them and instead swallowed mine. Then I coughed on the fiery liquid.

I cradled the glass in my hands and leaned against the counter, inhaling a ragged breath.

He was thinking of staying.

He was trying to stay. With me.

And yet, how could I be with someone who kept something like this from me? This wasn't about his past. What he'd done. What happened to his mother. This was now.

And he owned a brothel in Ireland.

I was drowning in a sea of withered daisies. The petals, heavy and suffocating, as they held me beneath the surface.

I loved Deaglan.

Loved him still.

Because love didn't drown. It treaded water. It fought to survive.

I just didn't know what to do with that love. How to keep it and hold it and trust it.

What made everything so much worse was that I heard about Deaglan from Curran's mouth, and that was like a fist straight to the heart.

I carried the three glasses over to the couch and sat as Ally walked in. "Kendra is coming first thing in the morning," Ally said as she dumped her bag on the floor.

She plopped down on the couch beside me and slung her arm around my shoulders, drawing me close. "Deaglan called me. I didn't answer, but I texted him that you'd call when you could."

I had a feeling that didn't go over well.

I nodded. "I know I have to talk to him, but I just can't right now." I wanted to be strong when I did it, stronger than I was in this moment, and not break into a million pieces.

Ally tightened her hold. "Uh, well, you have until morning, according to his last text."

Shit.

"Aunt Eva," Maddie cried as she ran into my bedroom and jumped on the bed. "Aunt Ally is here, too. And my birthday isn't for weeks and weeks." Sitting up, I looped my arms around her waist and dragged the five-year-old down next to me and tickled her.

Maddie squealed and giggled, struggling to get away. "Stop. Stop. Aunt Eva."

I stopped and kissed her on the cheek. "Hey, birthday girl."

She giggled. "Aunt Eva, it's not my birthday. Mom, says it's six-ty-five days away. And guess what?"

"What?" I asked, smoothing back her long blonde hair.

"She says I can pick my present this year." She scrunched her small nose. "But I can't decide because I like so many things."

"Well, what makes your stomach flip-flop and you smile so much it hurts?" I asked.

My heart clenched. Deaglan. Deaglan made me smile so much it hurt and caused my stomach to flip-flop.

Maddie blurted, "Annabelle."

"Who is Annabelle?"

She sat up and tugged on my hand. "Come on. Come on. You can meet her. She has twelve piglets and they're soooo fat and always eat-ing and playing. She is fat, too, but that's because she was in a tiny, tiny cage and couldn't move before Mommy stole her."

My brows lifted. "Your mom stole her?" But it didn't surprise me. Charlotte would do anything to help an animal being abused, includ-ing being arrested.

She nodded. "Annabelle likes to put her head in the red bucket and it sometimes gets stuck because it's not for her. But I help her get it off. Come on. Get up. Get up. There is a man with a gun who sounds fun-ny outside and another scary man with a gun, too. But I'm not scared of the scary man because the man who speaks funny said the scary man is afraid of dogs."

"Okay, birthday—" My body straightened and eyes widened. "Pardon?"

She crawled off the bed. "Come on, Aunt Eva, we're making pancakes."

She darted from the room like a little speck of fairy dust, and I heard her telling Ally that I was coming to see Annabelle and her ba-bies, too.

I fell back on the pillow and closed my eyes, feeling like I was go-ing to throw up.

That lasted all of two seconds before I scrambled from the bed, and with my back against the wall, I peeked out the window.

It was barely dawn, and there was Deaglan's car. The classy, silver, four-door car, and he was leaning against the hood with his arms crossed. I was unable to see his expression, but I saw the tension in his body and there was nothing casual in his limbs.

Shit. Shit. Shit.

He was here. Deaglan was at Charlotte's at six in the morning, and according to Maddie, so was Vic, although I didn't see him.

I had to pull my shit together. But it wasn't easy when all I wanted to do was run downstairs and leap into his arms.

I went to the washroom and brushed my teeth, then changed into jean shorts and a grey T-shirt before making my way downstairs. Ally was setting the table and Charlotte was stirring pancake mix in a stainless steel bowl. Maddie grabbed the cutlery out of the drawer as she recited all the names of the piglets to Ally.

The last stair creaked under my weight, and both Ally and Charlotte stopped what they were doing and glanced up at me.

"Maddie told me," I said. "How long has he been here?"

Charlotte shook her head. "I don't know. I saw headlights late last night, but it was the other guy you told me was coming—Vic."

Ally walked over and put her hand on my arm and squeezed. "Do you want me to tell him you don't want to see him? I will. If you need me to."

I shook my head. "No." And I had a feeling Deaglan wouldn't leave until he saw me.

Maddie dumped a pile of cutlery on the table and ran to the door with the dogs trailing after her. "I'll tell them it's breakfast time," she called as she darted out the door.

"Maddie. No," Charlotte called as she dropped the fork in the fluffy batter and ran to the door.

But it was too late. We all stared out the front window to see Maddie run across the yard to Deaglan. He pushed away from his car, and crouched in front of her, so they were eye level.

I choked back the wrenching sob that threatened to escape.

My heart cracked. It was like it had been frozen for the last fifteen hours and now it broke apart as I stared at him.

His eyes lifted from Maddie as if he sensed my eyes on him. My chest tightened and my heart stumbled, trying to find a rhythm. But like everything else inside me, it was unable to find steady.

I walked toward the front door, and Charlotte touched my hand and offered a reassuring smile. The screen door squeaked when I opened it, drawing Deaglan's attention away from Maddie.

He straightened, eyes on me.

Maddie tugged on his hand. "Come on, Mister."

Charlotte came up behind me. "Maddie, come inside, please."

"But he says he likes pancakes," she called, still holding his hand.

Deaglan said something to her, and she glanced at me before releasing his hand and running along the stone path and up the two front porch steps.

She stopped in front of me. "He said he wants to talk to you, Aunt Eva."

I swallowed and forced a smile. "Okay."

"Then can he come have pancakes? He said he used to make dog pancakes for his little brother a long, long time ago." My breath locked and my eyes shifted from Maddie to Deaglan, who stood watching me.

"Inside, my little care bear," Charlotte said, and ushered her daughter into the house.

The screen door slammed shut behind me and jerked my body into action.

I walked toward him, and part of me wanted to throw my arms around him, and the other part wanted to throw him a punch. I did neither.

I stopped a foot away from him and realized my mistake the second his scent slammed into me.

His jaw ticked. "You saw that bastard."

"Yes." I didn't know how he knew I saw Curran, but I guessed it was Greta.

"You saw the man who beat you. Who put you in the hospital and went to jail for assault, and you left town." He dragged his fingers through his hair. "Jesus Christ. That shit cannot happen again, Eva," he ground out. "Fuck."

Anger percolated, and I stiffened my back and raised my chin, which was a lot easier to do when his eyes weren't looking at me. Not because I was scared of him, but because vulnerability swam in the depths of his eyes and I wanted to take it away.

"What's Crown, Deaglan? Tell me it's not what he says it is." *Please tell me he was lying.*

He dipped his chin and stared at his feet for a second. "I can't," he replied.

I'd have fallen if he hadn't grabbed me as my world crumbled. It wasn't until he confirmed it that I actually believed Curran.

Because I also believed in Deaglan, I still had a sliver of hope.

Until now.

His arms wrapped around me and I shoved hard at his chest, pushing him back to pound my fists into him as tears streamed down my face.

It was true. Damn it, why? Why?

"Eva. Christ. Eva." His voice cracked as he held my wrists to try and stop me from hitting him. But it only fueled my anger.

Because I loved him. I goddamn loved him.

I staggered back, hands curled into fists at my sides. "Who the hell are you?" I shouted. "What are you? What are the cages? Are you a pimp? Do you pimp out the girls and take a cut? Is that how you make your money?"

The words tasted thick and raw in my throat. Wrong. They tasted wrong.

"You know who I am, Eva." His eyes remained on me, unflinching and hard. It was like a shield slammed shut over them.

"Obviously, I know fuck all about you." I swallowed, not wanting to ask, but knowing I had to. "Do you fuck them, Deaglan? Is that why you went home for five days? To fuck your girls?"

It took him three strides to reach me. He didn't touch me, but he towered over me and it took everything I had not to run.

"I'll let you ask that once, Eva. Once. Because despite what you think, you do know me. And you fuckin' know I'd never do that to you. I've never touched any of them. I've done things I'm not proud of. I've done things I hate myself for, but owning Crown isn't one of them."

My heart squeezed until it bled.

"My mom was a prostitute, Eva. It was her pimp who used her and beat her for years until he killed her." I choked back the sob. "Those girls were just like her, living with no protection from pieces of shit assholes who beat them when they didn't make enough money." He cupped my chin between his thumb and forefinger. "The cages. Yeah, I fought in cages. I did it since I was fifteen years old. But it earned me a name. A name that gave the girls protection. They have a safe place to live and they keep the money they make. All of it, Eva."

"They live in your house? He said they live in your house."

"My parents' house. When they died, I turned it into a place they could stay instead of the streets. But I don't live there, Eva."

I closed my eyes, willing away the tears. "I don't... Deaglan, I don't know what to think right now."

His hand dropped and he moved away, shoulders slumped. He raked his hand through his hair before turning.

He raised his head and our eyes locked. "I don't deserve you, Eva. I fuckin' know that. But I'm not giving up on us. And I'm asking you not to give up on me, baby."

I choked on the tears as his words filtered into me. I closed my eyes and tried to come up with some semblance of words to string together, but I couldn't.

Crown was there to protect girls like his mom. The one person he wasn't able to protect. But there was so much more of him I didn't know. But what really hurt was that it was Curran who had told me. He'd thrown it in my face and left me scrambling for air.

"I... Deaglan...." I inhaled a breath and started again. "I don't know. I can't... I can't... I need time to think."

He stepped toward me. "Eva..."

I shook my head. "Don't." He stopped. "I need time." It strangled me to say the words because the only person I wanted to hold me and take the hurt away was him.

I spun around to run back to the house, but he snagged my hand and pulled me into him. "Eva. Christ. Don't do this," he whispered next to my ear, his voice raspy and broken. "We can get through this, baby. I need you to try and understand."

But I did understand. I understood that he kept something so significant from me.

I pushed at his arms. "I had to hear it from the man who beat me. A man I hate. Do you have any idea what that's like?" He flinched. I shoved at his arms and stumbled away from him. "Go, Deaglan."

His hand jerked through his hair before he turned and walked to the car, and my heart slammed into my ribcage.

It shattered. It ruined. It destroyed. That was what my love for him did to me.

He opened the door and I thought he'd get in and drive away, but instead he bent, reaching inside for something. He straightened with a folder in his hand.

"Did Curran tell you how he knew about me? About Crown?" I shook my head. "That seven years ago he'd tried to steal a girl under my protection. That he tried to sell her."

My eyes widened. What was he talking about? Curran owned a shipping company in Toronto. He was a businessman. He hadn't even gone to Ireland as far as I knew.

He dumped the folder on the hood of the car. "The police report on your assault," he said. I tensed, and his eyes met mine. "I didn't look at the photos of you. I know you don't want me to. But I saw Curran Carrick's mug shot." He opened the folder and took out a photo.

He held it up. "This is the man I met in Ireland seven years ago. The man who tried to sell a girl to the highest bidder. This is Seth Garrett, Eva."

Twenty-Four

Eva

"AUNT EVA. MISTER. THE PANCAKES ARE READY. THE PANCAKES are ready. Come on," Maddie shouted from the front porch.

Deaglan's eyes shifted from me to Maddie. "Can you give your Aunt Eva another minute, hon?" he asked.

Silence followed a beat, then, "Okay," she said, and waltzed back inside.

He turned his attention back to me. "This is why after seven years Seth Garrett decided I'm a risk, Eva. Because I knew what he looked like. Because I'm with the one woman who knows his real identity. He knew I'd figure it out if I ever saw the police file. If I ever saw a picture you had of him. He wasn't going to risk it. Not after so many years of building his new identity."

It was like my body landed smack on the ground after jumping off the cliff. No breath. No heartbeat. Nothing except an ice-cold blanket lowering over me and I was falling under the weight of it.

And I would've fallen if hands hadn't grabbed my shoulders from behind me.

"Eva," Vic said.

I hadn't heard him approach, probably because my mind was drowning in a swamp of murky water.

Seth was Curran. *Seth is Curran.*

"You told her?" Vic said.

Deaglan nodded.

"He doesn't...." My eyes widened and stomach lurched. Oh God. I was with him. I was with a man who sold people. Girls. He hadn't only hid his personality. He hid who he was. That's why he knew about Crown. How he knew Deaglan.

Seth Garrett had disappeared for years. He'd disappeared because he became Curran Carrick.

My hand covered my mouth, smothering the gasp.

No. No, damn it. This couldn't be happening. I was a part of that. I was with a man who did that.

I'm going to be sick.

Deaglan swore beneath his breath and strode toward me, arm hooking my waist. Vic's hands dropped, and I heard his boots on the gravel as he walked away. "You didn't know. You couldn't have known, Eva."

There was so much spinning and colliding in my head right now that I couldn't think clearly.

"Eva, you couldn't have known." His thumb and forefinger held my chin as he forced me to look at him. "Give me your eyes, baby." He applied pressure to my chin and the haze lifted. "You couldn't have known. We didn't know. He disappeared as Seth Garrett and reinvented himself as Curran Carrick. After he was released from jail he's been renewing old contacts as Seth Garrett and that's why Frank Davidson was watching my place. We think he planned to use his shipping company for transporting girls." The pad of his thumb stroked back and forth over the subtle dip in my chin. "You couldn't have known."

I jerked from his hand, and he lowered his arm, sighing. "I don't want this. I don't want any of this." I stepped back, shaking my head. "Crown is important to you, Deaglan, and I understand why, but I can't be with someone who hides himself. Hides his past." Like Curran had done.

Everything was colliding in a murky swamp of quicksand that was sucking me under.

He stared at me a minute before he reached into his pocket and pulled out a cell phone and held it out to me. "You need a phone. This isn't about us, Eva. This is about keeping you safe."

I took the phone and put it in my back pocket. I wasn't arguing because I knew he was right, and no matter who Deaglan was, I knew deep down that he'd always look out for my safety.

"Does Curran know about the farm, Eva?"

I shook my head. "No. She bought it a year-and-a-half ago."

"Okay. Stay here until we find him. Vic will stay with you, and I'm sending Ernie, just in case."

I nodded without looking at him. I didn't want to go back to the city. Back to my house without Deaglan in it. To facing a life without him.

How did this happen? Why?

The gravel beneath his feet crunched as he walked to his car. "What are you going to do?" I called.

"What I do best. Kill him," he stated as he opened the car door and folded in.

The words to call him back were trapped in my throat as his car purred to life.

To tell him to be safe.

Tell him not to go.

Tell him that I loved him.

But instead, I watched as he drove away, taking pieces of me with him. I didn't know where those pieces would end up, except that I wasn't getting them back. He owned them.

I stood in the driveway, unable to move as the dust from his tires floated around me.

The screen door squeaked. "He's leaving?" Charlotte stood with her arms crossed on the front porch.

"Yeah," I replied.

"You okay?"

Instead of answering the question, I said, "Maddie must be starving." I turned to walk back to the house and caught a glimpse of Vic leaning his shoulder up against a willow tree.

But his eyes weren't on me. They were on Charlotte, and they weren't exactly friendly, but then there was never anything friendly about Vic.

I stepped on to the porch and Charlotte wrapped her arm around my shoulders, and we went inside and had pancakes.

Deaglan

"He was there. In the fuckin' hospital," I shouted into the phone. "Right in front of her. He could've grabbed her and...." I couldn't finish the sentence because the nightmare was replaying over and over in my head.

"He didn't," Deck said, his voice calm and steady, because he knew I was not calm and steady. I was in a convoluted web of fucked-up emotions. "And he doesn't know yet that we saw the police report. But he had to have someone on the inside to keep that sealed, and if they look into it, they'll know we saw it and Seth will disappear again." He paused, then asked, "Where's Eva at with Crown?"

"The entire foundation just blew the fuck up," I ground out. But I'd rebuild. I wasn't losing her, but first I had to deal with Curran.

"How long before you're back in town?" Deck asked.

"Two hours away," I replied.

"Good. Meet us at VUR. We go in Carrick Shipping at midnight."

"He's mine, Deck."

"He's yours," he confirmed.

I'd managed to bury who I'd been. The damaged kid who found his mom beaten to death. The teenager who fought in the cages. The man who hunted and killed without remorse.

He was being unearthed, and Curran was going to suffer for what he'd done to Eva.

Twenty-Five

Eva

"AUNT EVA, ARE YOU STILL SAD?"

I picked up one of the piglets and kissed the little pink nose that never stopped wiggling. "I'm still sad, sweetie. But Annabelle and her piglets make me happy."

My eyes were puffy and red this morning because I'd been crying—again.

It had been four days since Deaglan drove away and I thought each day would get easier. It didn't. It got harder.

Missing him. Worrying about him. Everything inside me hurt. Ached.

I spoke to my dad and told him everything, including all of the details about Deaglan and his mom and Crown. After a good minute of silence, he asked if I loved Deaglan. I didn't hesitate and said that I did. But that had never been in question.

The tears this morning were from my dad's words when he said, "I'm not saying what he did was right for keeping that from you, that's not for me to judge. I'm saying if you love him, then there's a reason you do, Eva. Trust in that."

Then he gave me shit for not telling him about the mugging sooner.

I placed the piglet back in the pen with the others and he oinked several times as he darted away with his back legs kicking up in the air.

"Did the man make you sad?" she asked.

Kids were so perceptive and Maddie was exceptional.

"I miss him, so yeah, it makes me sad."

Her eyes lit up. "Mommy says if I miss Kendra or grandma and granddad that I can call them anytime I want. So, you can call him and not miss him anymore."

I smiled. "I guess I could, birthday girl."

"Oh, Aunt Eva." She rolled her eyes.

I heard the low rumble of the tractor start up outside the barn. "Come on. Maybe we can ride the tractor with your mom again?"

"Okay." Maddie skipped to the half door and undid the latch and I followed her out.

My phone vibrated in my back jean pocket and I pulled it out as we walked outside. Ally and Kendra had returned to the city on Sunday night, but several times a day they texted to see how I was doing.

I staggered to a stop as my eyes hit the screen.

Deaglan: You done processing, baby?

I swallowed, staring at his words. No. Not really.

I wanted so badly to believe in him, and maybe I did already. Maybe I had never stopped, but he'd kept more from me than just owning Crown. He kept who he was. He knew I had trust issues after Curran, and now even more after finding out that Curran is Seth.

"Eva!"

I jerked my eyes from my phone and looked up at Charlotte sitting on the tractor with Maddie in front of her holding the steering wheel.

"Sorry, what?" I asked.

She half-smiled. "Deaglan?"

"Uh, yeah, he texted."

She squeezed her daughter's shoulder. "Honey, do you think you can go open the gate into Blaze's paddock by yourself?"

She vigorously nodded as she quickly hopped off the tractor. "Yeah. I'll do it. It's not hard, you know, Mommy."

She smiled. "Not for a strong girl like you. I'll drive the tractor over in a sec."

"Okay, Mommy." Maddie ran off.

Charlotte turned back to me, her hands lightly resting on the bottom of the steering wheel. "I swore to Deaglan I wouldn't tell you, but damn it, Eva, you need to know. He calls. Every friggin' day that man calls to ask if you're okay. It's short. It's to the point and there's no idle conversation to that guy, but I hear the concern in his voice. He's worried about you. And he should be, because I'm worried. You barely eat and you look like shit."

I felt like shit. I needed permanent cucumber slices for my eyes, and every time I ate my stomach objected.

She sighed. "I'm trying to stay out of this, Eva. But the guy doesn't call to gain points with you. He calls because he loves you."

I chewed my lower lip and leaned up against the enormous tractor tire, crossing my arms over my chest. "He owns a brothel, Charlotte. That's something you tell a woman you love. It's something you tell someone you plan to make a life together with. God, if Curran hadn't told me, he may have never said anything. What else is he hiding? Maybe I don't know him at all, just like I didn't know Curran. Or Seth. Christ, I don't even know which is his real name."

She sighed. "I know you're having trouble trusting your judgment, especially after learning about Curran, but what is your heart telling you?"

My heart wasn't telling me anything because it was broken and bleeding. How could I trust it? "I don't know."

"Mommy! Come on," Maddie called as she stood holding open the gate.

"Coming," Charlotte called and restarted the tractor. She offered me a half-smile. "Maybe it's not enough, I don't know. But that man loves you, Eva."

She slid the large gearshift into first and the tractor chugged forward. I glanced down at my phone still clutched in my grasp.

"Aunt Eva, Aunt Eva. Blaze wants to say hi," Maddie yelled as she stood on the fence and pointed to a chestnut horse trotting in her direction across the field.

I slipped my phone back into my pocket and jogged toward her.

Twenty-Six

Eva

THE CALLOUSED HAND SKATED FROM MY HIP, ACROSS MY ABDOMEN, TO settle on my waist. Goosebumps bumped along the back of my neck, then skipped down my spine to scatter like little embers of fire across my skin.

I sighed in the comforting warmth, my body finally relaxing after hours of restlessness.

A light kiss tickled the back of my neck, then a raspy whisper vibrated next to my ear, "Eva."

"Deaglan," I murmured. My eyes flew open and my body bolted upright at the sound of his voice. "Deaglan. What are you doing here?"

"I told you I'd be here," he said. He laid on his side with his head propped on his hand and his other hand resting on the mattress where I'd just been.

"Uh, not exactly. You asked if I was done processing." I must have looked at his text message a hundred times today as I attempted to type something back. But the words were never right and I didn't know what to say because I was still processing. Finally, I tossed my phone into the dogs' cookie jar and refused to look at it.

"You'll over process if I let you," he said.

He was right. I would.

I clung the sheet to my chest, even though I wore a camisole, and he'd seen me naked numerous times. "How did you get in the house?" I peered around the darkened room, as if he'd magically entered through some mysterious wormhole.

"Front door," he replied. "Vic saw me. Let me in."

Of course, he did. Apparently, Vic the machine didn't require sleep and had a way into the house despite the two locks on the door.

Unless Charlotte had given him a key, but I'd never seen him in the house, and he'd been using the loft apartment above the barn.

Jesus, I couldn't think clearly with him so close. All I smelled was his deliciousness and that had always been my Kryptonite. "You can't be in my bed."

He sighed. "You're still in your head."

"Yeah, Deaglan, I'm still in my head. It's a lot to think about."

"Eva," he said, curling his fingers around one wrist. "Look at me."

I kept my head down, knowing the tears would fall if I looked at him. I tried to will them away, but my willpower sucked when it came to Deaglan.

He sighed. "I'd give you the world, baby, but I can't give you any more time. Please, don't ask me to give you more time."

A tear spilled over the rim of my eye and slid down my cheek. "I hated that he knew. I hated that Curran was the one who told me. He didn't use his fists, Deaglan, but when he told me about you... God, it felt like he did. It felt like he plowed his fist into my stomach and I couldn't breathe."

"Jesus, baby."

"I felt alone, Deaglan. I felt blindsided."

But what I didn't say was that I'd gone over everything in my head a zillion times and nothing resolved except that I still loved him. And my dad was right, I loved him for a reason. Who he was now. This incredible man who had protected me. Who did thoughtful things for me like buy me a can opener because mine sucked. Who helped me pick out a fridge. Who took me to a hotel because he knew I wouldn't sleep after being scared. And my house. What he'd done to get my house ready so I could move in.

But there was so much more to Deaglan that I didn't know.

He shifted and the mattress creaked under his weight. I glanced up as he moved to sit on the edge of the bed with his back to me. His head dropped forward and his shoulders slumped as he jerked his hand through his hair.

There was a crushing vulnerability in his posture. Something I never saw in Deaglan. He was the definition of strength, and seeing him like this was what he'd hid from me. What was behind the shield.

This was a part of him I'd never seen.

It was all of him.

"My mom got pregnant with me at sixteen," he said, his voice crackling. He cleared it and inhaled a ragged breath. "Her boyfriend, Gregory Kane, asked her to marry him, but there was no way either of their parents would let that happen. Reputation was too important to both families and they wouldn't let them ruin their lives with a baby. They shipped her off to a convent in the north to have the baby and Gregory was sent to a boarding school out of the country.

"She was supposed to give me up and go home, back to her secure life. Her family. But she didn't. She refused to give me up. She ran away two days after I was born. But with no money and no place to go while raising a baby, it wasn't long before she became desperate. Fell in with the wrong crowd. But she did what she could to keep me fed and alive."

I dropped the sheet and crawled across the mattress. I perched on my knees behind him and curled my arms around his waist.

He didn't move for a second, his head still dropped forward and strands of hair hanging in front of his face. But I felt the tension in his back muscles slowly ease as I held him.

I pressed my cheek to his back and closed my eyes.

"She sold herself for me. To keep me. She did everything to protect me. Shield me from the abuse. All those years. She took whatever life threw at her and never complained. Fuck, she never complained. Even when I was old enough to understand what she did for a living, she said I was worth everything. That I saved her every single day."

Tears trailed down my cheeks, but I didn't bother wiping them away because there'd only be more.

"Even after that bastard killed her, she still protected me. My father never knew what happened to her or me, but she'd left a letter with a lawyer to find him if anything happened to her." He paused a minute, as if needing time to breathe. "I think she always knew the bastard would find her. Within a week, Gregory Kane showed up with a lawyer at social services and took me home."

He shifted to lean up against the oak headboard taking me with him. I curled into his side, one hand settled on his chest and my cheek resting against his shoulder.

"I was angry. That's when I started fighting. In school. Illegal fighting. Anywhere. The physical pain somehow eased the emotional pain of losing her. Of the guilt for not saving her and for the sacrifice she made for me. Fighting was my outlet.

"But as the anger grew, so did the revenge to find the bastard. It was all I could think about and it ate me alive. I didn't even know who I was fighting anymore. Myself, mostly."

"The cages," I whispered.

His muscles flexed as he hesitated for a second, and I slid my hand into his and linked our fingers. "Yeah. The worst of the worst came to those fights, and a lot of money exchanged hands. Maybe in some ways, it was me trying to protect her in that cage. Fighting to set her free."

"Or to set yourself free," I said.

He shrugged.

As if he was trying to find with the words, he was silent a few minutes and his jaw clenched and unclenched.

"I was twenty when I killed him." I stopped breathing and my body stilled. "Eight years. Eight years before our paths crossed again and I didn't hesitate. I beat him like he'd done to my mom for years. I beat him until he begged and cried for mercy. But I couldn't stop. Even after I left him in the alley dead. Killing him didn't stop the pain like I thought it would."

His chin dropped and his eyes closed. "I spiraled into a dark abyss filled with so much hatred for myself. Fuck, I don't even know how I managed to survive when all I wanted to do was die. The cage fighting became more dangerous. Huge stakes that included fighting to the death."

Oh God. No.

He didn't say anything for a while and I needed that time to absorb everything he'd told me. Tragic. A heart-wrenching and an unimaginable pain that led Deaglan done a path he's been fighting to get back from ever since.

"What's worse is that I can't remember the fighters I killed with my bare hands, Eva. I can't remember their faces. To me they all looked like one person—me."

My breath hitched and a choked sob emerged. "Deaglan."

"Every time I stepped in that cage, I was fighting myself. I killed myself. Over and over again. Until the last time. Until I met my match."

He peered down at me and gently wiped the tears from my face with the pad of his thumb. I clasped his wrist before he moved away and kissed his palm before slipping my fingers between his.

He squeezed me to him. "Deck got me out. Fuckin' guy showed up when I was near dead in what would've been my last fight. Not sure what he did to get me out of that cage alive, but it wouldn't have been pretty with a lot of money on the line."

The marker. Deaglan told me he owed Deck a marker, a debt. That was why.

He continued, "He threw my ass in some fuckin' basement for six weeks. Nothing to do but rage and pace and threaten anyone who came near me that I'd kill them. But if you're locked away long enough with fuck all to do except read books they toss you, and not knowing when, if ever, you'll get out, the dense fog of pain and rage slowly clears. It doesn't go away completely, but you start to see through it.

"There's acceptance on the other side. Far from forgiveness, but it was enough to get me out of the basement and find a way to live. And helping the girls, that was part of it. I'd built a name fighting and I used it to protect them. No one would fuck with them when they knew they were linked to me. If any of the girls want out of the business, I help them get out. But it's their choice, Eva. Always theirs."

I looked up at him with tears streaming down my face, and my heart lodged in my throat. There were no words to offer that would ease his pain. The word sorry felt wrong because it wasn't powerful enough.

It explained so much about him. Who he'd become. How protective he was. The shield he wore to keep all of this buried. Why he was controlled and determined in everything he did. He never wanted to lose himself again. He never wanted to love and lose like he had done with his mom.

I looked up at him and our eyes met. His were glassy and swam with unshed tears and tortured memories. "I'd do anything for you, Eva, but I can't change my past and I can't change who I am."

"I never asked you to change, Deaglan. I don't want you to change. I fell in love with you. With the man your past has made you into. All I wanted was to know what made you into the man I love. For you to trust me with yourself."

He inhaled a ragged breath, closing his eyes.

And then all the walls crumbled as I gave him all of me. "You don't pick and choose which pieces of a person you want to love. You love all of them." I curled my hand around the back of his neck and drew him closer. "And I want all of you. I want all your pieces Deaglan."

"Mo chroi, fuck, I love you so much." His mouth crushed mine.

Twenty-Seven

Eva

"BUT, MOOOOM," MADDIE MOANED WITH A FRUSTRATED STOMP of her foot. "Bucket wants to. Pleeeassse." The bundled swaddle in her arms moved and the wide nostril stuck out as the piglet sniffed the air. "See, he's hungry."

Charlotte lifted her eyes heavenward as she placed the bowl of hash browns on the table. "What piglet isn't hungry?" she muttered.

Ally laughed as she folded the napkins on the table. She'd arrived fifteen minutes ago, having surprised us by driving up to spend the weekend. Deaglan wasn't happy about it and neither was Vic, whom I noticed from the front window was currently leaning inside her car, checking it over.

"He can't eat breakfast with us, Maddie. Take him out to the barn," Charlotte said.

Maddie continued to argue with her mom while I came up behind Deaglan and slid my arms around his waist, kissing the back of his neck. "I'm not sure how you're going to make those look like a dog." He stood in front of the stove with a spatula in hand as he flipped the pancakes.

He pointed to the two oblong-shaped pancakes. "Ears. The big round one is the head and the small round pancake the muzzle." He nodded to the plate on the counter next to the stove. "Two blueberries for eyes. A strawberry nose and chocolate chips for the mouth. My mom used to make them for me every Monday morning before school. She said it was to start my week off right." I smiled, loving that he shared pieces of his mom with me. "I used to make them for Ronan. Even though I hated him following me around, but I guess it was my own way to be close to her."

"I'd like to meet Ronan one day."

"You'll meet him, Eva."

"And your hot, famous rock star cousin, Kite."

He grunted. "You're pushing it, baby."

I smacked his chest and he chuckled.

Last night, after he told me everything, we'd stayed up talking until the wee hours of the morning. Not about anything important, just talking as we held one another. He was leaving to return to the city after breakfast.

I discovered that the retired Navy SEAL guy, Ernie, had been watching the farm for the last five days since Curran went underground. Deaglan said his house was cleared out and his shipping business had been abandoned and there was no movement.

I knew Deaglan was anxious to get back and find Curran.

"Maddie. No," Charlotte said.

Maddie sighed and walked to the door, cradling Bucket.

I kissed Deaglan's cheek. "I'll go with her."

"No, I'll go, babe." He tried to pass me the spatula.

I shook my head. "You finish the pancakes."

I walked across the room to Maddie and crouched in front of her, tucking back the baby blue blanket so I could see the piglet's head. "So, Bucket is being bullied again?"

She nodded. "He gets pushed around a lot, and it's not very nice that they don't let him eat, too."

"Maybe we can feed him first, all by himself?"

Her eyes brightened. "Yeah, he'd like that."

I stood. "We'll be back in a few minutes."

"Babe," Deaglan called as I held open the screen door. "Take Vic with you."

I was going to argue that it wasn't necessary, but instead I smiled and nodded. "Okay."

"Here. You can hold him," Maddie said when we were outside. "But be careful, he wiggles sometimes." She handed me the swaddle, and I hitched the piglet in the crook of my arm before taking her hand in mine and we walked toward the barn.

"Vic?" I called.

He crouched near the front tire of Ally's car and reached out to examine something.

He shifted on the balls of his feet to glance over at Maddie and me. He didn't say anything as his hand continued to feel the underside of the wheel rim.

"Can you come to the barn with us? Deaglan is making panca...." My voice trailed off as his eyes shot back to the tire.

I didn't know what it was that triggered it, but the hairs on the back of my neck darted to attention at the same time as Vic abruptly stood, his neck twisting to shout at me. "Get down."

My heart stopped. It was like watching an action movie in slow motion as Vic ran and dove behind Kendra's car just as Ally's car exploded.

I dropped Bucket, and my arm hooked Maddie's waist. I shoved her to the ground and shielded her with my body.

Thick, black smoke filtered into the air as the crackle of metal melted under the heat of the blazing flames.

"Eva," Deaglan shouted as he tore from the house.

A spray of gunshots echoed, and the ping of splintered wood hit the beam beside his head. He dove for cover. "Fuck."

Charlotte ran out of the house. "Maddie."

"No." Ally grabbed her arm, but she yanked free.

"Charlotte," I screamed. "No."

She jumped off the front porch and raced across the yard toward me and Maddie.

I heard the bullets. Saw the divots in the grass behind her.

Vic ran across the yard, and with one swoop of his arm, grabbed her and dove behind the oak tree.

The bullets stopped, but the fire crackled and groaned as black smoke filtered into the air from Ally's car.

I heard Charlotte fighting Vic and screaming at him to let her go, but the tree blocked them from view.

Vic came out from behind the tree and shot in the direction of where the bullets came from. He looked at me. "Go. Now. The barn," he ordered. "I'll cover you."

I picked up Maddie and ran for the old collapsed barn. A slew of bullets sounded behind me, but I had no idea if they were aimed at me and Maddie or if they were Vic's bullets.

"Eva. Fuck," Deaglan shouted.

There was another sharp ping of bullets, and I glanced over my shoulder to see Deaglan jumping off the porch and running across the yard toward us. "Deaglan. No!" I shouted.

He dove behind his car and the windshield cracked like a spider web as bullets hit it.

I yanked open the barn door so hard the rusty hinges gave way. The door fell off the hinges and crashed to the side.

I rushed inside and placed Maddie on her feet. "A hiding spot, Maddie. Where can you hide, sweetie?" It was the unused barn that was partially collapsed, and had no animals in it.

There was a pile of rotting furniture covered in cobwebs and a loft of hay up in the rafters. Shafts of sunlight beamed through the cracks in the planks, illuminating the dust in the air.

Maddie choked on her sob as she stood trembling with tear-stained cheeks.

I squeezed her shoulders. "Maddie, I know this is scary. But we need to find a place for you to hide for a little while?"

"What about Bucket?" she cried.

"He'll be okay, sweetie." I wiped the tears from her cheeks with my thumb. "He got scared and ran away. We'll find him later."

She nodded, and with my hand clutched in hers, we ran through what remained of the center aisle of the barn.

It was the creak in the boards that warned me we weren't alone, but it was too late. Maddie's hand slipped from mine, as what felt like a log beam slammed into my throat and catapulted me backward into a hard, living wall. The beam was an arm and it quickly curled and locked around my neck.

My scream to warn Maddie was silenced from the hit to my throat. But I jabbed my elbow back into my assailant's abdomen and struggled to get free.

His hold tightened and cut off my air. My fingers clawed at his arm as I peeled at his skin with my fingernails.

"Don't fuckin' kill her. She's mine."

I gulped in a lungful of air as his grip eased. But sheer panic surfaced when I saw Curran walk out of the shadows with Maddie in front of him. He had one hand over her mouth to keep her quiet and the other holding her quivering shoulder.

"Curran. No," I cried. "Let her go."

He scowled. "Keep your voice down, bitch." His cold, hard voice sent a horde of shivers through me.

"Please, Curran. She's just a little girl," I begged.

My gaze flicked to Maddie. Her eyes were wide with terror as she stood in front of him.

"Boss," the guy holding me said. "There's movement."

"Take them both," Curran said.

My heart slammed into my ribcage. No. I couldn't let him take her. "You take her, you will have a war on your hands that you can't win."

His brows lifted. "I'm already in a fuckin' war because of you."

Maddie. God, He couldn't take Maddie. I knew what Curran was capable of, but what scared me more was what Seth was capable of. "I'll go with you. I won't fight you. I'll do whatever you want."

There was a slow upward curl of his mouth.

"Boss." The guy tightened his hold on me as I heard Deaglan's shout and another round of gunfire.

Curran released Maggie, and she fell to her knees before scrambling back to her feet and running to me. Her body slammed into mine. "Maddie, sweetie. You need to stay here. Okay? Don't move until Deaglan, Vic, or your mommy comes for you."

"You'll stay with me?" She peered up me.

"No, sweetie. I have to go with these men for a little while." I peeled her reluctant arms from around my waist.

"Aunt Eva," she cried.

I shook my head. "It's going to be okay," I soothed as my captor yanked me away from her.

"Cover us. Now," Curran barked into his phone, then turned to stride down the aisle into the darkness. My captor gripped my arm as we followed.

I looked over my shoulder at Maddie standing in the middle of the barn crying. She'd be okay. Maddie was safe.

Two guys appeared at the back of the barn where the boards were missing in the wall.

Curran ducked through the hole, followed by his two men.

"Go," my captor ordered and shoved me forward through the broken boards.

Deaglan. I choked back the tears because I couldn't break down. Not now.

Curran grabbed a fistful of my hair and jerked my head back. I winced, biting my tongue. "Don't make me regret my decision, Evangeline. Slow us down and I'm going back for the kid." He nodded to the tree line three hundred feet in the distance. "Run."

With my heart breaking and lungs screaming soundlessly, I ran.

Deaglan

"Maddie? Eva?" I shouted barging into the barn with Vic right behind. I didn't have my gun. It was upstairs in my jacket where I'd left it. But nothing was stopping me from getting to her, and besides, my hands were my weapons.

Maddie stood in the middle of the barn crying. Eva was nowhere to be seen. I rushed to her and fell to my knees in front of her. She wrapped her little arms around my neck and I picked up her trembling body.

"Where's Eva, honey?"

I didn't want to scare her anymore than she already was, so I tried to keep the panic from my voice. But inside it was like being pelted with bullets as my eyes continued to scan the darkness with no sign of Eva.

"Ernie," Vic barked into his phone as he approached us. "Do you see them? Can you follow?"

No. Fuck. No. She couldn't be gone.

Curran. Seth. He blew up Ally's car. He must have put a tracking device on her car.

Jesus.

"Maddie," Charlotte cried as she ran into the barn with Ally right behind.

I placed Maddie on her feet, and Charlotte crashed to her knees and pulled her into her arms.

"Where's Eva?" Ally asked, but I was already moving through the barn, my eyes on the floorboards as I studied the scuffle of disturbed straw that led toward the back of the barn.

I ran and Vic was right behind me.

My heart dropped when I saw the boards missing in the wall of the barn. I climbed through and stopped.

Nothing. Fuckin' nothing. We were too late.

"Ernie says there were two snipers." The distraction. "He killed one and left the other one tied to a tree for us to deal with later."

I swallowed the lump in my throat. "Did he see where they took her?"

He shook his head. "He was on the north side of the farm."

I slammed my fist into the side of the barn, and the wood splintered. "Jesus Christ. How the fuck did this happen?" But I knew how it happened. Curran had been patient and quiet for a week. He waited until Eva's friend led him right to her.

Vic's cell vibrated and he tapped the screen and put it to his ear. "Deck."

We moved back inside where Charlotte still held Maddie, while Ally slowly rubbed the little girl's back.

"I need to talk to her, Charlotte," I said. I didn't like to question the kid when she was so shaken up, but I had no choice. Eva's life was on the line. Seth had disappeared once before and I knew he'd do it again and take Eva with him. No way was I letting that happen.

She nodded and slowly eased Maddie from her tight embrace. "Maddie, do you think you can tell Deaglan what happened?"

She sniffled and peered at her mom. "Is Bucket okay?"

Charlotte smoothed her hand over the top of her head. "Yeah, Bucket ran to the stable. He's okay."

Vic had his back to me as he spoke to Deck. I couldn't hear all of it, but I heard the word interrogate. That's why Ernie left the sniper alive. For Vic to interrogate—his specialty. If the sniper knew where they were taking Eva, then Vic would get it out of him.

Charlotte placed Maddie on her feet, but kept her arm around her waist.

I crouched in front of the little girl and forced a smile. "You okay, Maddie? They didn't hurt you, did they?"

She shook her head.

"That's good, hon." I took my time, knowing I'd get more from her if she wasn't scared. "Did they hurt your Aunt Eva?"

She glanced at her mom, who half-smiled reassuringly before she turned back to me. "She went with the bad men."

My heart clenched. "Yeah." I inhaled a deep, ragged breath. "Did she go through there?" I pointed to the back of the stable. She nodded. "How many bad men were with her?"

She pursed her quivering lips together. "Two. He called her Evan… glin." Evangeline. Fuck. Curran came here himself.

"Okay." I squeezed her shoulder. "That's really helpful." I stood just as Vic pocketed his cell. "Sniper?"

Vic nodded.

I peered down at Maddie. "Why don't you see if your mom can heat up the dog pancakes I made you?"

I glanced at Charlotte and she nodded. "Come on, care bear. Let's find Bucket and see if he wants to share your pancake."

She scrunched her nose. "What about Aunt Eva?"

I lightly placed my hand on her head. "I'm going to find her, hon. I promise."

Maddie and Charlotte left, but Ally stayed, her eyes shifting between me and Vic. "You'll get her back, right? You'll find her?" She choked on a sob. "You saw what he's capable of. What he will do to her."

I clenched my jaw as my stomach churned. I hadn't. I never looked at the photos because I knew Eva didn't want me to.

"We'll find her," Vic answered for me. "Stay in the house. We need to use the barn for a while. Do not come out here. Understand?"

She nodded. "Yeah."

I clenched my jaw; hands curling into fists as I watched Ally walk out of the barn.

Only then did I finally lose it.

A tidal wave of rage and devastation ripped through me as if I was slowly being pulled through a meat grinder.

I picked up an old antique chair and threw it. The spindled legs broke off as it hit the side of the barn and fell in to a pile of broken pieces on the floor.

Eva. "Fuck," a loud roar escaped my raw throat.

Twenty-Eight

Eva

"INSIDE." A HAND SHOVED ME IN THE BACK, THRUSTING ME FORWARD. Blindfolded with my hands tied behind my back, I tripped over a ledge and landed hard on my knees. A loud, hollow vibration echoed in the room.

"Get comfortable. You're gonna be here a while," Curran's man said.

My body jerked at the whoosh then loud clang as if he slammed a heavy metal door.

A muffled sound escaped my mouth. Muffled because a piece of duct tape covered it. I inhaled through my nose and instantly gagged on the smell of urine and bleach. If I throw up, I'll suffocate on my own vomit.

I fell back onto my butt and pulled my knees to my chest. I rubbed at the blindfold using my knee. It wasn't tight like the coarse ropes cutting into my wrists, and after a few minutes I managed to push it off my head.

The relief didn't last when I realized I was just as blinded with it off. My prison was pitch dark, except for a hairline fracture of light where the man had sealed the door shut.

I shuffled on my butt like a caterpillar the few feet toward it. Pressing my nose to the crack, I inhaled several breaths before trying to peer outside.

Nothing. I couldn't see anything except sunlight. But that meant I wasn't in a building.

I leaned against the door, and slowly, my eyes adjusted to the darkness.

It was only about eight feet wide and equally as tall. I couldn't see the far end, but the walls were metal. The ceiling was metal. The door was metal.

That's when panic slammed into me, and my stomach dropped. I swallowed several times to keep the threatening bile from rising.

I was in a shipping container. They'd locked me in a shipping container.

I screamed. Or at least tried to scream, but the sound was a low, muffled moan. Not that it stopped me. I screamed and banged my body against the heavy metal door.

Logically, I knew it wouldn't do any good, but logic had spiraled into a dark murky hole.

I continually thrust my body against the side of the container and screamed until my throat was so raw it no longer emitted any sound.

Suffocating heat blanketed my body, and sweat dripped down the side of my face. My chest heaved as I sucked in deep breaths through my nose before I finally collapsed to the hard, unforgiving floor.

Where was I? Was the container on a ship? Or maybe it was an abandoned container in the middle of a field somewhere? God, I could be anywhere. The only thing I knew was we'd been in the car for several hours before they locked me in here.

I drew my knees up to my chest and laid my forehead on them. My arms were cramped and my fingers numb as I sat with my back against the door and waited. I didn't know what I waited for. Death? Did he plan to leave me here to die a slow agonizing death?

Why? Why would Curran do this? Why didn't he just kill me?

What did he want? Revenge for putting him in jail? Or was he using me to lure Deaglan into a trap?

Deaglan. God, Deaglan. I'd tried not to think of him, but as the hours passed, sitting alone in the darkness, I couldn't stop it.

He'd done everything to protect me. Everything.

He carried so much guilt over being unable to protect his mom, and now… now he'd blame himself for me being taken.

I sucked in a gulp of air through my nostrils as I swallowed back the threatening tears. I wouldn't cry. I refused to cry. I swore Curran would never make me cry again.

I'd fight. And I'd survive. No matter what he did to me, I'd never give up.

I stiffened at the sound of a clink of the latch lifting on the door. I pressed my back against the wall and pushed upward to scramble to my feet.

A scattering of pins and needles erupted in my legs and butt from sitting huddled in a ball for so long

The rusted hinges creaked as the door opened. The sunlight blinded me and I squinted against it. There was a sliver of hope that it was Deaglan. That he'd found me.

But that hope was crushed as my eyes adjusted to the light. My blood curdled and stomach coiled.

"Shall we get reacquainted, my love?"

Twenty-Nine

Deaglan

"**W**HERE DID HE TAKE HER?" I GROUND OUT.

Blood dripped from his broken nose and spilled onto his shirt. "Please, I don't know anything."

"Bullshit." I ploughed my fist into his jaw and sent him flying through the air and crashing into a pile of old dusty furniture.

I strode toward him, my control on edge. Rage tempting me to crack. Daring me to lose all the control and sanity I'd gained back.

Twenty-two minutes we'd interrogated this asshole and he refused to talk. But his shifting eyes, quick breaths, and jumpiness told me he was near to breaking.

I leaned over and grabbed the guy by his black tee and yanked him from the rubble.

Sweat dripped from the sniper's pulsing temples. His beady blue eyes jerked from me to Vic and back again.

We didn't tie him up. I wanted to hit the bastard when he had the chance to hit me back. And he'd tried. For the first ten minutes, he'd fought me, but not any longer. Now he was begging me to stop.

I stepped closer to him and heard the clang of his teeth as he clenched his jaw, as if bracing for a hit again. "Did your boss tell you what I used to do?" The sniper rapidly blinked. "Ever hear of the death cages, asshole?"

He swallowed and jerked his head side to side.

My brows lifted. "No? It's a fight to the death." He licked the blood from his upper lip that had dripped from his nose. "Slow. Painful. Agonizing, really. And I was exceptional at killing my opponents with my bare hands. I enjoyed dragging it out until my opponent begged me for mercy." I paused, letting him digest the idea. I nodded to Vic. "But if you don't beg, I'll let Vic have you."

The sniper's eyes briefly flickered to Vic, who stood with his arms crossed over his broad chest while leaning against a wood post in the barn.

"Vic's specialty is extracting information. I'm pretty sure I don't have to give you details as to what that means?"

I lifted my brows, and the sniper spoke for the first time. "No."

The guy looked barely twenty, which was to our advantage. The younger they were, the easier it was to get them to give us the information we needed. His loyalty was not yet cemented to Curran, or as he likely knew him, Seth.

"Where are they taking her?"

The sniper sniffed and his wide nostrils flared. His brows twitched, likely in pain from his shattered nose. He'd have a hell of a lot more shattered if I didn't get answers.

His gaze flicked again to Vic before he said, "He'll cut me up alive and sell me for parts."

"And what makes you think I'll be any nicer?"

He swallowed, and his head dropped. "Seth doesn't trust anyone. I swear, he doesn't tells us shit... but I heard he's leaving."

"No shit, asshole. Where's he going?"

He shook his head. "I swear, I don't know. Please."

I nodded to Vic, and he slowly walked toward us.

His eyes widened and body trembled. "His cargo ship. I don't know if that's where he'll take her, but containers were being loaded today." My blood ran cold. "He puts…. he puts people in them."

I glanced over my shoulder at Vic and he already had his cell out and to his ear. "Shipping yard. Port Authority. He's leaving on the cargo ship."

"What else?" I demanded.

"Yellow. He usually puts them in the yellow containers."

I turned and stormed out of the barn.

Thirty

Eva

MY BREATH LOCKED IN MY THROAT AS CURRAN STEPPED INSIDE THE container. My eyes shifted to the open doorway. To the possibility of freedom, but it was quickly eradicated when my eyes hit the two men standing guard outside.

I noticed the other containers, which meant I wasn't in the middle of a field somewhere. I could make a run for it. But a bullet was far faster than my trembling legs, and with my hands tied behind my back, it was unlikely I'd make it past Curran.

He approached me and I shifted back a step.

He scowled, brows lowering over his eyes. He moved quickly, snagging my arm before I could back up any farther.

He reached out to touch my face and I jerked my head away from him. "Don't be stupid," he growled, fingers biting into my arm.

My chest heaved and the duct tape over my mouth bubbled in and out.

He reached for my face again, and this time I stayed still. His fingers picked at the edge of the tape on my right cheek, then he yanked it off so fast it felt as if I had been slapped in the face with a wet rag.

I grit my teeth to swallow the hiss of pain.

Curran released me. "My apologies for the rather crude accommodations."

I spit in his face.

The saliva slid down his cheek, then dripped off the edge of his jaw. He clucked his tongue and shook his head as he used his thumb to wipe it away.

"I should've known you wouldn't behave." His voice was calm and smooth, yet underneath it was fingernails scratching a chalkboard.

"This is me behaving," I retorted. I was well aware of what this man was capable of, but there wasn't a chance I'd cower in front of him again. Not now. Not ever.

A slow grin formed. "You're going to need that strength where you're going." I kept my face expressionless, but I bit the insides of my cheeks so hard I tasted iron. "But first, we have things to discuss."

Hiding my fear failed as my stomach clenched and my eyes widened. I wasn't sure what he meant exactly, but it was the spark in his eyes that had my insides curdling.

He chuckled. Then, like a snake lashing out, he grabbed the back of my head and his fingers closed in the strands of my hair. He jerked, cranking my neck back.

This time I couldn't stop the gasp of pain.

"Do I have your full attention?"

"Yes," I hissed.

He jerked again, and I bit my tongue to stop the threatening scream. "Drop the attitude," he barked.

"You're a fucking coward. A pathetic, repulsive monster and Deaglan and his friends are going to hunt you down like an animal and kill you."

He nodded. "Yes, they've caused me a few difficulties, but I'm a very patient man. Evangeline. Very patient. I could've taken you a year ago, but I was waiting until I had my business back up and running. You fucking Deaglan Kane forced me to change plans. Do you know he is the reason I had to change my identity? Relentless bastard. You fucking him really screwed things up, Evangeline. And now I have to reinvent myself again. But, at least I'll have the satisfaction of knowing that he'll never have you."

I fought. I couldn't help it. My insides exploded into a war of emotions. Anger. Fear. Devastation. Strands of hair ripped from my scalp, and I barely noticed as I tore at the bonds on my wrists and flailed against his vicious hold.

I wanted to hurt him. Kill him. .

His grip on my hair released, and his palm wailed across my cheek so hard it sent me crashing to the unforgiving floor on my side.

I lay stunned for a second as my head throbbed and my cheek stung.

Black suit pants appeared in front of me, and I flung my hair out of my face as I sat up to face him.

He crouched, shaking his head. "It seems we've been here before, haven't we? Now, I've asked you politely to behave. I won't again." He propped his arms on his thighs, hands clasped between them. "I'd like to be able to have a polite conversation with you, Evangeline. Is that too much to ask?"

I glared, refusing to say anything because what came out of my mouth wasn't going to be polite.

"It was unfortunate you parted your creamy white thighs for that man. I may have kept you for myself."

Despite knowing it was better to stay silent, the words tumbled out. "You can kill me. Rape me. Torture me, but I will never regret being with him."

His fist snapped out and punched me in the jaw. A jarring vibration tore through my head as the impact sent me crashing to my chest on the floor again.

"Please be polite, Evangeline," he said.

Blood pooled in my mouth and I spat onto the floor. I sat up again, refusing to cower in front of this monster.

"I had no intention of selling you. Even after you had me thrown in prison. I don't normally lose control like I did with you, and it was a mistake. A mistake that almost ruined me."

Shivers raked my body.

He lowered his voice, tipping closer. "I had plans for us, dearest Evangeline." He reached in his inner jacket pocket and pulled out a square, blue velvet box.

My lips parts and eyes widened.

"You see, we were going to be married." God, he was delusional if he thought I'd ever marry him. He opened the box and held it in front of me. Inside was a stunning pear-shaped diamond with a white gold ring. "I had this made for you. Fourteen-karat white gold and a four-carat diamond."

I jerked when he snapped the velvet box closed.

"You would've made me a fine wife, Evangeline." He paused, his eyes roaming the length of me. "But you couldn't learn to behave."

"I'd rather be sold to the highest bidder than ever be your wife," I spat.

He nodded. "Ah, yes, there is that option. But now that I have you again, I haven't decided yet." His weight shifted as he straightened. "We will see once we arrive at our destination. That's if you survive the trip. Unfortunately, many don't. It's far, and with the sweltering heat in here…" he ran the tips of his fingers down the wall. "It's an excruciating journey. Or, so I'm told."

"He's going to kill you," I grit out.

He laughed. "Deaglan Kane. Yes. I have no doubt he will spend his life trying to find you."

"That's where you're wrong. He won't stop until he finds you. No matter what your name is."

It's what Deaglan does. He finds people.

He'll find Curran. It may be hours, days, months, or years. But one day he'll find him.

And I had no doubt he'd kill him.

There was a good possibility I'd die in this tin can, but I'd have some satisfaction knowing that one day Deaglan would find Curran and end him.

Deaglan was relentless, stubborn, and determined. He wasn't a man to give up. Curran knew that and it was why he'd changed his identity once already.

"We'll see. Where we're going has never been breached. Not once. Even I don't know where it's located yet. They tell me where to send their merchandise, and then they disappear." His voice lowered. "You, Evangeline, will disappear."

Curran turned and walked toward the entrance. He stepped off the small ledge, his hand on the door that would swing shut and seal my fate. "Beg me for forgiveness, Evangeline, and I'll consider a less painful journey for you."

I swallowed the bile in my throat and met his eyes. "Fuck you."

His eyes narrowed and thin lips pursed as he slammed the container door shut.

Thirty-One

Deaglan

COLD. STEADY. EMOTIONLESS.

That was what I needed. The detachment. It was the only way I'd survive this. Because if I thought about Eva in that bastard's hands, I'd lose it. And I couldn't afford to lose it again.

I'd let emotions control me before.

Revenge fed me. Blinded me.

And it destroyed me.

"Hey, man, you good?" Deck asked.

It wasn't a question as to whether I was good or not, because he knew damn well I wasn't good. He was asking if I was going to be able to keep my shit contained.

And Deck had every right to be concerned. He'd been there. He dragged my ass out of that cage barely conscious.

"You get me a visa to stay?" I asked.

The corner of his mouth tugged up. "Yeah."

"Then I'm good." Because Eva was mine and she wasn't going anywhere. And neither was I.

We were at Carrick Shipping watching the crane load containers onto the ship and unable to get on board without causing a mad minute and risking Eva's life.

Six fuckin' hours she'd been gone.

"She's in one of those fuckin' containers," I said. There were at least a thousand containers on that ship, and another five hundred or so on land. "We need to search the yellow ones, and we have to expect that he's likely ready for us."

Deck nodded. "Good chance he'll rig them."

I nodded. Open the wrong container door and we were likely to be blown into a million pieces. "It's been his M.O. And he has nothing to lose. He's done here. His identity. His business."

Eva. Fuck. Where the hell did he plan on taking her? Did he plan to keep her or sell her?

He knew I wouldn't risk her life, but he also knew I wouldn't let him take her out of the country without one hell of a fight. He'd tried before. He'd kidnapped Bria, the girl who was under my protection. He thought he could get away and sell her. He was wrong. And he was wrong if he thought he could take Eva from me.

We crouched beside a container near the cargo ship, waiting for the cover of darkness. But if the ship pulled anchor, we'd have to go in without it.

Ernie was on the roof of the warehouse with a sniper rifle, and Tyler was west of the shipping yard with Connor checking the containers that hadn't been loaded. Kai and Vic were to the east doing the same thing.

"Boss. Found a row of live yellow containers. Maybe twenty," Tyler's voice vibrated in the earpiece. "Bombs are triggered to the latches."

"Can you disarm them?" Deck asked.

"Take me some time," Tyler replied.

"How much time?" Deck asked.

"Thirty, maybe."

I glanced at Deck. "Gut says she's already on that ship. They're a decoy."

"And if they aren't and he blows them up the moment he sees us?"

I clenched my jaw and pursed my lips. "My gut's not wrong, Deck. She's on the ship. This is personal to him, he'd make it personal."

"Leave them," Deck ordered Tyler. "Circle back and meet up with us."

"Roger that," Tyler replied.

"Heads up," Ernie said in the earpiece. "One target on the ramp. Dockworkers' cleared out."

I lightly placed my hand on Deck's shoulder and moved past him.

I crept between the shipping containers toward the stern of the ship where the steel ramp onto the ship was located.

The ship's engine rumbled as it prepared to leave port. But it sure as fuck wasn't leaving without me on it. I was good at finding people, but if Eva disappeared in the cruel underworld of human trafficking, it would be like searching for a needle at the bottom of the fuckin' ocean.

I peered around a stack of five wooden crates.

One man guarded the ramp. I could easily take him out, but it would have to be silent. One mistake and this would all go to shit.

He pulled a pack of cigarettes out of his front shirt pocket and took one out, placing it between his lips. A click and snap of his lighter before a flame illuminated his craggily weathered face.

He shifted out of the direction of the wind and cupped his hands around the flame. .

I moved toward him.

He sucked in a long inhale, then exhaled, and smoke billowed all around him.

I took him out fast, hard and silent. My hands snapping his neck before he was able to emit a warning. His body sagged like a broken doll in my hold. I dragged him behind the crates and took his gun, shoving it in the back of my jeans.

"Clear," I said into the mouthpiece. "Going in."

Ernie warned, "Two cars approaching."

Fuck. "I'm going." I wasn't losing this chance. I kept low and ran up the ramp, crouching behind the railing. "On board."

A car door slammed and there was a murmur of voices, but I was too far away to hear what was being said.

I peered over the side and saw an SUV and a black van parked in front of the ramp. I counted ten men.

The driver got out and opened the back door.

My blood ran cold, and everything inside me stilled.

Curran.

It was as if I stood in that cage again.

Fighting the consuming darkness as sights and sounds faded around me.

Nothing existed except my opponent.

But there was one difference. This time I wanted to live.

And that made me deadlier than I'd ever been.

Thirty-Two

Eva

I SAT WITH MY BACK AGAINST THE DOOR NEXT TO THE HAIRLINE CRACK THAT teased me with the hope of freedom. The vibration of the ship's engine idling was a constant reminder that I'd soon disappear.

Would I become another statistic?

No. I was good at surviving. I'd survive him and whatever awaited me. And I'd fight until the end.

I'd never give up. On me. On Deaglan.

But that hint of hope was tested as minutes became hours. I'd tried to cut through the ropes on my wrists by rubbing them against a metal beam edge, but all I managed to do was cut into my wrists. I was numb to the pain. Even the ache in my jaw from Curran's fist had vanished.

It was thirst that ruled my every thought as my saliva dried up and my mouth felt as if it had a layer of sawdust in it. My only relief was that the sweltering heat had eased.

The adrenaline pumping through my body faded and I lay on my side with my knees curled up to my chest and closed my eyes.

I had no idea how long I slept, if it was one minute or five hours, but I woke to the sound of metal scraping metal as the latch lifted. I darted upright and scrambled to my feet, using the wall as a prop.

The door swung open and a wave of cool night air filtered in to me.

A bulking man with a shaved head stood in the doorway holding two bottles of water. In my head, my feet were already running toward him, and it took every ounce of willpower to not dive for them, crack the lids, and chug back the cool water. Not that I was even capable of it with my hands tied behind my back.

"Come here," he ordered.

I cautiously walked toward him. Cautiously because my legs shook and I was afraid they'd give out.

He tossed the two bottles of water onto the floor. My eyes followed them as they rolled into the wall before swaying to a stop. I looked at the bulky man again, then to the gun on his right hip, then the knife strapped to his tree-trunk thigh.

The water bottles told me that he wasn't taking me out of here. No, he was going to lock me in here. Days. Weeks. I didn't know how long, and that scared me more than anything.

I knew I had one chance at this. If I failed, I'd either die or suffer in this container for however long.

When I was within reach of him, he grabbed my arm and yanked me out of my prison. I stumbled on the ledge and he hauled me upright, fingers biting into my bicep. I kept my head down in submission, but from beneath the shield of my hair, I scanned the perimeter.

I was surrounded by a maze of cargo containers. There was no sign of anyone with him and the only light offered was from the half moon.

"Turn around," he ordered.

I did as he asked, and his hands jerked on the blood-soaked ropes as he untied them.

Tears pooled in my eyes when he tore the rough fibers from my raw skin. Circulation rushed into my hands, and pins and needles erupted with frenzy. I rubbed my hands together, desperate to get as much feeling back in them as fast as possible.

"Get settled in. You have a long ride." He pushed me toward the container.

I tripped on the ledge, but this time on purpose.

He bent to grab my arm, and I reacted.

I ploughed my elbow back into his chin as hard as I could. It was a move that Evan had taught us in our self-defense class. A jolt of electricity shot through my arm on impact. I heard the distinct crack of bone and the sound of his feet staggering backward.

He wailed in fury. "Bitch," he shouted.

I leapt to my feet and ran.

I had no idea where I was going, but I had the advantage that it was dark and I was in a maze of cargo containers.

His footsteps pounded behind me. "I'll fuckin' kill you."

My legs threatened to give way as they trembled with each step, but the adrenaline pushed me forward as I constantly switched directions, hoping to lose him.

I stopped and pressed my back against a container, covering my mouth with my hands to conceal my ragged breathing. I had no clue where I was going. God, I could be running in circles. I could run right back into his arms.

I held my breath, listening for his footsteps.

Nothing.

I lowered my hands from my mouth and crept alongside a container. I stopped and peered around the corner. It was dark, but I couldn't see or hear him.

I noiselessly weaved through the maze, hesitating to listen every few seconds. But it wasn't his footsteps I heard. It was the slosh of water lapping against the ship's hull.

My heart leapt. Escape. I could jump. I could jump into the water. He'd probably hear me, but by then it would be too late.

I moved quickly toward the sound.

Toward freedom.

When my eyes hit the railing of the ship, a wave of relief swept through me because it was hope. Jumping into the water was risky because I had no idea how far it was to the water's surface. But if the ship left dock, all hope would be lost.

I ran.

My hands curled around the railing and I heaved myself up. I couldn't see the water below, but I heard it. And that was enough.

I jumped.

A hand latched onto my arm. I flailed against the side of the ship.

"No. Let me go."

He hauled me back up and tossed me over the railing. I landed hard on the deck floor.

"Don't move, bitch." I stared into the barrel of his gun.

I didn't think, I reacted. I wasn't going to be locked up in that container again.

I swung my leg back toward his kneecap, but this time he was ready for me and jumped out of the way before his hand snagged a wad of my hair and yanked me to my feet.

My hands shot to my head as agonizing pain ripped through my scalp. I fell back against his broad chest with his gun pressed into my spine.

"Got her, boss" he said.

A crackle sounded on his radio, "Bring her to me."

I swallowed the bile at the sound of Curran's voice.

"Yes, sir."

He yanked on my hair. "Walk."

But I wasn't going to make it easy for him. Not while I still had breath in my lungs.

I flung my head back into his face, but he shifted to the side. "Jesus. Stupid bitch."

He kicked me in the back of the knee and my head snapped as I fell forward to the ground.

He reached down and grabbed a fistful of my hair. I tried to get to my feet, but he was already walking and dragging me behind him.

I twisted and flailed as I tried to get free. "You bastard," I yelled.

He ignored me as he kept walking and I saw my chance at freedom slowly slip away. Tears of pain mixed with desperation tipped over the rims of my eyes and glided down my cheeks.

He dragged me across the deck.

I kicked and screamed. Fingernails scraping at his arms. He jerked on my hair and I sucked in a lungful of air at the excruciating pain in my scalp.

My heart stopped and my body froze.

I stopped struggling as a familiar scent drifted toward me.

Deaglan.

My eyes frantically searched the darkness for him. Was it false hope? Was I imagining him? No, I'd never forget his scent. It was part of me.

When my eyes found his on top of the container, he put his finger to his lips with a shake of his head. I swallowed and choked on the sob that threatened to escape.

Deaglan. Oh God, Deaglan.

He found me.

Deaglan found me.

He silently moved parallel with us on top of the container.

I watched. Waited. My breath locked in my throat.

His eyes met mine with warning. There was a brief nod.

I curled my hands into fists, ready.

Deaglan's dark shadow pounced on my captor from above.

The two crashed to the floor and rolled.

The pressure on my scalp released at the same time my captor's gun slid across the floor. I scrambled away, diving for it.

The men crashed into the container emitting a loud clang.

My fingers curled around the gun. I flipped over and held it out with both hands.

But I knew if I fired it would alert the entire ship.

The two rolled and fought against one another.

Blood sprayed in a fan across the side of the container as fists flew. Bulky guy went for his knife and I was about to yell a warning to Deaglan when he slammed his fist into the guy's throat.

Bulky guy's eyes widened and both hands went to his neck as he struggled to breathe. Deaglan didn't let up. He punched him in the side of the head and the bulk crumbled to the ground in a motionless heap.

Deaglan towered over him, grabbed him by the neck and jerked with a twist, snapping his neck.

I stared at the lifeless body on the floor, then to Deaglan.

"Eva."

He crouched in front of me and reached for the gun. "Give me the gun, baby." He eased it out of my trembling grasp and tossed it over the side.

My eyes slid to his and that's when everything collapsed around me. "Deaglan," I choked out. "You found me."

He half grinned with his busted lip. "Told you I'm good at my job."

I threw my arms around his neck.

With one arm he held me tight to him as he stood, bringing me with him. He kissed the top of my head. "Babe, I'd hold you forever, but we need to get the fuck off this ship."

I released him and nodded.

He slid his hand in mine and squeezed as he spoke into his head-piece. "Eva's safe. We need a distraction to get off this tin can."

I couldn't hear the response, but it was comforting to know Deaglan wasn't here alone. "All hell is going to break loose," he said as he guided me between the containers. "Need you to stay close."

"Okay."

He pressed me up against the wall of a container, his body shield-ing mine just as a loud blast exploded into the air.

I jerked with the blast, and my heart jumped into my throat. Deaglan kept me locked to him for several seconds before he pulled back and tilted to look at me. "You good?"

I nodded. "Good."

He kissed me briefly on the lips. "Okay, let's get the fuck out of here."

I glanced at the thick, black cloud of smoke filtering into the sky as we ran. He stopped several times when voices and running footsteps drew close before we ran again, weaving in and out of the cargo.

"Fuck," he muttered. He grabbed me around the waist and shoved me behind a towering steel beam. "Deck. Ramp is a no go. We need an exit."

His eyes hit mine. Hard. Cold. Unyielding. There was no uncertainty in him. No fear. He was completely in control.

I jolted as a spattering of gunfire erupted.

"Stern," Deaglan said. "Water. Ten seconds." He tightened his hold on my hand and vaulted to the right. I stumbled after him as we ran toward the railing. He glanced over his shoulder as he stopped. "You need to jump. Connor is in the water. He'll help you get clear."

My eyes widened. "What about you?"

His jaw clenched and he shook his head. "I need to end this, Eva."

I shook my head, hand sliding from his grasp. He was going after Curran. "No. Deaglan, no. We jump together."

He reached for me, arm hooking my waist. "No time to argue. Go."

There was a thunder of footsteps and shouts.

I knew Deaglan. I knew he needed to do this for him as much as for me, but I wouldn't leave him. "Deaglan. I'm not leaving you."

He grabbed me around the waist to lift me over the railing. "Push away from the ship," he ordered.

"One move and she dies," Curran's voice vibrated behind us.

Thirty-Three

Eva

"PUT HER DOWN," CURRAN ORDERED.

Deaglan's hands tensed on my waist as he slowly lowered me to the deck. "Be ready," he whispered under his breath.

I stiffened, but kept my face emotionless as I faced Curran.

He waved his gun at me. "Come here, Evangeline."

Deaglan's hands curled into fists as he stepped in front of me. "That's not happening. Do you think I came alone, Curran? That I'd take the chance you'd escape me again."

Curran tensed and his brows furrowed. "You forget. I'm the one with a gun. Evangeline, do as your told," he barked.

I lightly placed my hand on Deaglan's back. I wouldn't risk him being shot. Not ever.

His hand snagged mine before I could move past him. "No."

"You promised," I whispered, looking up at him. He promised not to get shot. It was a ridiculous promise, but I was holding him to it.

"Do not move," he said, shielding me with his body.

"Wrong answer," Curran said, and fired.

"Now." Deaglan shoved me to the ground and landed on top of me.

A barrage of bullets pelleted the container near Curran. I didn't know where they came from, but I knew it was Deck and his guys.

Curran dove for cover between the shipping containers and Deaglan ran after him.

"Deaglan." I jumped to my feet at the same time as he lunged for Curran.

Curran raised his gun again, but Deaglan was already on top of him and knocked it from his hand. The metal hit the deck and slid under a container.

Deaglan didn't hesitate as he slammed his fist into Curran's jaw, sending him staggering back.

Curran gained his balance. "I'll fuckin' kill you."

Deaglan smirked. "You can try, asshole."

It was hard to tell who was who in the shadows as they fought. Blood sprayed. Grunts bounced off the deck into the night air. Bone pounded bone.

And thumps echoed as bodies smashed into the hollow metal containers.

Curran's fists swung wildly. But Deaglan was calmer. Precise. Methodical. Every blow a precision missile.

Deaglan continued to pound into Curran, who tried to escape the relentless blows by staggering back farther and farther.

I held my breath. Heart pounding as I watched Deaglan.

This was Crown. This was the man who fought in cages.

This was the man who fiercely protected. And fiercely loved.

The man I loved.

But it was also the boy who lost a mother to a monster like Curran. A mother who gave up everything for him. Whom he loved and couldn't protect.

"Get back," a deep, raspy voice growled.

Vic.

His arm hooked my waist and pulled me farther from Deaglan and Curran. I hadn't realized I'd been slowly moving closer.

I glanced away from Deaglan and Curran for a second to see Deck and Tyler, too. No one moved to help Deaglan, although he didn't look like he needed much help.

"He needs this," Deck said, as if knowing what I was thinking.

Salty iron pooled in my mouth as I bit the inside of my cheek. Tears pooled. My heart pounded. It wasn't because I was scared Deaglan would lose. It was because I imagined him fighting as a kid. Fighting to end the guilt. To end the pain that drove him.

Deaglan plowed his fist into Curran's throat. He staggered, hands to his neck as he struggled to inhale. His eyes widened before he fell to the ground like a cement block.

My fingers dug into Vic's arm as he kept me locked to him.

Deaglan straddled Curran's body. He grabbed him by the shirt and half-lifted him as he watched him take his final breath.

Curran went limp and Deaglan tossed him aside like garbage.

He stared at Curran's lifeless body. His chest heaving and blood dripping from his damaged fists.

"Let me go," I said, prying at Vic's hold.

His arm unlocked and I ran for Deaglan.

I slammed into him and he grunted as he staggered back a step.

My arms hooked his waist and I pressed my cheek against his chest, hearing the distinct thump of his heartbeat. His arms remained at his sides for a second as if he didn't know who I was.

Then… then he enclosed me in his embrace. "Eva," he whispered in a ragged breath.

I sagged against him. God, I loved this man. All of him.

Because love wasn't about loving only the best pieces. It was about loving all of them.

He pressed his lips to the top of my head. "Cuisle, moi chroi." His hand cupped my chin and our eyes locked. "You're the pulse of my heart, Eva."

Epilogue

Eva
2 months later

"HIS FEET SMELL LIKE PANCAKES AND BIRTHDAY CAKE," MADDIE said while holding the five-week-old, black-and-white-spotted puppy, she'd aptly named Polka-a-dot, in her arms.

We were in my backyard on the patio with the remnants of a busted piñata scattered across the grass that had hung from the large oak tree. Everyone was here except for Kendra, who was in Niagra Falls covering the hockey training camp. But Deaglan's brother Ronan was flying in tomorrow, and she was coming back to interview him.

Hope's eyes widened and Skye gaped as she stared at the oversized puppy paws.

Deaglan crouched in front of Maddie and cradled the pup's paw in his palm. He brought it to his nose. "She's right. They do smell like birthday cake and pancakes."

Maddie's grin broadened. She had insisted the pup blow out the candles with her. Polk-a-dot had other ideas and squirmed out of her arms and dove head first into the horse-shaped vanilla cake Ally had brought.

Within seconds, he was covered in white and pink icing.

"Really?" Skye asked, shifting closer.

"Reckon it's good enough to eat." Deaglan opened his mouth and pretended to put the paw in his mouth.

The three girls burst out laughing.

This was the man I'd met at the charity event... casual, charming, and playful. The dangerous, bossy, and overly protective demeanor was still a part of him, but it had eased without the threat of Curran lingering.

"Go ahead, smell." Deaglan winked at Maddie as he straightened. She giggled and readjusted her hold on what looked like a mastiff cross pup. Someone found it on the side of the road in a garbage bag when it was a few days old. Charlotte was handraising it until it was old enough to be adopted.

Skye and Hope leaned in to smell Polk-a-dot's paw.

I laughed, as did London, Georgie, Charlotte, and Ally, who sat at the patio table with me.

The screen door slid across the tracks, and Kai strolled out with three juice boxes in his hand.

London's eyes swung to her husband. "Uh-oh."

Kai's brows dipped as he looked over at the girls and Deaglan. "What the... Hope, don't put your face near that filthy animal's paws."

"But, Daddy, his feet smell like pancakes and birthday cake," Hope said. "Deaglan tasted."

Kai's glare flashed to Deaglan, who shrugged with a smirk. "Yeah, because he ran through the fuc... fridgin' cake." He dumped the juice boxes on the patio table. "Sweetie, dogs walk through their own—"

"Skittles," Tyler blurted as he came out of the house.

"Uncle Tye Tye, that's just silly," Skye said, rolling her eyes.

"It's not silly, you little monster." He made a low growl and dove for her. She took off running with a squeal of laughter.

The restless puppy wiggled out of Maddie's arms and clumsily galloped into the backyard. Hope and she went running after him, while

Deaglan sauntered over to my dad and Vic.

It was late afternoon, and my dad and Deaglan had barbequed hamburgers and veggie burgers, and the girls had brought salads and chips. It was Deaglan's idea to have a get-together before my women's center opened in a few weeks. The house was finished along with the detached, two-car garage that was insulated and renovated into a quaint space for group counseling.

Two social workers from the Treasured Children's Center, who had also personally escaped abusive situations, were volunteering at my center part-time. I'd cut back my hours at the hospital in order to focus on the center and spend more time with Deaglan.

He had his visa and was officially part of 'Vault's Unyielding Riot'. He'd also officially moved in with me. He was flying back to Ireland with Ronan when he left next week to 'deal with things', and those things included Crown.

He suggested he find someone he trusted to take it over, but I knew Crown wasn't only important to him, but important to the girls he protected, and I wanted him to keep it and continue to help them.

It was a lot like my center, in that sometimes the path isn't always the one a girl has chosen, but the path they're given.

And when that path cracks and bleeds beneath her feet, it's not the fall, it's how she survives it. How she finds her way back. I didn't know how the girls at Crown came to be on that path, but Deaglan helped them survive it and gave them a chance for a new beginning if they wanted it.

"Deaglan is really good with kids," Charlotte said, interrupting my thoughts. She placed her white wine on the patio table. "You guys talk about having any?"

"Uh, no. Not yet." I wanted kids, but I didn't know how Deaglan felt.

"That man is a gift from God." Ally's eyes roamed the length of Tyler as he jogged over to Deck and Connor with Skye perched on his shoulders. They were in the backyard cleaning up what was left of the piñata the three girls had beat up with a baseball bat. "And God wrapped him up in a big red bow of deliciousness."

I smacked her arm. "Don't even think about it. Tyler's a total player."

Georgie sipped her sparkling water. "So was Deaglan until he met you. And Tyler needs a woman to come home to after killing bad guys."

"What's Vic's story?" Charlotte asked. "Besides being seriously scary."

Vic stood leaning against the wood railing, arms crossed and an untouched beer cradled in the crook of his arm. His scowl was fierce, but then it was rare it wasn't.

Deaglan told me they were working on finding Curran's connections and who he'd planned to sell me to. Vic interrogated one of Curran's men, but had obtained nothing from him yet. It could explain the numerous cuts on his knuckles, though.

Georgie caressed her palm over her swollen belly. "That guy needs a woman to teach him how to dance in the rain."

I laughed because I couldn't imagine Vic dancing and I'd heard he hated the rain.

"Hey, did you hear Tear Asunder's new hit song?" London asked.

The girls chatted about the rock band, mentioning they were coming back from their North American tour next weekend. Deaglan had informed me yesterday that we were going to Logan's house, the lead singer of Tear Asunder, for a get-together so I could meet his cousin Kite.

My eyes shifted to my dad as he barrelled out a laugh at something Deaglan said and slapped him on the back of the shoulder before shaking his hand. Deaglan grinned and Vic's mouth twitched.

I smiled to myself as warmth settled over me. God, I loved that they got along so well and I knew it meant something to Deaglan. He'd never had the chance to form a relationship with his real father when he'd been so consumed by rage and hatred.

As if sensing my eyes on him, Deaglan's head lifted and he looked at me. My heart squeezed like it always did and I snagged my lower lip with my teeth. His eyes flicked to my mouth and heat blazed in the depths.

He said something to my dad and Vic then pushed away from the railing and stalked toward me.

Goosebumps rose and tingles scattered.

"I know that look," London said as her gaze went from me to Deaglan and back again. "I think it's time we head out." She stood. "Hope, sweetie. Time to go."

I knew that look, too, and an ember ignited in my belly.

The other girls stood, too, and Charlotte snagged the pup as he ran by her with a shoe in his mouth.

"Hey, sweetpea," Georgie called to Deck. "Deaglan wants his girl."

I felt the heat burn in my cheeks, but I wasn't sure if it was from her comment or the fact that Deaglan was looking at me like he was going to strip me naked and fuck me right here on the patio.

When he reached me, he pulled me into the cocoon of his arms. "I do want my girl," he drawled against my neck as he trailed kisses. "Naked. Moaning. Begging."

A twinge squeezed between my legs and I shoved at his chest. "Stop. My dad is here."

He chuckled. "Your dad knows we fuck, baby. And he wants grandkids."

My heart stopped and my fingers curled into his white tee as I looked up at him. "He said that?"

"Mmm," he murmured.

"What did you say?"

He smirked, eyes twinkling. "I said we'd work on it."

My breath locked in my throat. We'd work on it. We'd work on having kids.

"You want kids? I mean, you'd be an amazing dad, I just didn't... I mean, we've never talked about it and we should talk about it. I want kids. Two, really, but I'm good with—"

"You're babbling."

I totally was.

His heated breath wafted against my neck, causing an army of goosebumps to invade. "And just so you know, baby." His voice lowered. "I'm marrying you first."

I tried to swallow, but I couldn't. I couldn't do anything but breathe, and even that was hard to do because Deaglan wanted kids. He wanted to marry me.

I didn't have to time to respond or think or process as I was swept up with goodbyes as everyone filtered out. As soon as the front door closed behind my dad, whom to my utter horror had winked at me knowingly, Deaglan corralled me against the wall in the foyer.

"I'm marrying you, Eva, but I'm going to give you some time to process that. Because when I give you the ring, the processing is over. Your dad's good with that."

I jerked. "My dad? You asked my dad?" The words barely passed my lips.

"I asked him weeks ago when we were having a beer after working on your garage." My mouth dropped open. My dad hadn't even hinted that Deaglan asked him. "But, baby, tonight we have some unfinished business we need to deal with."

That unfinished business was the name of my center. I promised I'd make a decision on what to call it by tonight. And I had decided, I just hadn't told Deaglan yet.

He locked my wrists in his hands above my head. "What's the name, Eva? Or would you rather I fuck it out of you on a bed of your sticky notes."

I smiled. "Tempting."

"Mmm. Or hazardous."

I ran my tongue over my lower lip and his eyes flared. "For you or me?"

"Babe. Fuck."

I inhaled a breath. "I'd like to call it Caitlyn House."

His body froze and his eyes glassed over with emotion. "Caitlyn House," he repeated.

I nodded. I'd been a little concerned that he wouldn't like it. That naming it after his mother was too personal, but she was important to him and he had meant the world to her.

"Jesus, Eva. It's beautiful. She'd have loved that." He released my wrists, and his hand curled around the nape of my neck. "Fuckin' rare."

There were no pieces he hadn't given me. Some may be ruined and damaged, but they fit. We fit.

"Going to fuck you now and show you how rare," he said. "I want you off the pill, baby."

"Okay," I whispered.

"Love you, Eva." His lips met mine.

THE END

Want to read about Deaglan's friends?
Deck's Story: *Perfect Chaos*
Kai's Story: *Perfect Ruin*
Connor's Story: *Perfect Rage*
Coming: Vic Gate's Book

To the readers,

Thank you for reading *Irish Crown*. I hope you enjoyed Deaglan and Eva's story.

I'm always humbled by the kindness book lovers have shown me throughout my career and thank you is never enough, but know that it means the world to me.

Happy Reading,

Nash xo

Acknowledgements

Thank you to all the readers for waiting so patiently for Irish Crown. I don't know if this book would be here without you. Your patience, support and amazing words, were my driving force. You believed in me, when I struggled to believe in myself.

Nash's Naughty Fillies', I'm so lucky to be able to chat with each of you. When I pop into the group, I know I'll leave with a smile on my face. Thank you from the bottom of my heart for all your support.

Thank you to my editor, Becky at Hot Tree Editing. You totally rock as always. I'm still laughing at the Adam's apple comment.

This cover, I love this cover so damn much. Thank you to Sara Eirew Photography and model Mike Chabot for bringing this to life.

This book's interior is beautiful because of Stacey at Champagne Book Design. There is a lot that goes into formatting a book and I know I can always trust Stacey with my words.

Elaine, love you. You find those pesky mistakes that I somehow hop, skip and jump over while you easily lasso and bring to my attention. Thank you.

And to my amazing Beta readers, Midian, Susan, Snow, Lana, Jill, Yaya, I put you girls through the ringer with this one. Bits and pieces then twists and turns and oops, nope let's do it again. Thank you for sticking with me and reading this twice.

And as always thank you to my family and fur babies for being patient when I disappeared into my cave for days at a time.

About the Author

Nashoda Rose is a *New York Times* and *USA Today* International bestselling author of over twelve novels, including the Tear Asunder series, the spin-off Unyielding series, and her paranormal Scars of the Wraiths.

She lives outside of Toronto where she enjoys hiking with her Newfoundland dog and riding her horses.

Goodreads: http://bit.ly/1PbiWHa
Twitter: http://bit.ly/2iecrYP
Amazon: http://amzn.to/2yC43IV
FaceBook: https://www.facebook.com/authornashodarose/
Instagram: http://bit.ly/1Slj8WG

E-mail: nashodarose@gmail.com

CPSIA information can be obtained
at www.ICGtesting.com
Printed in the USA
BVHW031909010421
603947BV00006B/73